By the Sea

By the Sea

Claudette Renalds

Copyright Notice

By the Sea

Cover and Interior Design: Derinda Babcock

Editor(s): Judy Hagey, Deb Haggerty

Author Represented by the Seymour Agency

PUBLISHED BY: Elk Lake Publishing, Inc., 35 Dogwood Dr., Plymouth, MA 02360, 2019

Library Cataloging Data

Names: Renalds, Claudette (Claudette Renalds

By the Sea / Claudette Renalds

264 p. 23cm × 15cm (9in × 6 in.)

Description: Reclusive author adopted by twin boys.

Identifiers: ISBN-13: 978-1-950051-00-7 (trade) | 978-1-950051-01-4 (POD) | 978-1-950051-02-1 (e-book.)

Key Words: Beach Read, Romance, Contemporary, Twins, Family, Single Mothers, Cancer

LCCN: 2018968304 Fiction

ACKNOWLEDGMENTS

Any good manuscript takes more than a lone writer. Without the inspiration and anointing of the Holy Spirit, there wouldn't be a story. His Divine guidance led me to Deb Haggerty and the team at Elk Lake Publishing Inc. Deb saw potential and believed in me after reading only the first chapter and has been a source of encouragement since. She helped me find my agent, Jessie Stover, from the Seymour Agency. Jessie's enthusiasm keeps me young and energetic, and I know she has my best interests at heart.

My editor, Judy Hagey, not only corrected my mistakes but patiently fed me a wealth of information comparable to a college-level creative writing course. Thank you, Judy, for making my book better and more enjoyable with each read.

I am blessed with a host of friends scattered throughout the world. They represent many different denominations, cultures, and life choices. Some have been a supportive presence for many years; others arrived in my life more recently. What they have in common is they love God and me. Several have read my manuscript and offered their comments and edits. Others are waiting patiently for the final product while showering me with prayers and love. My thanks to all of you, including my social media friends who say they can't wait for a signed copy.

Special thanks to Johnese Burtram and the members of the Northern Virginia Christian Writers' Fellowship. Through their critiques and workshops, I received the confidence to pursue publication of my first novel. I'm grateful for the prayer and emotional reinforcement I receive from my "Juliets" friends (Joyful Unique Ladies Incredibly Eager to Socialize), my Dominion Valley Community Bible Study ladies, and my dear Christian family at Thursday night life group.

My sister, Paulette Zawadzki, drives from North Carolina when I need her, critiques my writing, and offers medical advice for my book and my family. I am grateful for her loving care and inspiration.

Lastly, I am thankful for my family. For my husband, Charlie, for loving me for over fifty years and for our two children and their families. Without their love, patience and support I would not be where I am today.

DEDICATION

By the Sea is dedicated to the loving memory of my mother, Hazel Ogden Sharpe. Hazel loved a good story. She passed on her love of reading to her children, grandchildren and great-grandchildren and we are forever grateful.

CHAPTER ONE

Late September 2010

"Bailey, come."

The golden retriever scampered ahead sniffing the sea breeze and investigating the open spaces between the dunes and the ocean. He occasionally stopped and looked toward the dunes as if his fine-tuned sense of hearing deceived him.

Lured by the Frisbee thrown into the surf and his natural instincts, the dog momentarily dismissed the misplaced sounds, changed course and headed toward the swelling tide. With his prize captured, he rushed to shore, kicking up sand in his wake and sending his master on a sudden retreat.

"Bailey, look what you did."

Alex laughed and brushed the wet sand from his shorts. He continued his early-morning walk unaccompanied by the canine who seemed more interested in a convention of seagulls. The disturbed birds complained in loud protest when forced to move their congregation farther up the beach.

The waves beat a steady rhythm as the sun made a gradual appearance, turning the horizon into a portrait of pinks and reds. Alex faced into the brisk wind and picked up his pace while his thoughts turned to the nonexistent book outline he'd promised his literary agent. Remembering her frantic email brought a self-satisfied smile. No way would she like his answer. Let her stew a while. The wait would do her good.

These walks along the shore inspired much of his successful writing career. Today, however, Alex's mind wandered without a creative thought in sight. He had no ambition but to romp with his pet and bask in the early morning sun still low on the horizon. He'd found the perfect life.

"Bailey, come. Now!"

Bailey stopped, wagged his tail and barked excitedly. The dog ran back and forth between his master and the object of his latest interest.

After sprinting to catch the wayward dog and grabbing him by the collar, Alex found himself near the row of cottages beyond the dunes. As he searched the area, he spotted a scene so unusual he removed his sunglasses for a clearer view. This late in the season, it was rare to find anyone stirring so early in the morning, but there in the sand sat two young boys—not more than three or four years of age. Concerned for their safety, he scanned the area for adult supervision. Why are these boys out alone? He vacillated between investigating further or ignoring the interruption and resuming his walk.

As he focused on their energetic play, Alex's imagination kicked in. The otherwise deserted area came alive with the animated scenes flashing through his mind. A little boy building roads and sand castles with his father while his mother plays nearby with a younger child. Could this be a scene from his own childhood? Shaking his head and halting the flow of creativity, he wondered why he hadn't considered the characters of children before.

Alex dismissed previous concerns while his thoughts took yet another detour. Perhaps he might experience a glimpse of fatherhood through the pages of his next novel. The idea appealed to him, although it probably didn't meet his mother's desire for grandchildren. Despite her best efforts at matchmaking, not one recommendation came close to improving his idyllic life. Marriage might work for others, but he had no room for the interruptions and complications. The only romance he cared to pursue appeared within the pages of his novels, dispersed in the right increments to satisfy female readers.

Alex never knew what might inspire him next, but this surprising scene pricked his mind with possibilities—perhaps a young widow struggling to survive the hardships of the depression era ....

Drawing closer, he heard the young boys talking. "Let's make a road for our cars. You be the dump truck, and I'll be the one with the scoop on front. If Daddy was here, he could be the backhoe."

"I wish he hadn't gone away."

Whining, Bailey broke free from his preoccupied master and rushed toward the pair, wagging his tail, and running in circles around the wide-eyed boys. Alex stood glued to the spot, unable to intervene even when Bailey knocked one of the boys into the sand and showered him with wet kisses. As he watched the giggly boys chase the dog around the dunes, he marveled at the effect his pet had on the children.

After the exhausted romp, they hugged Bailey between them and stroked his damp, sandy fur. "Do you think God already sent us a dog, Jonathan?

"Since Mama said we can't have another daddy, I prayed for a dog."

With the intention of claiming his dog before the boys and his pet adopted one another, Alex moved into their line of vision and approached the children. The child closest to him stopped mid-stroke, stood in slow motion, and looked with fearful confusion toward the nearby cottage. In contrast to the reception they'd given Bailey, the boy looked at Alex as if he were an intruder about to spoil their fun. The child shifted uneasily before he spoke.

"Is this your dog, Mister?"

Alex heard the longing in the child's voice and noticed the admiring look he cast Bailey's way. Though he sympathized with him, he could never give up his furry companion. To Alex's surprise, the two youngsters lingered. They continued petting the dog, ignoring the woman who now made an appearance on the porch steps. While shielding her eyes from the sun, she held fast to the railing as if needing the support.

"Yes, this is my dog Bailey. I hope he's not interrupting your play. We're out for our morning walk. Are you vacationing in the cottage?"

When Alex pointed toward the house, he noticed the mother's look of alarm and her frustrated effort to descend the few steps down to the sand. He wrinkled his brow in sympathy as she bent over and held her fat belly. She seemed unable to catch her breath.

As Alex made a move toward her, she made a quick recovery. She put her hands on her hips and glared at him. He didn't need to be a genius to get the message. Despite his intent to greet her and welcome her family to the neighborhood, he grabbed Bailey by the collar and fumbled to attach the leash. The uncooperative dog resisted confinement and barked with disapproval, but the woman's look gave him no choice. He pulled the dog along before the furious mother called the police.

The boys had no such thoughts, however. "We like Bailey, don't we, David? Can he play with us again? We won't hurt him, and he likes us, too."

"Yes, he does seem to enjoy you, but I'm afraid he's messed up your road."

"You could help us build another one. You could be the dump truck. It's the easiest."

Alex laughed at their offer as he glanced at the agitated woman and eased toward the surf. "Bailey and I live down the beach and walk this way every morning, but you need to ask your mother if it's okay for us to stop by."

"She likes dogs. If we promise to be good, I think she'll let us. Don't you, David?"

Alex hastened on up the beach wondering about the unusual encounter. Their mother may like dogs, but she didn't seem to like him. Though he could read her concern from the distance, she avoided a confrontation. He shook his head at his own cowardly actions. Perhaps he should've approached her and given her a piece of his mind for neglecting her children. At the sound of her voice calling the boys, he discontinued his ridicule and took one last look at the frightened woman. An uncharacteristic ache welled inside his chest accompanied by a deep longing, leaving him confused and annoyed.

When he passed the cottage on his way home, Alex continued to fret over the young family. An element of mystery surrounded them and their recent arrival. Were they here for a short vacation or an extended stay? Where was the father? Why were the children outside alone? It was true, they'd played within sight of the cottage, but he'd want to be with his boys. His boys? What on earth prompted him to think such thoughts and what difference did it make? He wasn't a parent and didn't plan to be. So why the sudden concern?

The unsuccessful attempt to separate fact from fiction bothered him. Whether for curiosity or research, he began plotting how he might become acquainted with this mysterious family. His earlier resolve to avoid disruptive relationships had washed away on the tide.

CHAPTER TWO

Sarah trembled as she called the children inside. Thank God, the stranger left before she had to waddle out on the beach. Though the man appeared harmless, she refused to take a chance. Scattered up and down the strand were a few large, upscale homes, but Shell Island, off the coast of North Carolina, mostly appealed to middle-income families with modest second homes. Only a handful of residents remained past Labor Day. Despite the peace and tranquility of the place, the island had its share of vagrants up to no good. She wouldn't put it past their early morning intruder to use that dog as bait. Much to her disappointment, the children acted as willing fodder.

"Why did you make us come inside? We met a man with a dog, and he's the best dog ever. Did you see him? Can we have a puppy like Bailey?"

"Slow down, Jonathan. I think you've forgotten our discussion about talking to strangers. Do you realize how scary that was for mommy?"

"I know, but he's a really nice man, and his dog's the best. He said he'd stop again and let us play with Bailey if you say it's okay."

"Well, nothing will convince me to say it's okay. You're not permitted to talk with strangers. Period. You'll have to stay inside until I find out more about the man. You guys are my family, and I'd feel terrible if something happened to either of you. No more discussion for now. Go wash your hands, and I'll make breakfast."

Jonathan, her opinionated, headstrong son, went off in a huff while his quieter twin, David, followed in compliance. If her husband, Tom, were here, he'd know what to do, but he wasn't. She'd have to face this problem alone. Sarah decided to give her mother a call after breakfast. Although she hadn't stepped foot on the island for over two years, the woman knew the residents and would help her sort things out.

Thoughts of Tom reminded Sarah of the circumstances leading to their arrival on Shell Island. Before leaving for Iraq, her husband had suggested she and the boys move into her mother's large home in Raleigh, but Leslie had refused to consider the idea, citing every possible excuse. Her mother's excuse still grated on Sarah's nerves.

"You don't understand, Tom. These last two years have been horrible, and I don't think I can deal with another change. I love my daughter and the boys, but I like the peace and quiet of an organized home. They would keep my house in a constant state of turmoil. I know that sounds selfish, and I'm sorry. Perhaps later. I still can't get over the loss of Sarah's father."

Appalled at her mother's attitude, Sarah suffered in silence until they were home. When the boys were down for naps, she ranted.

"I can't believe she said that about the boys. They aren't disruptive or noisy. Just active children who would bring a little joy to that sad house."

Anger gave way to tears as Sarah thought about Tom's leaving and her mother's rejection. Her dad had been bigger than life in their family and losing him had been difficult for her as well. Though she missed him, she tried to imagine how she would feel if forced to live without her husband. She found out soon enough.

Sarah's fantasy of an executive officer chained to a desk, far from danger, brought a measure of relief until she discovered that those same desks and their occupants were required in war-torn Iraq. A week after her husband's departure, a military car stopped in front of her Raleigh townhouse. Two Army officers from Fort Bragg destroyed her life with the dreaded news. On his return to headquarters, Tom's jeep had run into mortar fire. He had not survived.

The officers sent to deliver the news were kind and sympathetic, but Sarah didn't want their kindness or their sympathy. She only wanted the bearers of unwelcome news to disappear so she could release the fury building inside her. In that one painful moment, at the age of twenty-seven, her status changed from married to widow.

Sarah managed the arrangements and the funeral in a daze. In the days that followed, whenever someone offered comfort, she lashed out in anger, blaming the politicians, the army, and even God. No one wanted to be near her, and nothing suited her more than to be alone. The only person she longed to see had deserted her. When her tirades abated, she found herself making the early morning rush to the toilet bowl.

What a dirty trick for God to play on her! First, he took her husband, and then left her with not two, but three children to raise—alone. Not long into the pregnancy, the doctor discovered an additional heartbeat. Now there would be four mouths to feed. Sarah went from a thankful heart to paralyzing fear and insecurity. Sorrow became a full-time companion, making her sick with grief. No matter how determined she was, she had no energy to accomplish even the simplest task.

The morning she emerged from the fog was the day she accepted her fate and the almost impossible responsibilities thrust upon her. After another sleepless night, she hauled herself downstairs in search of a cracker to settle the lingering nausea. Moving in slow motion toward the kitchen, she heard the boys talking as they poured themselves a bowl of dry cereal. The kitchen looked as if a tornado had come through leaving empty take-out boxes and dirty dishes in its wake. Not noticing her in the doorway, the boys continued their discussion about *her*.

"We need to pray for Mama. She's sad cause Daddy's not coming home. She misses him."

"But she said he's in heaven. Maybe God will let him come back sometime to see us. That should make Mama happy. If we pray real hard and be real quiet maybe he'll come soon. I miss him too."

Sarah couldn't stand to hear another sad word. She slipped back upstairs and fell to her knees. Neglecting herself and the house didn't bother her, but that she'd disregarded her most precious possessions shamed her. After a sincere prayer of repentance and a quick fix up in the bathroom, she returned to the kitchen and joined her boys in a conversation more focused on her children than herself. Her anger with God evaporated when she ceased dwelling on the loss and remembered to be thankful for what remained.

After she had met with the military representatives, Sarah had realized the entitlements assigned widows fell far short of Tom's meager salary. As much as she disliked moving, she and the children couldn't afford their townhouse near her mother.

When the lease expired, and her mother continued to resist sharing her home, Sarah had no choice but to move to her parents' vacation home on the island. Despite her mother's strong objections to returning to the shore, Sarah was surprised when her mother made the generous offer. Since her father had died, her mother panicked at the thought of even crossing the bridge to Shell Island. Too many happy memories stolen by death waited on the other side.

The jangle of the telephone interrupted Sarah's preoccupation with the past. "Mother, I'm glad you called. How are you?"

After a few minutes of routine chatter, Sarah remembered her earlier concern and relayed the incident to her mother. "Do you know anyone who fits that description?"

"Although it's a bit out of character, he sounds a lot like Alex Caine, your neighbor to the south. He's a reclusive, but harmless, author, and according to his mother, he takes early morning walks with his dog."

From there, her mother's conversation became disjointed into something unreal. "He'd be a good catch for someone if that individual happened to be interested. My book club chooses his latest historical fiction as soon as it's available. I haven't heard from his mother lately, but I know she speaks highly of him. Besides, his parents are wonderful Christians."

"Don't go there, Mother. I'm glad his parents are believers, but that doesn't mean he is. Regardless, Tom remains very much alive in my heart. He's only been gone a few months, and you're already trying to find me a husband? I can't believe you'd even suggest such a thing. Besides, do you really think his own mother would give him a poor recommendation?"

"You're too young to be single forever, Sarah. I realize it's way too early to consider another man, but I only wish for you to be happy."

"I know, Mother, but I doubt a reclusive author would be interested in me."

She hung up and thought again about the dangers on the island. When they had first arrived, and she'd noticed the high, pounding waves in the distance, Sarah had set strict boundaries. The boys could play near the house provided they stayed within her sight. If she didn't feel up to going out with them, she'd watch from the porch. In all the scenarios, however, she never considered that someone would leave the beach, walk between the dunes, and approach her children.

CHAPTER THREE

As Sarah mulled over her mother's favorable recommendation, she recalled a conversation with the boys a few nights before. They were donning their pajamas when Jonathan looked at her with the most serious expression. "Mommy, David and me want a daddy to play with us."

As Sarah saw the longing on her little boys' faces, she tried to hide the shock and disappointment on her own. "I know you miss your daddy. He loved playing with you and giving horsey rides, but you know he's now in heaven. When the new babies arrive and are old enough, Mommy will play on the beach with all of you. You can help me with your brothers or sisters. Won't that be fun?"

"But the babies will tear up our sand castles and roads, and you're not a daddy. We need a daddy." Jonathan continued to argue in defiance while David stood nearby, nodding his agreement.

"Since God took our daddy away, we're going to ask him to bring us another one."

"You know, boys, God doesn't always give us what we want."

They both thought for another moment or two. Then Jonathan replied, "Well, can we have a dog then?"

Sarah marveled at her son's persistence. "I'll think about the dog, but not right now. Mommy doesn't feel well, and you should be grateful that we're here together. You know a dog is a lot of work."

"We can take care of him. Can't we, David?" Her excited son jumped up and down as he envisioned a dream come true.

"I know you will, but we must wait until after the babies are born to consider a dog. By then, I'll feel much better. Do you think you can wait?"

Jonathan lowered his head as if he'd lost all hope until another idea surfaced. "We could pray for you to get better like you pray for us."

Before Sarah could answer, Jonathan and David bounded over and put their hands on her head. "Dear Jesus, heal our mommy so she can play with us, and please give us a daddy. We need one so-o-o much. If you can't get the daddy, could you help us find a good dog? Help those babies come out of Mommy's tummy soon, and I hope they won't be a lot of trouble. In Jesus name, Amen."

Sarah turned away from her boys as she wiped the tears clouding her vision. She cleared her throat and changed the subject before they noticed her own sadness. "Before you go to bed, I want you to pick up all your toys. That would be a tremendous help to Mommy."

The boys scrambled to do her bidding. If she remembered correctly, surprise visits were a regular occurrence with the full-time island residents. Regardless, she preferred a bit of order—the one thing she could reasonably control in her chaotic life. Although others might not appreciate the intrusion, she longed for adult conversation over a cup of coffee. The problem with that scenario was she didn't know the first person on the island and hadn't been anywhere to encourage future friendships.

As for the boys, she prayed that God would meet their needs, both emotional and physical, but she would not remarry only to satisfy their desire for a "Daddy." Furthermore, what man would want to be encumbered with a woman with four small children?

Though the twins might be satisfied with a dog, Sarah couldn't see how to make that work. As it was, she worried about feeding and clothing her children. How could she afford the expenses of a pet? The small cottage closed in on her as she envisioned four children and a dog scuffling for space.

The boys' wakeup calls the next morning seemed more exuberant than usual. "Can we go play on the beach?" Jonathan held her face in his hands demanding an answer while David bounced steadily on a corner of the bed.

Hoping to deter them until their neighbor finished his morning stroll, Sarah said, "Why don't you wait until after breakfast? It'll be warmer by then, and perhaps I'll feel like taking a walk with you."

"We can't go later. If we don't go right now, we'll miss the nice man and his dog. He promised to let us play with Bailey."

How could Sarah compete with such an enticement? She moaned at their enthusiasm while resisting the stranger's intrusion into their lives. With the trek through the sand too much for her anyway, she gave her usual warnings and surrendered to their pleas.

Sarah grabbed a handful of crackers along with her Bible and journal and moved to a comfortable chair on the screened porch. Though she didn't feel up to trudging out with them, she would follow their every move, especially if the dog man made an appearance. *I only wish they'd given me time to make coffee before they raced out of here.*

Feeling sorry for herself and her sweet, fatherless boys, she observed her children. They laughed and played together, so happy and carefree—such a contrast to her negative attitude. *Please help me, God, and forgive me. I should be thanking you instead of complaining. The day is beautiful, and the boys love it here. Protect them from harm and give me the wisdom to teach them about you.*

Seeing the boys' pleasure brought back a bittersweet memory. Tears streamed down her face as she recalled Tom and her father playfully chasing the toddlers on the beach. An image of the boys running on their short, stubby legs, squealing with delight as they tumbled in the sand filled her memory. Perhaps the boys didn't remember their grandfather, but they would never forget those special moments with their daddy. Amid all the wonderful memories, she prayed the island would be a place of healing for both herself and her children.

Her jumbled thoughts were interrupted when Bailey made a sudden appearance and pushed Jonathan over into the soft sand. Sarah struggled to her feet, prepared to intervene when she heard her child giggle. The excited dog smothered him with wet kisses before moving on to a surprised David. The boys were soon chasing after Bailey, laughing and yelling as he darted from one to the other. She couldn't help but smile at the happiness on her children's faces.

Sarah's momentary pleasure vanished, however, when the dog's owner rounded the dune. What a shame the sweet dog couldn't show up alone. As she stewed in frustration, she saw the man's amused grin as he ruffled the boys' hair and gave them fist bumps. After his initial greeting, he stood back with his arms crossed, watching the children with Bailey.

The stylish man appeared average in height and well-built as if he worked out on a regular basis. Expensive-looking shorts and a logo sweatshirt complemented his well-tanned skin. His designer sunglasses obscured his eyes, but he had light brown hair with highlights—possibly due to the sun.

Almost as if he knew she admired him, he looked at the porch with a questioning expression. Not certain he could see her through the screen, she cringed at the thought that he might choose this time to introduce himself. In their rush to get outside, the boys hadn't given her time to change out of her nightgown and robe. She didn't think her hair had seen the brush in a while nor her teeth felt the strokes of a toothbrush. The house might be prepared for drop-ins, but not her. Far from it. *Lord, please make him move on down the beach.*

To her horror, God chose not to answer that frantic prayer. The man took one more look her way, said something to the boys, and started toward the house with them all in tow, including Bailey. The boys' expressions of happiness as they led the parade didn't outweigh the nightmare playing in real time before her eyes. If not for her concern for her children, she'd have run inside and locked the door against the presumptuous man.

Jonathan rushed ahead, burst through the screen door and proudly made the introductions, "Mama, this is our friend and his dog, Bailey. He wants to meet you."

Sarah gulped. "I'm sorry, but I'm not prepared for this. I'm not even dressed. Please, I can't meet anyone." Distraught? Awkward? Petrified? All that and even more described Sarah at such an invasion of her privacy. When talkative Jonathan looked at his mother in dismay and became speechless, his shoulders drooped along with his fading excitement. Sarah cringed at her ill manners and her child's discomfort.

The silence didn't linger, however. Though Sarah couldn't move, the man didn't seem the least offended as he stood holding the open door. He ignored her discomfort, removed his sunglasses and approached her with an outstretched hand.

"Good Morning, Mrs. ..." He cocked his head, waiting for the speechless woman to fill in the blank.

Glued to her chair, Sarah could only stare at the handsome stranger. She couldn't help comparing his good grooming to her recently-tumbled-from-bed look. The man looked as if he'd just completed a beachfront shoot for *GQ*. Surely, he must realize her embarrassment.

When she didn't physically or verbally respond, he continued, "I'm your neighbor, Alex Caine. I don't mean to disturb your morning, and I understand your reluctance, but I must talk with you about your children."

Stunned, Sarah didn't have a coherent thought in her head as her assertive visitor continued, "I don't want you to think that I have inappropriate intentions toward your boys. Though I don't have children of my own, I've always been interested in people of all ages and your children are certainly fascinating. They're twins, aren't they?"

With only a slight hesitation, her visitor plowed ahead even though Sarah's tongue refused to cooperate. "I've never seen Bailey so excited as yesterday when he heard the children on the beach. When the three met, it was almost as if they belonged together. If you approve, I thought I'd stop by a few minutes each morning and give the boys some time with Bailey. Do you think that would be agreeable, Mrs. ...?"

Sarah tried to focus on what the man said as he rubbed his scruffy shadow of a beard. His index finger tapped the doorframe in sync with her heartbeat. "I understand if you're uncomfortable, but you could check my references. I assure you, I mean no harm to your children."

She took a deep breath and adjusted her robe before feeling calm enough to answer. "Of course, I'm concerned, Mr. Caine. Is that your name? Although I've warned them about talking to strangers, my boys are too trusting. They couldn't seem to resist your friendly dog though. Was that part of your ploy to kidnap them, sir?"

The man ignored Sarah's accusation as a knowing smile spread across his face. The frustrated scowl he'd worn moments before now resembled a look of admiration and interest. Sarah wrinkled her brow and wondered if her visitor had been out in the sun too long. What on earth could he find attractive about a woman who resembled a beached whale?

Finally, he asked, "Is your husband with you, Mrs. ...? I would like to meet him."

When Sarah didn't answer right away, he raised his voice in frustration, "For goodness sake, Mrs. ..., can you not at least share your name? It's not as if I'm trying to accost you or steal your children."

Mr. Caine rubbed his hands through his hair leaving behind a messy hairdo that looked even more appealing. "Forget it. I probably don't need more complications in my life anyway. But if I were you, I'd return to civilization soon so that baby isn't delivered on the dunes."

Sarah cringed as Mr. Caine turned to leave, obviously frustrated by her lack of cooperation—probably a first for a man unfamiliar with a woman's rejection.

"My name is Sarah, Sarah Stuart."

At the sound of her voice, the man turned around, shook his head in disbelief and gave a frustrated sigh. Sarah watched his exasperated expression as he ran his fingers through his hair. He was probably pondering whether to let his anger go or go himself. He peered at her through narrow eyes and in the next instant, the confident, arrogant man who'd insisted on an audience with her had reappeared.

His good humor returned with the distraction of her giggly children hugging his pet.

"My boys are Jonathan and David, and they're quite taken with your dog."

Mr. Caine chuckled as they jumped back and forth to avoid the excited swats from the canine's tail. "As you can see, Bailey is also fond of them. He won't be satisfied with my company after that little romp with your boys."

After his comment, the man lowered his gaze and rubbed a hand over his beard. Sarah fidgeted in the uncomfortable silence until he turned sad eyes toward her. "I'm so sorry, Mrs. Stuart. I can't believe I barged in on you like I did. I've upset you, and that wasn't my intention."

Though Sarah agreed that her new neighbor owed her an apology, she liked him and wanted to put him at ease. "I'm sorry, too. Please forgive my distrust, sir, but my boys are about all I have left of the wonderful life I'd planned. You see, my husband died in Iraq a few months ago, and I don't think I'll ever recover. I'm living here in my mother's house quite legitimately, if that's your concern."

"No concern there, Mrs. Stuart. Please accept my condolences on your loss. That must be difficult for you and the children. I don't wish to increase your stress. The boys seem excited to be with my dog, but I don't want to stop without your permission. Would you mind?"

He sounded sincere, but Sarah remained guarded. "Yes, I guess that would be okay. You and Bailey may visit with the boys on your walks, but please don't encourage them to leave my sight. I must know they're safe."

Her ire returned as she remembered his cautionary remark about her delivery plans. She rubbed her belly. "And don't concern yourself about when I'll leave the island or where I'll have my baby, Mr. Caine. I have a qualified midwife to airlift me to a mainland hospital, if necessary. Will that give you peace of mind concerning my delivery on the dunes?"

Sarah looked away and bit her tongue at the sarcastic retort coming from her mouth. Thank goodness, the boys had gone inside to get a ball and didn't hear. When she heard the man laughing, she glared back at him, more furious than ever.

"I'm glad you're enjoying my discomfort, Mr. Caine."

The words were barely out of her mouth when Alex knelt before her. Surprised by his invasion of her personal space, she retreated as far back into the chair as possible. With her temper rising, she prepared to give him a piece of her mind when his smile faded to a look of distress.

"Please forgive my rude remark about your pregnancy. I don't know what possessed me. I'm sorry for upsetting you, but I wanted to make certain we have permission to spend time with the boys. You have wonderful children, and you should be proud of them." He paused and chuckled under his breath as the children hurried past with Bailey. "I would buy them their own puppy, but I'm certain you don't need additional responsibility. Thank you for agreeing to my short visits. I'll try to earn your trust."

Sarah stiffened, afraid to breathe lest she touch him, but as quickly as he'd knelt, he stood. There was that annoying look of admiration—again.

"If you require assistance with anything, call me. I live down the beach and will be happy to help."

He retrieved a card for her from his shorts pocket and waved goodbye as he called Bailey from his game of catch. The disappointed boys stood with drooping faces and watched the departure of their new playmate.

With her emotions on edge and confusion rendering her speechless, Sarah struggled from her chair to watch the man and his dog saunter toward the beach. Unable to control her fragile feelings, she burst into tears—tears she hadn't shed since coming to the island. How could this arrogant, pushy individual transform into a caring, understanding man after the way she treated him?

The attention and kindness of her neighbor brought back memories of Tom. Sarah could almost feel her husband's presence, whispering words of encouragement and love. Though she longed for his strong embrace, she was resigned to accept a life without his comfort.

What is happening to my resolve? How can a man reduce me to tears with a few kind words? And how could she compare him to Tom? Nothing about Alex Caine resembled her husband, and she wouldn't allow her wayward thoughts to continue. Sarah had responsibilities, and despite her out-of-control hormones, she intended to meet them without Tom or any other compassionate man who happened along. She looked at his card again and tossed it on the table. Alex Caine would be the last person she'd call. She didn't want his sympathy or his charity.

Sarah took a few slow breaths and fanned her flaming face with a magazine. Her mind returned to the neighbor's request and the pleasure his dog brought the boys. Perhaps Bailey would be the answer to their desire for a pet. They could enjoy him for a brief time on the beach each morning without the added expense and responsibility. That first, disastrous encounter with the dog's owner should've been enough to negate further interest. She shook her head in disbelief as she replayed the most confusing, irrational conversation ever.

Before she dismissed him completely, she remembered her neighbor's appearance when he invaded her space. Although he was not nearly as handsome as her husband, she saw an awareness, a sensitivity as he studied her with searching blue eyes. He had that rugged look with his strong jaw and shadow of a beard. Any casual shopper would recognize his distinctive image smiling from the covers of magazines at the grocery store. She understood why his fans considered him a catch and wondered why he wasn't married.

Instead of the eligible bachelor, Sarah would've preferred a visit from one of her friends from Fort Bragg, but deployments had uprooted and scattered them throughout the country. In her present state, she dreaded even the thought of leaving the house. The last few months had been a whirlwind that left her floundering. If she could only survive the next few weeks, then perhaps she would look for a new church community where she might find supportive friendships.

Sarah's musings ended with an unexplainable longing to be held and comforted. Not only had the man put ideas into the heads of her sons, but his nearness made her miss the love and intimacy of a spouse. Even God felt as far away as her beloved husband.

CHAPTER FOUR

Alex's life was ruined. He hadn't produced a creative thought in weeks. His daily walks proved fruitless. Unless the weather kept them inside, those toddler boys met him on the beach and interrupted his morning stroll along with his peace and concentration. Like powerful magnets, they drew him into their miniature world. He regretted the unproductive hours but marveled at the joy and pleasure the children generated.

No longer the casual observer, he became one of them—building roads, castles, and moats. They assigned him a dump truck complete with a front loader and welcomed him into their realm of make-believe. In New York, he was forced to socialize with the rich and famous. Here, he eagerly chose the company of a couple of youngsters.

The boys impressed him with the way they played together and the extent of their imaginations. Their ingenuity held him captive as he tried to remember a similar time from his childhood. The lack of such memories bothered him and prompted him toward a serious discussion with his mother.

"Tell me something, Jonathan. Are you and your brother named after someone in your family?"

Jonathan huffed as if Alex should have known the answer. "Mama and Daddy named us after Jonathan and David in the Bible 'cause they were good friends."

Since David generally gave preference to his brother, the boy surprised him by adding, "And Mama says that friends stick closer than brothers. So, we're brothers and friends. Don't you think that's a good idea, Mr. Alex?"

The children said little without bringing God into the conversation. Their names and the idea of picking them from a Bible story stirred his interest and curiosity. The story of David and Jonathan sounded vaguely familiar from attending Sunday School as a child. Perhaps the neglected Bible he'd received from his mother would provide the answer. The boys talked about the Book as if it represented a great deal more than a few fictitious stories.

One day when Alex joined the boys, David gave him a studied look. "Mr. Alex, do you think we could build heaven? Did you know my daddy's up there?"

Reluctantly, Alex played along. As far as he surmised, heaven signified a place Christians dreamed up when they weren't happy with their earthly life. Since he considered himself well satisfied, he didn't require an imaginary crutch.

"Mommy says that Daddy is looking down on us. Is heaven a beautiful place, Mr. Alex?"

Alex hesitated in search of a reasonable answer. Even though he refused to believe the myth himself, he preferred not to confuse his little friend. Unless, of course, he wanted an excuse to infuriate their over-protective mother.

After a few gulps to hide his discomfort, he finally responded. "My mother used to tell me that heaven is more beautiful than we could ever imagine. I think she mentioned streets of gold and gates of pearl. Sounds as though it would be hard to describe much less replicate here in the sand."

"What's *repacate* mean?"

"Replicate means trying to build something like the real thing, Jonathan. Why don't you and David explain to me how you think our heaven should look, and we'll try to find ways to build it."

The boys went to work but seemed more interested in talking than creating. "Mommy says that when we die, we get to go to heaven and be with Daddy, but that's a long time from now. I wish Daddy still lived with us and not so far away."

"I wish he did too, David. Dads are special to little boys and even to big boys like me. I really love my daddy too."

"You have a daddy, Mr. Alex? Could we meet him sometime?"

"Yes, I do. He lives in Virginia. The next time he comes for a visit, I'll introduce you."

"Do you have any children?"

"No, Jonathan. I'm not married. You should have a wife before you have children."

"Our mommy doesn't have a husband. Maybe you could marry her and be our daddy. We need a daddy down here, and we like you. You could make her happy again."

"And if you were our daddy, Bailey could be our dog. 'Member, Jonathan, how we told mommy we wanted a daddy or a dog? This way we could have both." David stroked the affectionate dog.

David and Jonathan had it all figured out. Fortunately, before Alex could respond to their enthusiastic plans, their mother called them inside for breakfast. At his cue to exit, they once again invited him to stay. He winced as he imagined the inevitable conversation around the table. No desire to be included trumped the relief at his escaping such a scene.

Although the boys could be quite convincing, and the mother tempting in more ways than one, he refused to entertain such a proposal. Not only would their idea not benefit him, but a relationship would also bring disruptions of catastrophic proportions. They had already disturbed his peaceful, quiet life more than should be allowed, which reminded him of his original resolution: to remain single. Regardless of what he thought, the appealing, but uncooperative mother would no doubt agree.

Alex chuckled to himself when he remembered his first and only meeting with Mrs. Stuart. Uncomfortable didn't begin to describe her. Throughout their conversation, she adjusted her oversized robe and struggled without success to control her curly, messy hair. From a distance, he'd thought her overweight, but in her presence, the enormous bulge almost rendered him speechless. He couldn't look away.

Alex couldn't believe how he had treated her. He'd first considered her an overweight negligent parent, and then he intruded on her early morning privacy. He cringed at the rude remark about her pregnancy. The woman's sad story of losing her husband filled him with deep compassion, causing his protective instincts to surface. He wanted to rescue her or at least make her life easier. Despite her disheveled appearance, those sparkling green eyes, and the fine lines of her face outlined by a profusion of messy blond hair captivated him. Her vulnerability and love for her children appealed to him in a way he'd never imagined. Mostly, he admired her courage and fortitude as she faced the birth of yet another child without the love and support of a husband. The woman seemed determined to make the best of her circumstances. Illogical as it was, he felt drawn to her in a way he'd never been attracted to other women.

Although the boys considered him a friend and a "prospective daddy," their mother exhibited signs of distrust, apparent even from a distance. He laughed as his imagination caricatured her like a mama bear. She never left the porch when he played with the boys but watched him with intensity. At the first wrong move, she'd have come flying, lashing him with her sharp tongue.

Perhaps afraid he might approach her again, Mrs. Stuart appeared more groomed when she nervously opened the screen door to call the boys inside. If he didn't feel so drawn to her family, he would've ended the unusual relationship long before. But for some reason, he couldn't seem to escape the awkward situation.

Out of consideration for the young mother's concerns, he often cut the play time short. She had his phone number, and if she required assistance, she could call. Her independent streak, however, would likely keep her from relying on him or anyone else, for that matter.

In the meantime, he had more important business to consider as he struggled to come up with material for a new book. His agent, Lori Sharp, pressed him daily for the outline, overdue by a few weeks, and he didn't have the first idea on paper. He dreaded her next phone call that would again find him groping for a plausible excuse. *God help me!*

Alex's spontaneous prayer gave him pause. He hadn't thought about God since junior high when he attended church with his parents. Could he be mimicking his little playmates? Every few sentences were interspersed with some religious nonsense gleaned from their mother. He wondered about the Bible in her lap the morning he met her on the porch. No doubt she ranked up there with other religious fanatics who thought that little Book possessed all the answers.

The idea annoyed him, but he didn't care. His mother also kept religion front and center. She too believed the words written in that erroneous Book and loved her church and neighborhood Bible studies. "Living her faith," she called it. Despite his mother's strong influence, he'd never embraced the idea for himself. As a teen, he'd debated almost nightly with his parents and had finally concluded God didn't exist, and church attendance was a waste of valuable time. Although he'd studied the Bible from various perspectives, he viewed the Book as fiction with perhaps some historical facts thrown into the mix. Sort of like his novels, come to think of it.

Alex's mother had called the night before, wanting to know if something happened. She said God awakened her in the middle of the night to pray for him. After asking the usual, "Are you sick? Are you sleeping well? How's the book coming along?" She tackled the main reason for her call. "Have you met anyone special lately?"

"*No. No. No.* and *Yes.*" The pitch and volume of his voice rose with each curt response. "What do you want me to say, Mother? If I can't figure this out myself, how are you going to help?" He hated that he came across unreasonable and rude, but he didn't appreciate her interference into his spiritual life or his marital status. Somehow, he'd regain control and stop this gradual downward spiral. His mother aggravated him when she insisted God awakened her or told her something, especially when it concerned him. He refused to acknowledge anyone who notified his mother concerning his life.

"I didn't call to help, son. I only wanted to know how to pray for you. Thank you for being honest with me, and when do we get to meet the young lady? I haven't seen any rumors about a new affair."

Alex refused to get into this with his mother, or anyone else for that matter, so he avoided her question and ended the call. Over the last few years, he'd become an expert at dodging questions, especially when they related to God or women.

After he hung up, he couldn't suppress the thought, *Boy would she ever be in for a surprise if I did introduce her to my elusive, beautiful neighbor.* He could just hear the conversation. "You're a widow with two children? Pregnant with a third?" His mother would think he'd lost his mind. The fact that the woman had a strong Christian faith would please her, but that bit of information was Alex's primary objection to the otherwise attractive Mrs. Stuart. He didn't need another woman pushing religion down his throat.

Alex couldn't understand why he acted so obsessed with the woman. His typical dates included classy models, celebrities, or Wall Street executives. Not one of them claimed to be a Christian, nor were they pregnant with toddlers in tow. Only the fact he loved his mother enabled him to tolerate her God talk, and if her children were any indication, Sarah Stuart believed something similar. Besides, he didn't know her, and she didn't know him or show any interest in getting to know him. Why should he waste his time and energy even considering the complicated woman?

Rain came in a slow drizzle the next morning, preventing his usual walk. Bailey made a quick visit to the doggy run on the side of the house and hurried back inside dripping wet. He managed to spray water all over the lower level mudroom before Alex could towel him off. To keep the peace with Anna, his housekeeper, Alex confined Bailey to his kennel.

Anna came after lunch each weekday, straightened the massive house, shopped for groceries and supplies, and prepared Alex's dinner before she left for the day. Once a week, she supervised the crew he hired for a more thorough cleaning of the four levels. Fate had apparently given him yet another of those God talk people. Anna couldn't carry on a conversation without throwing in something religious.

"Praise the Lord for the rain!" or "Look at this beautiful day. God is so good." Sometimes, "Thank you, God, for this wonderful job and for Alex who's so good to me." God had nothing to do with any of it. Finding Anna was a stroke of luck. His ambition and successful career provided the salary for the "wonderful job."

The line that disturbed him most went something like, "Alex, I'm praying God's blessings on you. Someday he will use you to bless others." A bunch of poppycock, if he ever heard it! The only one who would bless him would be Alex Caine or Stephen Jacobs—the writer Alex masqueraded as when he left the island. Despite his aversion to the subject, he fiddled away the entire day rehearsing his spiritual conversations with his mother, Anna, and now, two sweet little boys. All people he had come to know, respect, and love.

The rain moved out by the following day, and the elusive sun of the day before crept over the horizon. The air felt a bit crisp for the second week of October, but Alex and his dog were back on their walk. Bailey wasted no time finding his buddies and raced ahead anxious to play. Despite the appealing morning, Alex resisted the idea of interacting with anyone. Instead, he slumped onto the sand and mulled over his situation. Why did he feel so antisocial and discontent? Although the boys were happy with

Bailey, they tried numerous times to engage him in both conversation and activity.

David left his brother a few feet away and leaned against Alex's shoulder. "Are you sad, Mr. Alex?"

"No, David, I'm just not up to playing today. Thank you for asking, though."

"Maybe you need Jesus to help you. Mommy says he'll be our friend and help us when we feel sad. You should ask him to be your friend."

"Perhaps I should. I'll think about it. How's your mother?"

"She's okay."

David shrugged and gave the usual answer to Alex's persistent inquiries. The boys could talk all day about building roads, heavy construction equipment, and sand castles, but nothing concrete about their mother unless it concerned her lack of a husband and their need of a daddy. The uncomfortable subject often surfaced in their conversation along with imagining their father up in heaven. They even interspersed their fantasies with God, angels, and stories from the Bible.

This time, however, David came too close to invading Alex's comfort zone. He refused to discuss his spiritual condition with anyone, much less a child. Disliking the irritable feelings and his inability to glean anything new regarding their mother, he stood to escape further torture.

"I'm glad your mother is well. When you go in for breakfast, tell her I asked about her. Right now, Bailey and I must go. I'll see you tomorrow."

Two sad, bewildered youngsters stared after him as he forced Bailey onto his leash and made a quick exit. Despite the pain to his bare feet, Alex kicked every scattered shell that crossed his path on his way home. He could worry as well in the solitude of his study, a place he'd recently come to despise. *God help me.* Once more he caught himself in prayer to a God he refused to acknowledge. What had those children done to him?

Alex now thought of the boys' mother by her given name and dreamed about her often. Sometimes the dream took the form of a nightmare. She screamed for him, and as if his legs were rendered immovable, he couldn't get to her. The uneasy feeling the dreams invoked made him wonder if he shouldn't go away, at least until she delivered her child or left the island with her little preaching crew.

After Alex showered and changed, he settled himself in the upper-floor study with the intention of outlining a book idea. Unable to focus, he paced the floor debating the feasibility of various plots. Alex worried about his state of mind. He despised the unproductivity but had little or no concentration to write the first sentence. The ache he felt as he rubbed his chest didn't help. Thoughts of Sarah had escalated into a nagging worry. Not merely concern, but obsession with a woman he knew only through her young sons.

His thoughts were interrupted, however, when frantic screaming sent waves of fear up and down his spine. From the floor-length window, he searched the area and caught sight of David running from the beach.

Alex kept his eye on the child as he rushed down the four flights of steps on the outside decking. He didn't stop until David sobbed in his arms. After a few comforting words and reassuring gestures, he was able to calm the hysterical boy enough to understand what he was saying.

"You've got to come help Mama. She's bleeding all over the floor, and we can't wake her up."

A chill ran through Alex as he visualized the child's description. "After you left, we didn't see Mommy on the porch. We can't play outside unless she's watching, so we went to find her."

She must have been in pain, or she wouldn't have left the porch. What if she'd gone inside knowing he would be with the boys? Had she trusted him for the first time? Alex continued berating himself for his self-centered ruminations as he gathered the child in his arms and entered the house. He grabbed his keys by the garage door, threw the boy into the rear seat, and quickly backed the SUV out of the garage.

Between sniffles, David protested. "Mama says the car doesn't move until everyone is buckled up and this belt doesn't even fit me."

"It's okay, David. Just buckle it the best you can. We have to get to your mother."

Alex took the steps to the front door of the cottage two at a time. Locked. In frustration, he slapped the door with his hand. Jumping off the end of the porch, he sprinted around back.

"Sarah," Alex called as he entered the house through the screen porch. The only response was a faint whimpering. David followed Alex to the front bedroom where they found Jonathan on the floor with his arm around his mother. His eyes were red and swollen from crying. Jonathan slumped against the bed when he saw Alex. "You came."

Blood soaked the carpet near Sarah's head. Alex placed two fingers on her neck. If there were a pulse would he be able to feel it? He relaxed a little when he saw the rise and fall of her chest. Retrieving his cell phone, he called 911.

"Yes. My neighbor fell and hit her head. She's pregnant, but I don't think she's in labor." When the operator asked for the address, Alex had to run outside in search of the house number. Most of the additional questions, he was unable to answer. How would he know how far along the woman was?

After he disconnected the call, his thoughts turned to the boys who watched their mother in wide-eyed fear. "It's going to be all right, boys. She'll regain consciousness soon and be fine. In the meantime, please play out on the screened porch."

"Can we have something to eat?"

"How about a glass of milk and a few cookies?"

When Anna arrived at one o'clock, he'd ask her to pick up the boys and feed them lunch. He couldn't think beyond getting them settled and waiting for the ambulance.

"Mommy doesn't like it when we eat cookies before meals."

"It'll be okay this time, Jonathan. I should stay with your mother until the paramedics arrive. I won't be able to make breakfast. Will you be responsible young men for me? Can I trust you out here by yourselves?"

Streaks of tears marred the faces of the distressed children who seemed relieved that someone would take care of their mother. Alex's nightmare had become a reality.

CHAPTER FIVE

Alex returned to the bedroom but stopped at the threshold. "I can do this," he prompted himself as he watched the injured woman. Sarah had regained consciousness, but she moaned and held her head as she struggled to get up.

When she saw Alex standing in the doorway, panic filled her eyes, and she gave a frightened scream. "It's okay, Mrs. Stuart. I'm your neighbor, Alex Caine."

Alex watched her terror-filled expression give way to relief. "Oh, Mr. Caine. Thank God, you're here. You said you'd help me, and I need you right now. Please don't stand there gawking. I can't do this on my own."

Alex hesitated, then stammered as the frantic woman pulled herself into a fetal position and gave a muffled cry. "What in the world? Mrs. Stuart?"

"*Oh, God, this is awful.* I'm in labor. It's too soon, and it's happening fast. I don't suppose you ever delivered a baby? Well, you're about to deliver two. Here, please help me up before another pain hits."

Before Alex could leave the threshold, the woman cried out with another pain. He reluctantly moved into action. After a couple of awkward movements, he scooped her from the floor and rushed toward the bed. Even before he released her, she stiffened, and he felt her stomach tighten against his abdomen. She panted and held her stomach while he pulled the covers from under her. In between the muffled screams and erratic breathing, the orders flew from her mouth like an angry sergeant. He would rather stand back and watch the scene unfold, but her desperate directives kept him moving.

In his confusion, Alex looked around the room and tried to focus on her incoherent instructions. "Go boil some water and sterilize the kitchen scissors. No. Don't wait for the water to boil, throw in the scissors, and hurry back."

As Alex made his way into the unfamiliar kitchen, he scratched his head and struggled to make sense of the crazy morning. A sharp pain made its way up his spine and settled in the back of his neck and shoulders. He didn't want to be here. If not for the urgency of the situation, he'd walk out the door and flee to his sanctuary down the beach.

Alex pawed through every messy drawer until he felt like dumping them one by one in the middle of the kitchen floor. He looked up in frustration and noticed a knife holder sitting on the counter. He slapped his forehead when he realized the elusive scissors were in plain view. Alex leaned against the counter and took deep breaths, trying to remember his next order of business. *The pot for boiling water.* With another search of the cabinets, he completed his task and returned to Sarah's side.

Alex's voice sounded shaky and hesitant as he made a feeble attempt to calm and reassure Sarah. "The EMTs should be here shortly. I'll do what I can in the meantime."

In the past, he'd endured stressful situations with confidence and self-control but never anything like this. *Two babies?* Surely, he'd misunderstood. Alex scratched his head in disbelief. What on earth would she do with two more children?

Alex stewed as he longed for some competent person to free him from this nightmare. In his wildest imagination, he could never conceive such a scenario, especially with himself as the main character. Seeing Sarah falling apart had him seriously worried. With each painful contraction, her body seemed to grow weaker. What would he do if she didn't have the strength to deliver her babies? What if no one came? *Oh, God, help us!*

At each short lull, Sarah pulled irrationally at her clothing. "Here, let me help you. What are you trying to do?"

"These clothes. Get them off me. A gown. I need my gown."

"Where, Sarah? Where's a gown?"

"I don't know. Top drawer, somewhere. Please hurry. I can't stand the pain."

Sarah continued tugging at her oversized shirt while Alex frantically tossed clothes around the chest searching for the missing gown. When he looked her way again, he almost choked. In her exhaustion, she'd collapsed on the pillows, holding her clothes in a frail attempt to hide her exposed body. Tears ran down her face. Never had he wanted to gather a person in his arms, calm her fears, and relieve her pain as he did at this moment.

Alex cleared his throat and searched for an appropriate response. If doctors could look past unclothed bodies, he'd put aside his embarrassment and focus on her stressed, but beautiful face.

Sarah had a faraway look in her eyes as she stared past him. "What am I going to do? Where are you, Tom Stuart, when I need you? You left me with all this responsibility. I can't do it alone. *Oh, God, please help me. You're all I have left.*"

She fixed her gaze on Alex. "Why are you standing there as if you're about to faint. I don't like this either, but you're the only one here. You're going to have to help me."

Her demanding attitude got the best of Alex. The compassion he'd felt moments before disappeared in a rush of anger and resentment. How did he find himself in such an awkward situation?

"What happened to the wonderful midwife who promised to keep you from having the babies on the beach? Why would a woman in advanced pregnancy come to this secluded area in the first place? And where is this wonderful God of yours?"

Sarah burst into tears. Between sobs, she tried to explain, "The midwife went away for the weekend. I felt fine when she called on Friday, and I'm not due for another three weeks and why am I explaining this to you? *Oh, God, help me. This is awful.*"

Alex watched as she moaned and arched through another wave of pain, and then forced herself to return to the determined young mother. "We don't have time to argue, Alex. Go wash your hands with the antibacterial soap in the bathroom. Hurry."

Alex slumped his shoulders and gave an exaggerated sigh as he left to comply with Sarah's wishes. What else could he do? As his compassionate heart resurfaced, his rattled, creative mind could think of but one thing: *Boy, is this great material for my next book.* No sooner had the irrational, unsympathetic thought entered his mind than he gasped in horror. Sarah needed him, and he had to focus no matter how much he'd rather be elsewhere.

When he returned to the room, Sarah looked miserable. She sobbed into the bundle of cast-off clothes she held in her arms. "Please hold me."

That he could do. He'd been dreaming of this for the last month. She obviously visualized him as the deceased husband, but he welcomed the momentary pleasure. He sat on the bed beside her and pulled her toward him. She fit perfectly against him until his wayward mind pictured her unclothed body. Unfortunate timing, indeed.

While he struggled to control the physical attraction, Sarah arched her back and pushed him away. "The baby's coming. Go catch him. Why are you sitting here? The EMTs aren't coming. Help me."

In an instant, Sarah transformed from a needy, sweet beauty to a beast of the worst kind. When she pulled her legs wide apart and pushed furiously, he screamed at her. "No, Sarah. You cannot do this to me. Please wait for somebody who knows what they're doing. What happened to all those hours of intense labor and controlled breathing, and where are those medics anyway?"

"The babies won't wait, Alex. You're all I have, and you must help me," she groaned.

Alex couldn't move. He couldn't think. For the first time in his life, he felt lost. Amid the confusion and hopelessness, strange words came to mind. *Look to me.* The command came with such authority, no explanation was necessary.

Oh, God, please. If that's you, I need you right this moment. I can't do this. The prayer may have been desperate, but he was dead serious.

Almost immediately, he stopped shaking, and a peaceful calm filled the small bedroom. For the first time since he'd arrived, he felt capable of the task thrust upon him. He bravely moved between Sarah's legs in time to see a little bald head emerge from the birth canal. With Sarah's next push, the tiny, wet thing slipped into his hands so fast he almost dropped her. The slimy infant screamed with displeasure at finding herself thrown so quickly into unfamiliar territory.

Alex cried in relief as he wiped some of the mucus from her face and wrapped her in a blanket found stacked on the dresser. As he held the tiny child, his emotions gave way to joyful laughter that bubbled from deep within his chest. An unfamiliar presence filled the room and immersed him in peace and love. He had participated in a miracle. *Is it possible that God orchestrated this whole scenario to prove himself to me?*

As he cuddled the sweet baby, Sarah interrupted. "Don't take her far. She's still attached."

"What?"

Alex opened the blanket and saw the umbilical cord binding the baby to her mother. "What am I supposed to do about that?"

"Bring her to me while you grab the scissors."

Alex laid the baby on Sarah's tummy and did as she asked. He searched the entire kitchen before finding a pair of tongs but failed to realize the effect of boiling water on metal. In his haste, he reached for the scissors with his bare hands. A few painful howls later, he gathered his supplies and returned for additional instructions.

Sarah explained how to tie the cord in two places and cut between them. After he checked the baby over and assumed his work was finished, Sarah cried out with another excruciating pain. "The other baby's coming!"

"What are you talking about?"

Hidden beneath the frantic orders, he remembered her mentioning twins. How did he transform so quickly from relaxed, quiet author to novice obstetrician? He took a deep breath and prayed for strength. When he felt his body relax and the courage to continue, he looked around the room, surprised at the sudden calm.

"Alex," Sarah panted. "We aren't done here. Please put the baby in the crib and go wash your hands."

A few pants and smothered screams later, a second little girl slipped into his arms. This time, he tied and cut the cord without Sarah's direction.

After a few moments, Sarah called out again. "Please, help me."

What on earth could be wrong now? Her whole body buckled in pain as she massaged her swollen abdomen. *Surely, not triplets? When would this ordeal end?*

"You are *NOT* having another baby, Sarah. I forbid it!"

What happened to his quiet, serene life? He preferred the dramas of his imagination—not this real-life spectacle. She shooed him to the foot of the bed where a glob of blood appeared. The placenta. "Ugh. What a mess."

With the babies snuggled together in their crib, Alex wrapped a sheet around Sarah and helped her into the bathroom. Back in the bedroom, he searched again for the nightgown. He found one in a basket of clean laundry along with fresh sheets, which he used to remake the bed.

Alex knocked on the bathroom door. "Sarah, are you okay? I found your gown."

"Could you hand it to me? I'm fine."

Alex cracked the door enough to pass the garment to her and waited in case she needed him. When Sarah finally opened the door, she collapsed.

"It's okay. I've got you." Alex lifted her into his arms and carried her to the clean bed. Not only the physical attraction but admiration for her courage and strength hit him full force. He felt as if his body would explode and burn if he didn't control his emotions. He hurried to remove her from his arms and hide her tempting body under the sheet and blanket.

"What are you doing, Alex? Get some of this cover off. Are you trying to smother me?"

"No. Merely protecting your modesty. I'm not used to all this nudity. You are way too attractive you know."

"Are you kidding me? You're blushing? I've read the supermarket tabloids. You seem to have an affair of some sort going all the time. What is it with you, Alex Caine?"

"I know it looks that way, but my parents taught me to respect women, and I've never had the desire to play around as those articles suggest. I can honestly say, this is the closest to intimacy I've ever been."

"Well, you're certainly the exception these days. I appreciate your concern, but please take off the blanket. The sheet and nightgown will be fine."

"So, you were checking up on me in the rag magazines, huh? I wouldn't think you'd waste your time on such nonsense. Am I that appealing to you, Mrs. Stuart?" Alex needed something to lighten the mood and teasing Sarah seemed to work.

"Don't flatter yourself. My sole interest was whether you were really on the up and up. Can't have my boys spending time with some weirdo."

"Well, you satisfied your curiosity. Did I meet with your approval? I told you I'd give you references—legitimate ones."

"You'll do. Will you help me wash the babies?"

Alex liked holding the babies, but he wasn't sure about bathing them. "Are you certain you're up to that. Couldn't they wait until you've rested a bit?" Perhaps dragging his feet would produce the overdue emergency personnel and get him off the hook.

"The EMTs won't bathe them. We should clean them up now."

Now, the woman could read his mind? Alex muffled a protest as he filled a plastic baby bath with lukewarm water and brought it to Sarah.

With shaky hands, he held each of the fragile babies over the tub while Sarah gave them a quick bath.

"Look at her, Alex. She seems so calm after all that drama. Turn her over for me to wash her back."

When Sarah's motions slowed, Alex's attention moved from the child to the mother. Tears ran down her pale cheeks, and she looked weak with exhaustion. He offered to finish without her, but she declined, probably not trusting him with the tiny infants. He couldn't blame her. He didn't trust himself.

Alex carefully dried the baby and listened as Sarah gave him a quick lesson in applying disposable diapers. Though her instructions were thorough, he soon wished for more, along with a second set of hands. How could a freshly birthed child have that much energy?

"Do you think the girls can see me? They're following me with their eyes."

"They're merely adjusting to the light, Alex."

"Well, I choose to disagree. They're getting to know their papa."

"Perhaps you require a lesson on the birds and bees, sir. Delivering a child doesn't make you their father."

"Don't burst my bubble, Sarah. My imagination puts food on the table. Regardless, they're beautiful." He looked from one baby to the other, then to the woman across the room. "I do believe they favor their mother."

"Don't you think that's stretching it a bit. It's hard to tell this soon. They'll change a lot the first few years."

"We'll see. You look great, by the way. You'd never know you just gave birth to twins."

"I wish I could say the same for you, Mr. Caine. You look slightly frazzled." He thought he saw her wink. At least he hoped so. Given his insecurity around women, he couldn't be sure what went through their complicated heads.

Alex laid the sweet-smelling newborns next to their mother. They made little mewing noises while opening their mouths toward Sarah's breasts. Amazing instincts. As she prepared to feed them, Alex excused himself to check on their big brothers.

"Bring the boys in to see their sisters, Alex," Sarah called after him.

"Are you sure you want them in here while you feed the babies?" Breastfeeding made him uncomfortable, and he wondered how the boys would react.

"It's okay, Alex. Just give me another blanket. I must see my boys."

Alex found the boys huddled together on the swing on the back porch. He checked his watch and realized they'd been alone over two hours.

"Did the babies come yet, Mr. Alex?"

"Yes, the babies are here, and Mama wants you to see your sisters."

"Aww. Why did she have to have girls? We wanted boys, didn't we, David?" Dried tears streaked David's cheeks. His dazed look told Alex he was still trying to process the morning's excitement.

Alex pulled David to him and addressed both boys, "I'm sorry that I didn't check on you sooner, but I'm proud of you for staying out here and waiting. You are obedient young men."

"Mama scared us. We could hear her screaming and crying and shouting at you. Why was she mad at you?"

Alex couldn't explain the rapport he'd established with the boys these recent weeks. He loved them as if they were his own children, and he hated that they overheard their mother's distress. With a child under each arm, he pushed the swing with his foot and wondered how he might comfort them.

"Your mother wasn't mad. Having babies isn't easy, but she's fine now, and she wants to see you."

Alex could hold them back no longer. They jumped from the swing, raced into their mother's room and climbed up on the bed. Though the infants were hidden under the blanket, Sarah gave her boys kisses and reassurances. A few moments later, she pulled the baby girls from her breasts and placed one into the arms of each big brother. Warmth and desire filled him as he observed the exchange. As his mind drifted, he refused to deny the unrealistic scene invading his mind. The picture expanded to include himself, smothering them with love and affection.

When Alex rubbed his eyes to clear his vision and shake himself from the fanciful dream, his thoughts returned to the boys. He couldn't imagine how they must have felt being alone on the porch. He slapped his forehead when he remembered he hadn't called Anna.

"Do you think it would be okay if my housekeeper came and took the boys to my house? They haven't had much to eat today, and I'm sure she'd love to feed them and put them down for naps. She's a grandmother herself and would take excellent care of them. What do you think?"

Sarah looked at Alex through narrowed eyes. "And what will you be doing, Mr. Caine?"

"I'll be staying here with you, of course. Sarah, you trusted me to deliver your girls, don't you think it's time to trust me with your boys?"

Alex wanted to scream at the ungrateful woman. But then he remembered her trauma that had ushered two new lives into the world. He sighed and swallowed his anger. She was right, delivering the babies didn't give him the right to intrude. Sarah still saw him as a perfect stranger.

"It's okay, Sarah, I know you've been through a lot. I understand your concerns."

Alex saw tears glazing her eyes as she turned toward him. "You're right. How can I ever thank you? Please forgive me. I do trust you. Do what you think best."

While Alex called Anna to pick up the boys, they snuggled with their mama and kissed their baby sisters. He overheard Sarah talking about how special they were to have twin sisters and what terrific big brothers they'd be. The woman managed to convince even Jonathan.

A few minutes later, he heard sirens in the distance. "Are you telling me the paramedics are just now arriving? I can't believe it. You could've died before they got here. Why do we need them now?" He wanted to hit someone as he stomped from the room. The front door hit the wall with a crash when the medics arrived along with Anna and Bailey.

"Is this what you call an emergency response? I telephoned over two hours ago. Where on earth have you been? Mrs. Stuart could've died while you took your time showing up."

"I'm sorry, Mr. Stuart, but we ran into a five-car collision on the way with multiple injuries. We had to respond to the accident first. Usually, births take several hours, so we expected to be here in plenty of time. If you were that concerned, you should've put her in the car and taken her to the hospital."

Alex didn't respond to the young man who looked to be fresh out of high school, nor did he correct him for calling him "Mr. Stuart." Sarah could give them the details while he worried about their lack of qualifications.

"Well, you are way too late, but you might as well check them over while you're here. In addition to delivering the babies, she suffered a cut on the back of her head."

Alex took several deep breaths to suffuse his anger. Anna looked at him and shook her head. "What's the matter, Mr. Caine? This too much drama for you?" She patted him on the back and pulled an excited Bailey away from the medics.

Alex showed the two young men to the bedroom and stayed long enough to see the astonished looks on their faces as they waited for Sarah to hug the boys. To avoid further embarrassment, Alex excused himself while the medics examined Sarah and the infants. His relief at overhearing the suggestion to transport all three to the hospital turned to annoyance when Sarah refused. He returned to the bedroom to protest.

"You ought to consider their suggestion, Sarah. The babies seem so small and vulnerable. Didn't they arrive sooner than you anticipated? Besides, that fall could've done more damage than you realize."

"We're fine, Alex, and I can't afford the additional expense."

"Sarah, you and your children are dependents. Don't you qualify for military insurance?"

She glared at Alex. Through clenched teeth she reiterated her stance. "We're staying here."

Alex froze in place as he watched the medics pack their gear. He wanted to grab them by their shirttails to keep them from leaving.

Sarah didn't fool him. She refused to leave out of concern for her other two children. *She doesn't think I'm a reliable caretaker. And who else could she ask to watch her sons? The stubborn woman has a trust issue a mile wide. But she's stuck with me until someone can replace me. And I'm stuck here.*

The unwelcome feelings he'd harbored toward Sarah for the last month rushed to the surface, along with a vivid realization—Sarah belonged to him. Now that he'd spent time with her, his dreams of her paled compared to the real Sarah Stuart. He loved her two sets of twins, and he loved her. *How could he fall in love with a woman he barely knew?* What he did know of her suggested they had little in common. They hadn't even attempted a rational conversation. Regardless, he and Sarah had experienced something over the past couple of hours that would forever bind them together.

The giddy Alex felt like a ninth grader with out-of-control hormones. In one of his novels, he had written about this "love at first sight" condition, but never in his wildest dreams had he expected he would be a victim. Up until this moment, he had viewed the phenomenon as a fantasy to attract female readers—not something that could happen to a level-headed, mature person like himself.

Regardless of his feelings, his sanity finally returned. The woman would think he'd lost his mind if he didn't slow down. Alex would have to win her affections one moment at a time. Now that she'd allowed him into her home, he would carefully find a way into her heart.

With the medics gone and the boys under Anna's care, Alex went into the bedroom to check on his patients. All three were sound asleep. The girls, tummies full, snuggled safe and warm next to their mother. As for Sarah, her tranquil, relaxed posture contradicted the trauma he'd witnessed earlier. Alex lingered inside the doorway. He didn't care if he ever wrote another book. At this moment, his life felt complete.

As Alex continued to gaze at the sleeping trio, Sarah stirred and noticed him watching her. A slight smile creased her face, followed by a question in her eyes when she saw him wipe his cheeks. He looked down in surprise at the dampness on his fingers.

"What's wrong, Alex? Did something happen to the boys?"

"No, they're fine. When I last checked, they were having a terrific time with Anna and Bailey. Her arrival with my dog did the trick. Sometimes I think Bailey belongs more to Jonathan and David than he does to me. Anna certainly knew what would appeal to children—those two anyway.

"I don't know what came over me just now. I guess I got caught up in the moment. You three girls looked so beautiful."

Alex cleared his throat to continue. "Can I get you anything? Oh, by the way, I asked Anna to drop the boys off when she leaves at six. She'll bring the dinner she usually prepares for me, if that's okay."

"You don't know what a blessing you've been today. I imagine this is quite a stretch for you. You must be exhausted. How will I ever repay you?"

"I'll think of something, Sarah." He bent over to make eye contact and lowered his voice. "In the meantime, I think you should start trusting me and allowing me to help you more. I'll be sleeping on the couch tonight and all the nights hereafter until you're able to manage on your own or someone comes to relieve me." He straightened his back and stretched, relieving the tension that had been building in his neck and shoulders since he'd seen David running toward his house that morning. "You're right. I am tired, but this day has been incredible."

"It has, hasn't it? The boys were born at the military hospital in a sterile, almost perfect environment. Their delivery took hours, Tom helped me breathe through the contractions. Between the pains, he rubbed my back to relieve stress and encouraged me to relax. My parents were both there, walking the halls, anxious for their first grandchildren to arrive. It seemed nothing compared to today.

"This time, my labor went too fast—so fast, in fact, I felt unprepared and panicked. Please forgive me for the way I treated you. You must have thought me a mad woman, screaming orders, and acting the shrew. Despite my emotional outburst, I'll treasure this time as an amazing, wonderful experience, and you helped make these births special."

"Thank you for letting me be here to do what I could. My inexperience probably caused even greater stress." He stepped back and folded his arms. With a twinkle in his eyes, he said, "I am a bit disappointed not to have had time to rub your back, though. Any time you require a good rub, I'll be happy to oblige."

They laughed at the truth behind his teasing. Sobering, Alex said, "Sarah, don't you think it's time to call your mother. She should be here with you. If nothing else, she'd want to know that the babies arrived safely."

The look Sarah gave him bordered on panic. Since he'd first met Sarah and the boys, he had wondered about the absentee mother. Jonathan and David rarely talked about their grandmother and never mentioned a visit. What was the big deal about calling one's mother anyway? Sarah should appreciate his reminder. Her expression told him to take the advice he often gave his mother, "to mind her own business." To avoid further stress for Sarah or himself, he would refrain from interfering.

Sarah resented Alex's reminder. She hadn't even thought to call her mother. What gave him the right to tell her what to do? *I suppose he earned the right.* Although they were practically strangers, Alex'd arrived when she needed him and endured a gruesome morning with few complaints. Despite her original aversion to the man, she felt grateful for his involvement and sensed a feeling of camaraderie developing between them.

"You don't understand, Alex. My relationship with my mother is complicated. I don't have to talk to her to know what she'll say, but I'll call her eventually."

Sarah should get over feeling hurt at the thought of her mother. From past experiences, she knew exactly how the woman would react. Tom would say she ought to forgive and love her, but that wasn't always easy. Alex was right, her mother should be here with her, *not* some stranger.

Picking up the receiver, her hands shook, and perspiration filled her palms. She returned the phone to its cradle so fast one of the babies jumped beside her. While she played the conversation in her mind, she watched Alex gather the soiled linens, and thought about his caring for her as a mother would. That was all the motivation she needed.

"Thank you for the reminder, Alex. I'll call my mother, but I'm not getting my hopes up."

Sarah stalled a few more minutes, hoping her mother's response would surprise her. Although she spoke to her mother regularly, the fear of rejection weighed heavy on her. She finally dialed the number. Leslie answered on the fourth ring just as Sarah prepared to leave a message.

"How are you, Mother? I wanted to let you know that the babies came today .... Yes, little girls, pretty—beautiful really .... Oh, I'm not in the hospital. They came without warning, and we didn't have time to get to the doctor .... My neighbor helped me with the delivery. Remember you told me about him .... Well, there were no women here, and my midwife went out of town."

So much for best-laid plans, Sarah thought amid her mother's ranting about the indecent, dangerous situation. The longer Leslie complained, the more guilt Sarah heard in the woman's voice. Her mother had convinced herself the babies could've died and Sarah along with them.

"Yes, he says he lives next door. You know, Alex Caine .... I don't remember his pen name .... You know, the writer. Although he doesn't seem to be doing anything other than delivering baby girls and playing with the boys .... Yes, I'll remind him that you, along with others, are waiting for his next novel .... When can you come see the babies?"

Sarah pulled the phone away from her ear and impatiently rolled her eyes while her mother reiterated the familiar excuses intermingled with short panicky breaths. She was obviously having a bad day. "I know it'll be hard to return to the cottage without Dad, but the boys would so love a visit from their grandmother. Think about it. Please." The hurt her mother inflicted added to the pain she'd just experienced and kept her from prolonging the conversation. "Okay Mother, I understand. I love you."

Alex couldn't help hearing Sarah's end of the conversation, and he didn't have to hear the other end to know Sarah's reluctance to call her mother was well founded. His heart ached further when he heard her weeping following the call. He didn't understand how Mrs. Warren could be so hurtful. If he called his mother right now, she would come in a heartbeat. *God, please show me how to comfort Sarah in the loss of her parents. I don't know why I'm praying so much, but there don't seem to be any other answers. Sarah believes in you, God, so I know you'll hear prayers on her behalf.*

Not only had Alex fallen in love within a few short hours, but this crisis with Sarah had blown an enormous hole in his unspiritual viewpoint—a position he had held irrevocably for the past fifteen years. It's true he felt on the verge of panic while preparing for the first baby, but when he sincerely prayed, God intervened and surrounded him with confidence and peace. Maybe he should give the Christian faith another look.

CHAPTER SIX

Alex amazed Sarah. This reclusive writer made her a sandwich and brought it to her room along with a banana and a glass of milk. Although her husband had treated her with kindness and concern, he had rarely had time to serve a meal or help with the children.

Each time the babies cried, Alex changed their diapers and brought them to her. Sarah almost felt guilty staying in bed while this surprising man took over her responsibilities. Despite her desire to dislike him or for him to disappoint her in some way, he did the opposite. Her unbalanced hormones suggested "love," but the voice of reason rejected such nonsense.

Though embarrassed herself, Alex's claim of discomfort with her unclothed body was hard to believe. She estimated him to be a few years older than her, and he confessed no interest in God or the church. Most men his age, if they didn't object for moral reasons, were in a sexual relationship either with their wives or a significant other. His embarrassment presented an oxymoron with the image she gleaned from pictures blazing on the front of magazines or the accompanying articles. Sarah didn't understand.

Her mother said Alex wrote historical novels under the pen name of Stephen Jacobs. She'd heard the name mentioned on talk shows but didn't remember reading anything he wrote. His books were not in her current library, which consisted predominately of Dr. Seuss books along with pregnancy and childcare magazines.

This overly-sensitive man was too obsessed with her family, however, and she didn't like that. Sarah cringed at the notion she might've encouraged him. Her husband remained a strong presence in her thoughts, decisions, and emotions. If she did decide to remarry one day, Alex wouldn't be a candidate. They stood at opposite ends of almost every spectrum of the marriage compatibility scale. Raising her four children was her sole concern, and she didn't need a good-looking man sidetracking her.

Sarah knew she shouldn't be alone and would have preferred a family member or friend instead of her more-than-willing neighbor. This first night she had no choice, but tomorrow she'd take care of her own needs and those of her children. When Alex helped her to the bathroom the first few times, she wanted to hide in embarrassment. That alone was reason enough to send him down the beach.

While Sarah mused over her dilemma, she heard his cell phone ring. "Hello, Mother" Perhaps now would be an opportunity to discover more about "Mr. Nice Guy." Nothing like a conversation with one's mother to bring out the best or worst in a person.

"Did Anna tell you where I am? .... No, well I guess she thought it my story to tell. I had an amazing day. You'll not believe what happened .... Okay, if you insist. I want you to know that I delivered twin baby girls this morning. Quite the experience. I'm thinking about changing my profession." Sarah could imagine his mother's response. She loved his playful sense of humor.

"I cannot begin to tell you how it felt. Truthfully, this has been the most fulfilling day of my life. Although I did get a little embarrassed with the naked part. Why are you laughing at me, Mother? .... What? .... Of course, they're not my babies. You know I'd never cause you that kind of grief .... Well, they are about the prettiest little girls I've ever seen, and I'd be proud to be their daddy. In fact, they feel like my babies and so do their big twin brothers .... No, their mother's still grieving the loss of their father.

"If I haven't confused you enough, I'd love for you to see them. They are sort of like little trophies or masterpieces. Sarah can't seem to talk her mother into coming. You know Mrs. Warren, don't you? .... She could use your prayers. Sarah said she's having a tough time since her husband's death and is unable to face the memories of the island .... Yes, I know, it must be hard, but I hurt for Sarah. I'm sure she'd rather have her mother here instead of me .... Of course, I'm spending the night on the couch. You taught me better than that, Mother."

After a long pause, Alex continued, "Since I required his help this morning. I was surprised he answered my prayers when I haven't acknowledged him since eighth grade. Though he probably responded due to Sarah's faith. She knows him like you do. Well, enough about me. You would like to come, wouldn't you? ... Let me know when you can drive down, and I'll talk Sarah into it. She's a bit in my debt right now, and I'm hoping she heard our conversation since I eavesdropped when she talked with her mother. Well, I must go. Duty calls. Love you, Mother. Be good and tell Dad not to get his hopes up. I'm still considering how I might obtain equal custody of the children without marrying the mother .... She won't have me .... I know, Mother, you think I'm wonderful, but not everyone agrees. I'm hanging up for real this time. Bye!"

Alex appeared in the doorway with a smug smile on his face. He reminded her of one of her boys anxious to share a secret.

"Well, did Sleeping Beauty wake up? I hope my telephone conversation didn't disturb you. Was I too loud?" Sarah swallowed her laughter when Alex's expression suddenly turned into something too difficult to define.

Sarah ignored the serious look and continued the banter. "You are about the most arrogant man I've ever met. Who do you think you are, telling your mother that those babies are yours? If you aren't nice, I might move away and never let you see our babies again." The moment the statement came out of her mouth, Sarah regretted her word choice. Alex would never let her forget the fact that she said *our* instead of *my.* A little slip like that wouldn't faze most people, but she'd learned in the last few hours that he would take it and run with it.

Alex continued to stand in the doorway, grinning as if he'd opened a special gift. "My point exactly, Mrs. Stuart. Oh, by the way, did you hear the part where I invited my mother to meet her grandchildren?"

Though she attempted an angry expression, laughter spewed from her mouth. How did she end up indebted to this kind, witty neighbor? No wonder he boasted a sizable fan club. At a time when her emotions were so raw and fragile, his teasing lightened her mood. *Thank you, God, for Alex. But give me the strength to guard my heart.*

"Your mother's welcome to come, Alex, but make sure she knows that they're not your children. I heard what you said to her, teasing both of us at once. You're something else."

A while later, Alex came into the room for about the fifth time, checking to see if the babies still breathed. "Sarah, are you sure the babies are okay?

They haven't nursed lately. Shouldn't they be eating every two or three hours?"

"The babies are fine, Alex, merely a little tired from the trauma of the birth canal. They'll probably sleep most of the next couple of days but be prepared for a sleepless night. You should rest while the boys are with Anna, or better still, how about making a run to the grocery store? I'm certain we could use a few items. I realize you aren't used to that sort of thing, but do you think you might manage?"

"What are you trying to do, Sarah, get me out of your hair? Well, that won't work. I'm not leaving you alone. If you need groceries, Anna can shop tomorrow on her way to work. But don't worry about me. I often get by on little sleep. You're the one who should rest while you're able."

Sarah couldn't begin to describe her reaction. When the temptation came to fantasize about a future with him, she reminded herself of their vast differences. His sudden interest in Christianity sounded more like teasing than a genuine conversion. A little begging for God's help didn't make a believer, but she was glad somebody prayed. When she awakened from the fall in excruciating pain, she'd panicked. Relief came moments after she noticed Alex standing in the doorway. No matter the condition of his heart, her neighbor arrived in answer to prayer.

Alex fed the boys dinner, supervised their baths, and helped them into their pajamas. Sarah strained to hear their soft voices as they described their afternoon with Anna and Bailey.

"Miss Anna took us for a walk on the beach and showed us a turtle nest. She said when the baby turtles came out of the eggs she saw the whole thing. Will you take us to see them next time?" Sarah heard Jonathan's excitement as he related the story.

"We'll have to check with your mom, but I think it's a possibility. But you'll have to wait a long time before the turtles lay their eggs again. Summer has to be almost over before the babies hatch. Sometimes it's late at night when they decide to show themselves and make their way back to the ocean. We'll see."

Alex's morning visits with the boys seemed to bind the three of them together in comfortable, mutual affection. She was amazed at his patience. Thank goodness he hadn't promised them a campout on the beach without checking with her. Knowing her boys, she'd never hear the end of it. With their delay tactics exhausted, Alex herded them into her room for a story and prayer.

When Sarah finished the story surrounding the birth of Samuel, Jonathan asked to pray first. "Thank you, Jesus, for my baby sisters even though I wanted baby brothers. Thank you for letting Mommy be okay. And thank you for Mr. Alex who plays with us and takes care of us. Don't let anything bad happen to him like it did to our daddy. Amen."

David prayed, "Thank you, God, for letting our babies come today without too much trouble. I'm glad Mr. Alex came to help, even though he didn't buckle me in my seat belt like Mama said. Bless all the little children in the world and keep them safe. Amen."

Sarah rolled her eyes at Alex who stood at the door. His solemn expression changed abruptly into an amused shrug followed by an unmistakable wink as he left the room. The audacious man was flirting with her, and she didn't know whether to laugh or groan.

A few minutes later, Sarah heard the opening of cabinets and the hum of the microwave. She wondered how he managed in an unfamiliar kitchen and longed to rescue him, but she felt too weak to get out of bed. Sarah forced a smile when he entered the room bearing a tray with two plates of delicious-smelling food. She recognized a shy, insecure look as he handed her the utensils wrapped in a napkin.

"Is it all right if we eat together? Perhaps I'm overstepping my bounds, but I eat alone so often, and since we've had such an amazing day, it only seems right."

Sarah didn't mind. In fact, she expected it of a sensitive man like Alex. With the food before her, she'd bowed her head to pray when he interrupted.

"Would you like me to bless the food?"

"Why, yes, I'd be interested in your conversation with God, especially after hearing the boys' prayers for you."

Alex laughed, but bowed his head and remained silent for so long that Sarah thought he'd changed his mind.

"God, I know I haven't talked with you much in my life, and I'm sure it's unusual to hear from a person like me, but I want to thank you for these beautiful baby girls and the amazing experience. When I see such a miracle, I'm unable to deny your existence. Thank you for taking care of them and Sarah and for protecting the boys while they waited alone on the porch.

We're grateful for this food that Anna prepared. Also, please encourage Sarah's mother to come. At times like this, a woman's mother should be with her. In Jesus's name, Amen."

"Thank you, Alex."

Whether from her raw emotions or the trauma of childbirth, she felt tears gathering below the surface. Physically, she ached. The abnormal cramping and blood flow left her light-headed and dizzy. Despite her weakness, the dinner looked good, and for the sake of the babies, she'd force herself to eat. She didn't dare mention her problem to Alex.

"Are you okay, Sarah? You look pale to me."

"I'm fine. This tastes delicious. You'll have to thank Anna for me."

"She delights in feeding others. I'm lucky to have her in my employ. She's more like family, a devoted friend as well.

"You know, Sarah, we've grown rather close over the past few hours, but we've never had a real conversation. While we eat, do you think we might get to know one another? For instance, why don't you tell me what you know about me, and I'll tell you something you might not know. I gathered from your end of the conversation with your mother that she knew something of my writing. When we finish with me, then we can discuss you. Does that sound like an acceptable plan?"

"Why do men always require a plan? Couldn't we just talk about what happened? Are you trying to pry into my personal life? You ..."

Sarah stopped mid-sentence when she noticed Alex's hurt, bewildered expression. During the silence, she rehearsed her jumbled remarks. "Alex, what's wrong with me? I'm not usually like this."

Alex scratched his head at Sarah's confusing behavior which left him scrambling for a response. However, he managed to overcome the hurt when he thought of what she'd endured and chose not to upset her further. Even though they were both tired and wore fragile feelings, he disliked having to tiptoe around her—one of the main reasons he'd avoided relationships with the opposite sex. The little reminder went far in returning sanity to his romantic thoughts.

While he searched for an opening to this "unplanned" conversation, Jonathan stumbled into the room looking white as a sheet and holding his stomach. "I don't feel so good." Alex set his plate aside and picked up the boy. He didn't feel hot, but he collapsed in his arms.

"Rush him to the bathroom, Alex, right now!" The previously weeping, repentant Sarah reacted with a little too much force. At the same time, Alex wondered what else might go wrong in this unending day.

Before Alex had time to question Sarah's urgent directive, he heard the gush. Then felt something slimy and wet oozing down the back of his shirt. Between the smell and the feel, he gagged.

Jonathan cried out and clutched him tighter. Alex wanted to cry with him. "What can we give him, Sarah? Is there medicine in the cabinet that might help?"

Sarah had already struggled out of bed and headed to the kitchen for something to settle her son's stomach. Nothing kept the woman in bed when one of her children needed her. Another attribute in the extensive list of things to admire about Sarah Stuart.

By the time she returned with ginger ale, Alex had removed his shirt in the bathroom. "Can you believe he's as dry as can be? The mess went over my shoulder and down my back. At least it'll be easy to settle him back in bed. Let me get the wastebasket from the bathroom, Jonathan, in case you throw up again. Come to think of it, let's put it between your two beds. David might decide to copy you. What do you say, buddy?"

Jonathan soaked up the attention, especially the idea of ginger ale, the nearest thing to cola his mother allowed. The pale boy nodded, "Can you stay with me for a while?"

Alex noticed that Jonathan addressed him instead of his mother and wondered how she felt about the slight. "Of course, let me see if anything got on the rug. Maybe Mommy has one of her big shirts I can wear. Wouldn't that look funny, huh?"

Although Jonathan seemed better, Alex covered the carpet between the boys' beds in the event of a reoccurrence. Sarah returned to the room carrying what looked like a man's T-shirt. *Go Army* read the caption. He shook his head as he thanked her then left to scrub the bathroom and tackle a few places on the bedroom carpet which he'd already pronounced a disaster after her bloody fall.

At his return to sit with Jonathan, he found Sarah holding her son and checking him over. She quietly encouraged him to sip the drink as she pushed his hair back and kissed his forehead. The domestic scene filled

Alex with a longing that made him want to gather them both into his arms. At least he had sense enough to hide his emotions and take her place when the babies' cries forced her to relinquish her post.

With Jonathan back in bed, Alex returned to Sarah's bedroom to remove the dinner trays. He'd barely touched his food while Sarah's had disappeared.

"I see you managed to finish your dinner. You must have licked the plate. I won't even have to rinse it before putting it into the dishwasher." Sarah threw a pillow at him.

"If I didn't know better I'd think you arranged that little episode to get out of a serious conversation with me. I'll let you off the hook for now, but tomorrow is another day, and I suggest we continue. What do you think?"

"I believe you enjoy torturing me, Alex Caine, but I don't mind. What Jonathan did to you bordered on brutal. Let's call a truce for tonight. Okay?" Although Sarah looked tired and pale, her attempt at humor lightened the tension between them.

"Truce. Hope you can rest and sleep well. I'll take care of the boys, but if you need anything, let me know. Goodnight, Sarah."

CHAPTER SEVEN

Early the next morning, when the sun hadn't yet made its way over the horizon, Alex woke from a fretful slumber and looked in on the boys. They appeared fine each time he had checked during the night and slept peacefully now, but a niggling worry wouldn't leave him.

As he entered the front bedroom and heard the frantic cries of the babies, he knew something had to be wrong. They kicked and screamed with no response from their mother. Alex frowned as he approached her bed and noticed the tears sliding down her cheeks. "Sarah, what's wrong?"

"Oh, Alex, I hated to call out, but I need to go to the bathroom, and I feel so weak, I'm afraid to attempt it alone. Could you help me before I feed the babies?"

When Alex put his arm around her to help her up, she went limp. As he lifted her, he discovered the backside of her gown and the sheets covered with blood. He couldn't think past the paralyzing fear. His fragile nerves would take little more. Praying under his breath, he carried her to the bathroom, doing almost everything for her.

"Sarah, this can't be normal. I'm going to call the EMTs, and I pray to God we get prompt service this time."

Sarah didn't argue. She nodded and almost fell off the toilet as he maneuvered to get his phone. *Oh, God, please help us.* While holding Sarah with one arm, he called the emergency number. "911, What is your emergency?"

"I'm with a hemorrhaging mother who just hours ago gave birth. I want you here now. Don't you dare take your time like you did the last time I called."

"Calm down, sir. What is your location?"

Alex gave the woman the address and hung up before he said something he shouldn't. He carried Sarah back to bed and threw a folded clean sheet over the soiled area. In one swift movement, he swept up the squalling infants and placed them on Sarah's chest. "Sarah, please try to feed the babies before the medics arrive. I don't know what else to do."

"Keep praying, my friend."

Tears streamed down Sarah's face as she prepared to nurse her little ones. She was so weak, she couldn't hold them to her breast, and he had no choice but to help her. As he sat on her bed and leaned over her, his heart filled with warmth and love. Never had he experienced such frustrated intimacy.

After about fifteen minutes in the awkward position, he felt relieved by the blare of the siren and lights flashing through the window. He took the babies from Sarah and prayed they had sufficient nourishment for at least a few hours. Without delay, the EMTs assessed their patient and prepared her for transport to the small mainland hospital.

As the paramedics rolled her out, Alex grabbed her hand and whispered assurance in her ear. "Don't worry, Sarah, God and I are speaking again, and I know he'll take care of us."

Standing on the front stoop and watching the taillights disappear in the early morning darkness, doubt and fear slapped him in the face. *What was I thinking? What will I do with four children?*

Inside, Alex fell on his knees in the living room. He wanted to lash out, but his love for Sarah turned his thoughts toward God. He knew no other source. *God give me wisdom. Show me what to do.* He remained on his knees in quiet meditation until he had an answer.

Alex rose on shaky legs, determined to take care of Sarah's children. He made three telephone calls—the first to his mother.

"Mother. Something terrible has happened, and I need you."

"Oh, Alex. I can hardly believe this. You sound so upset, of course, I'll come. The trip will take a while, but I'll be praying as I drive."

"Thank you. I knew I could count on you."

Before she hung up, Grace gave him the telephone number for Leslie Warren and prayed a quick prayer for Sarah, Alex, and the children.

"Father, give Alex wisdom and compassion as he telephones Sarah's mother. And please help my friend, Leslie, to rise above her paralyzing grief. Her daughter needs her."

Alex concluded the call echoing his mother's prayer and dreading the call to Sarah's mother. He'd hated to ask his mother to drive that distance alone, but knowing Mrs. Warren's attitude, he'd run out of options. For the first time since moving to the island, he felt isolated and helpless.

The next few minutes were spent building a case of resentment against the person he was about to call. By the time he dialed the number, he nearly choked to prevent the venom from escaping his mouth. "Mrs. Warren, I hate to tell you this, but your daughter has been rushed to the hospital with excessive bleeding. If you care anything about Sarah, you need to come. She needs you."

"What? Where are the children?"

"They're with me, ma'am. Who else does she have?"

"How could you let this happen, Mr. Caine. Why didn't you insist they take Sarah and the babies to the hospital?"

As the woman continued to rant at him, her voice weakened into a quiet sob, and Alex cringed at his lack of compassion. "I'm sorry, Mrs. Warren. Please forgive me if I sounded abrupt. Things are a bit shaky here."

The emotional woman sniffed a few times and blew her nose. "I'll join Sarah at the hospital as soon as I can. Thank you, Mr. Caine, for letting me know."

Next, he called Anna, his sole friend in the area, and asked her to stay with the children until he checked on Sarah and found a pediatrician at the hospital. He thought about taking them all with him but nixed the idea considering the babies were merely a few hours old. Anna agreed and arrived in record time.

Alex blasted through the ER entrance on the run and made his way to the reception desk. "Could you tell me where to find Sarah Stuart?"

"Sir, if you'll give me a moment to finish helping this person, I'll be happy to answer your question."

Alex hadn't even noticed the woman next to him filling out paperwork. He pushed his hair back and drummed his fingers on the counter, tension building in his chest.

"Now, sir, who is the person you wish to see?"

"Sarah Stuart. She was brought in a few hours ago by ambulance."

"Are you her husband?

"No, but I need to know what's happening to her."

"If you aren't a close relative, our privacy policy prevents me releasing information to you. I'm sorry."

"You don't understand. She has four children at home that have been left in my care. You have to help me." The last thing he needed was to draw attention to himself, but he noticed people beginning to stare and murmur.

The authoritative woman wrinkled her face into an uncooperative frown, folded her arms across her chest, and pierced him with sharp dark eyes. "Would you kindly move aside so I can assist the next person in line."

"You are not going to brush me off, lady. Sarah just gave birth to two of those children a few hours ago, and I haven't a clue what to do with them. Their mother is somewhere in this hospital, and she is the sole source of their nutrition. Do you really want to be responsible for two baby girls starving to death because of some privacy malarkey?" Every word increased in volume until both staff and visitors were casting annoying stares his direction.

As Alex looked about wondering what to do next, an official-looking woman walked up to him carrying a clipboard. "I'm Maggie Rice—in charge of patient relations. Let's step over here so we can talk privately. If you will calmly explain your problem, I'll see what I can do to help."

Alex let out a long breath and described his situation along with a confession of his lack of knowledge. When he finished his desperate plea, the woman smiled and started toward the reception desk "I believe you need to talk to a pediatrician. Let me page one for you."

Alex only had to wait a few minutes before an attractive woman walked up with an outstretched hand. "Mr. Caine, I'm Dr. Scott, the pediatrician on call today. The ER nurses tell me you're rather upset with us. Can you explain?"

Alex drew in a deep breath and slowly repeated his dilemma. Dr. Scott nodded. She paged the nursery and ordered a supply of formula. Pulling a pad and pencil from her pocket, she wrote detailed instructions for which formula to buy and how much and how often to feed the infants. The doctor promised to check on Sarah and provide him with as much information as permitted.

Dr. Scott discussed the merits of admitting the babies to the hospital, but since they had care at home, she decided they'd be better off without introducing them to hospital germs. If Alex could be assured of Sarah's recovery, he felt confident he and his mother could manage at home.

When Dr. Scott returned, she didn't have good news. Sarah had been prepped for emergency surgery. The doctor asked for Alex's cell number and promised to keep him informed as she sent him home to take care of the little ones. Alex stood in the hallway watching Dr. Scott disappear into the elevator. He massaged the stress pain emerging from the vicinity of his heart and took deep breaths to relieve the pressure. Leaving Sarah proved more difficult than he imagined as he forced himself to move toward the greater responsibility.

Alex prayed all the way home as he called both mothers with an update. Thank God, they were on their way. When his mind started to drift toward the worst-case scenario—Sarah's death—he chose to hope for a more positive outcome. Even with all the complications, Alex couldn't imagine life without Sarah. Being with her made him want a future that looked the opposite of anything he ever envisioned. *How could I lose her when I've just found her?*

Anna greeted him with both girls in her arms—walking and praying and singing. If she sang, they were quiet, but when she stopped, they howled. While the poor babies were hungry and wanted their mother, Anna seemed more concerned for the older two.

"The boys woke up a while ago asking about their mother. After we feed the babies, Alex, please spend time with them. They were frantic when both of you were missing."

Anna directed Alex toward the back porch where he found the boys huddled together on the swing. "Hey, guys. Sorry I had to leave before you got up."

"Where's mama?"

"She's at the hospital, but the doctors are taking care of her. We'll talk more after I help Mrs. Anna feed your sisters. Before breakfast, how about creating something with your blocks?" During his attempt to settle the boys, Alex had noticed the plastic crates of toys stacked in the corner. He picked up the one with multiple shaped building blocks and dangled it before the boys. Jonathan grabbed the block from his hands and dumped the rest on the colorful outdoor rug.

At first, the babies made funny faces as if the formula tasted vile. Their tongues repeatedly pushed the foreign nipples from their mouths. The scene would've been comical if not for their obvious frustration. Alex winked at Anna when the little sweethearts finally got the hang of it.

As he fed one of the twins, he felt some of the pleasure Sarah must feel with the babies at her breasts. An unexplained love for these tiny girls nearly undid him. He rubbed his finger over their soft skin and breathed in the scent of their mother. Nothing compared to such a moment—not even the satisfaction he felt after writing a perfect paragraph he knew would connect with his audience.

With the babies settled, Alex sent Anna home to rest while he made a late breakfast for the boys. They wanted to know more about their missing mother. "We were scared when we couldn't find you or Mama."

"I know, but your mama's very sick. We need to pray and trust God to take care of her."

David didn't waste any time. "God, please don't take our mommy away, too." His prayer was drenched in tears, and it took all Alex's fortitude not to join him.

A little after eleven o'clock, Sarah's mother called with an update from the hospital. The surgeon was unable to stop the bleeding without doing a complete hysterectomy. Alex's initial disappointment gave way to relief that her prognosis was good, and she'd soon recover.

When the silence stretched a little too long, Leslie asked, "Are you okay, Mr. Caine?"

"Yes, I'm fine. I'm just glad she's alive. Do you think they'll let me see her in a few hours?" Fine would never be an accurate assessment of his feelings, but he preferred not to discuss his emotions with Sarah's mother.

Leslie Warren wasn't sure why Alex Caine asked to see Sarah unless he wished to talk about the children. How he managed to be watching them remained a mystery. Domesticated didn't describe the young writer who hired someone to attend to his own needs. How would he ever take care of her grandchildren? From what she'd gleaned over the years, he seemed a bit self-centered, lacked involvement in the lives of others, and spent little time with his family. She caught herself when she realized how unfair she was to judge him based on information gained from the tabloids and brief conversations with his mother. Considering her own situation, who was she to criticize?

"How are the babies and Jonathan and David?"

"They're fine. A pediatrician at the hospital gave me formula along with instructions for feeding them. The boys are concerned about their mother, but I think they'll be all right. When my mother gets here, I'm going out for diapers and formula and plan to stop by the hospital."

"Your mother is coming from Virginia?" Leslie couldn't imagine how he'd managed to get Grace Caine involved. She had always liked the woman, but to come that far to help with a stranger's children? Was something happening with her daughter that she didn't realize?

"I had no choice, Mrs. Warren. Sarah said you refused to come to the cottage, and I can't handle this alone. My housekeeper came early this morning to stay while I went by the hospital. As you probably know, this isn't something I do every day. In fact, it's a first for me, and I need all the support I can muster. I'm glad you're there for Sarah. She needs you, Mrs. Warren. I'm a poor substitute for anyone's mother."

"I know, Mr. Caine. I'll try to do better for everyone. It's tough losing someone you love." Leslie didn't appreciate the reprimand, especially from someone young enough to be her son. Alex might be right about some things, but he couldn't begin to understand her paralyzing loss.

"Well, you almost lost someone else you loved today, and that would've been a double tragedy. But I know it means a lot to Sarah that you've come. I'll see you later." Leslie broke down in tears as she rushed out of the waiting room doubled over with guilt and worry for her family. She rubbed her chest in a futile attempt to relieve the heaviness pushing against her lungs. The secluded spot at the end of the hall became her cocoon of self-pity and remorse.

CHAPTER EIGHT

Relief arrived along with his mother. Caring for the children overwhelmed Alex—not to mention the mountains of laundry. No one—especially Sarah—needed to know he Googled for instructions on infant care along with laundry procedures. So far, he'd managed to move ahead, one task at a time. Whoever complained the loudest got his attention.

His mother did a double take as she scanned the cottage.

"Alex, I'm amazed. Under the circumstances, I expected to find a chaotic mess. Looks as though there might be hope for you after all."

"Thank you for the vote of confidence, but believe me, this isn't easy. I've never been so happy to see anyone. You're probably exhausted from the drive, but I appreciate your coming to my rescue."

Grace Caine more than lived up to her name as she made friends with the boys. She came prepared with gifts of puzzles and books resurrected from Alex's childhood along with a couple of gently used construction toys she rescued from the attic. Neither toy looked familiar to him, but the boys thought they were great. They danced around him pleading to play outside. For lack of supervision, Alex denied their unceasing requests. He promised them beach time when he returned from checking on their mother.

In no time, the babies captured his mother's heart. While she held them, she carried on a sweet conversation that kept Alex smiling despite his exhaustion. She had an unusual technique with a little swing of her body and hum in their ear. It appeared so natural, you'd think she attended lessons on infant childcare. How did she make it look so easy? Perhaps he should take that same class.

Alex stood unobserved in the doorway watching his mother. She squinted her eyes behind the reading glasses trying to make out the fine print on the carton of dry formula. Bottles and a measuring cup were scattered over the counter.

"You don't have to measure the water, Mother. Just scoop the formula into the bottle, pour in the filtered water and shake. It's not quite as easy as the ready-to-serve bottles, but less expensive."

"Your dad will be happy that you remember something from his lectures on budgeting and finance. Must be left-over from the days of a struggling writer."

"I've always been careful. You know that."

"As to the formula, I'm quite capable, and if I've forgotten anything, I'll manage to read the small print. Guess this wasn't meant for mature eyes." His mother smirked at him. "How do you suppose you and your sister survived?"

Alex put his arm around the feisty woman and nuzzled her neck. "I wonder how you put up with either of us, but thank you for everything."

She pushed him away and playfully hit him on the shoulder. "There's never a dull moment with either of you, that's for sure. You said these children are my grandchildren? I cannot fathom how this all came about, but I'll treat them accordingly. All I can say is, you've been quite busy."

Their banter ended abruptly when he realized the boys were too quiet in the next room. Before he could check, they came running.

"You're our grandma?" David asked. His eyes sparkled as he bounced on his toes.

Without a hint of hesitation, Grace stooped to the boy's level. "I'm Mr. Caine's mother, but you can call me Grammy. Do you think that would be okay?"

David turned and ran to his brother. "Jonathon! We have three grandmas.

With the children down for naps, Alex made his way to the hospital, uncertain if he'd be allowed in Sarah's room. When he stepped off the elevator, he recognized Mrs. Warren standing outside a door near the nurses' station. He didn't know her, but they'd met briefly once or twice when his parents visited.

"Mrs. Warren, how is she?"

"Mr. Caine, are the children doing okay?"

Sarah's mother didn't appear to be any more interested in chit-chat than Alex. He filled her in on how her grandchildren were adjusting under the care of his mother and Anna. She seemed to relax when he mentioned the additional help.

"Sarah's doing well, considering how much blood she lost before she arrived at the hospital. Why on earth didn't you call 911 sooner, and why didn't they bring the babies in with her?"

Alex's shoulders drooped under the weight of her criticism. The pressure he was under had him near the end of his patience and good manners. "Mrs. Warren, I'm doing the best I can, but I must see Sarah. Would you please make arrangements for me to do so?"

Mrs. Warren seemed confused at his abruptness, but he saw no point in delaying the conversation. Any need to defend himself took a back seat to his desire to see Sarah, and he refused to leave until he'd seen her.

"I made arrangements with the doctors when I first arrived. They know you must communicate about the children. Sarah wants to see you, but please don't upset her while you're in there. She doesn't need anything else to rock her world."

"I'll do my best, Mrs. Warren. Thank you." Alex held his temper and shook his head at the woman's cold demeanor. Rock her world? What more could he add to her misery? With that, Sarah's mother opened the door and motioned for him to enter the room. Rather than closing the door to give them privacy, she left it slightly ajar. Was she so concerned about his involvement with her daughter that she eavesdropped at the threshold? At this point, he didn't care.

When he turned his attention toward Sarah, he gasped when he saw how pale and fragile she looked. He straightened his spine and filled his lungs to keep from throwing himself on the bed and declaring his love. Instead, he bent over and kissed her lightly on the forehead, perhaps lingering longer than necessary. As he backed off, she looked questioningly at him. "Are the children okay? Who's watching them? Please tell me you haven't abandoned them."

"Still the trusting little mama, I see. They're doing fine. Didn't your mother tell you that my mother came to the rescue?" He couldn't believe Leslie hadn't filled her in on the details to relieve her fears.

"She may have. Alex, I've been so out of it, I don't know what I know or don't know. The births went so well, and I thought everything would be fine—then this nightmare."

Suddenly, her mood shifted to amusement. "I guess your mother came to see her grandchildren. What did she think? Does she adore them?"

Then, like that, she changed the subject again. "Oh, Alex, I forgot. What are you doing about feeding the babies? They must be starved. The nurses have been helping me pump, but with the strong medications, the babies couldn't have my milk if they were here. Are they really okay?"

Alex pushed her hair back and enjoyed the feelings she stirred. "You're not to worry. After they took you away, Anna arrived to stay with the children while I came to the hospital and talked with a pediatrician. She even managed to get me an update on you. Can you believe they wouldn't tell me anything about your condition? Not knowing almost drove me crazy. Thank God, this Dr. Scott understood our situation and requested some formula from the nursery. She spelled out the instructions nearly as well as you would have.

"As long as they had plenty of care, the doctor thought the girls would fare better at home. Dr. Scott seemed relieved when I told her that the EMTs had checked them shortly after birth. When you're better, she suggested we find a pediatrician to give them a thorough examination."

"I see you've been busy, Alex. You've certainly gone way beyond the requirements of a good neighbor. I'm sorry we've taken you from your writing, but I don't know where I'd be without you. You're truly a gift from God. Do you realize that, Alex Caine?"

Although Sarah couldn't be more serious, Alex enjoyed the opportunity to tease, "Oh, you won't believe the ideas emerging for my next book. There are a few moments you have to experience for yourself before you describe them to others, and I've developed an arsenal over the last few hours."

Alex basked in Sarah's teasing smile as he waited for the inevitable comeback. "Don't you dare put my personal life into a book, Mr. Caine. From the moment we met, I suspected you'd turn out to be a scoundrel."

She didn't mean a word of it, except maybe the part about forbidding his use of their experience in a book. He loved her feistiness and thought of the fun they'd have in the future. She looked beautiful even while fighting to recover her strength.

"Well, I hate to cut this visit short, but my Mr. Mom duties await, and those girls certainly go through the diapers." He took the lone hand unobstructed with needles and held it briefly before kissing it. After looking at her for a moment, he closed his eyes and enjoyed the feel of her fingers against his mouth. What he wouldn't give to have her lips there instead.

"I'm praying for you, Sarah. Even though I feel frantic at times, I'm trying to picture you coming home to us. In the meantime, please do all you can to recover. We need you. Goodbye, love."

As he turned to go, he heard her quiet response. "Goodbye, Alex, and thank you for the roses." In the stress of the day, he'd forgotten about ordering them. Without acknowledging her reply, he looked back, feeling blessed to have found such a woman.

Sarah sighed as she admired the red roses. When did he have time to consider such a thing? The brief card left her wanting more. "Love and Prayers, Four Munchkins and Mr. Mom." His thoughtfulness encouraged a wistful stirring in the pit of her stomach.

That sense of being cherished quickly evaporated when she rehearsed his visit and realized how pathetic she must've seemed. She'd reveled in his lingering kisses and gentle touches. They felt wonderful at the time, but now that she could breathe and reason, the significance of such intimate actions made her cringe. That hungry look coming from Alex scared her enough without feeling the pressure of his lips against her fingers. He even called her "Love" as he left. How did a man advance from a perfect stranger one moment to expressing romantic love the next? Maybe he thought after seeing her completely bare, both soul and body, he had the right to her heart.

From their first meeting, Sarah recognized Alex as a man with deep feelings and emotions. She didn't know why he reacted so toward her nor why she weakened at his nearness, but she couldn't allow these irrational feelings to continue. Once back on her feet and possessed with better judgment, she purposed to discourage Alex's involvement in her private life. Until then, she'd guard her heart with all the strength she could muster.

Not wanting to continue the previous conversation with the woman's accusations and concerns, Alex checked the hallway for Mrs. Warren. When the coast was clear, he slipped through the door and headed toward the elevator. Just as he pushed the down button, Sarah's mother appeared out of nowhere and caught "Romeo" moments before he heard the ding.

Hands on her hips, she glared at him. "What are your intentions toward my daughter, Mr. Caine? She lost her husband only a few months ago, and she doesn't need further complications."

Seeing his way for immediate escape, he jumped on the elevator. As the door closed, he quickly declared, "I plan to be your son-in-law one day, Mrs. Warren." Let her chew on that for a while. Too bad he couldn't stick around to see her reaction.

As Alex entered the grocery store, he pulled his baseball cap down and removed his sunglasses. Grocery shopping ranked among Alex's least favorite things to do. Anna had assumed the responsibility when she first came to work for him, freeing him of the chore. At his mother's insistence, he searched the aisles for the unfamiliar items on the list of snacks and foods preferred by little boys. Sarah didn't seem to stock up on the extras, and that bothered him. He hoped the empty pantry stemmed from an objection to junk food instead of the low budget he suspected. The few items he did find were wholesome organic foods. To stay in her good graces, he searched the aisles for healthy snacks along with fresh fruits and produce.

What he thought would be an easy assignment soon turned into a complicated game of hide and seek. Each item took longer to find than he planned while his fellow shoppers enjoyed the entertainment. He knew the moment his cover was blown. Two women with their heads together whispered loud enough for him to hear. "Isn't that the writer over there? What's he doing in the baby aisle?"

Ignoring his audience, he focused on the task at hand. The assortment of disposable diaper sizes left him standing in aisle eight scratching his head. Sarah didn't have a baby scale, so they hadn't weighed the babies. He had no idea what to purchase. They were a few weeks early and looked small to him, but what did he know? After talking to himself and discussing his dilemma with every passing mother who wasn't ogling him, he opted for the small. Even if the diapers were slightly large, at least they'd work until he found the proper size, or they grew into them. At the rate and frequency of their eating, that shouldn't take long. Their newborn tendency toward sleeping for prolonged periods had fled the house along with their mother.

Even when surrounded by crowds of admiring fans or obnoxious paparazzi, Alex had remained cool and collected. Now, he broke out in beads of perspiration as he squirmed under the raised eyebrows and inquiring looks of his fellow islanders. As he stepped into the check-out line, he felt as trapped as the hero in his latest novel who found himself surrounded by the enemy with no means of escape. What would this little grocery store visit do to his reputation? He wiped his brow with his arm and fidgeted with his credit card while the clerk took her time examining each of his purchases. With a grin similar in magnitude to his discomfort, she held the questionable items for all to see. Alex frowned at her and bagged the groceries himself to speed the process. Without waiting for a receipt, he grabbed the bags and fled for the car.

When Alex returned to the cottage, he heard nothing but the roar of the waves lapping the shore. The open windows caused the sheer curtains to dance in the strong breeze filling the room with the fresh scents from the ocean. Alex closed his eyes and inhaled the calming invasion of his senses. Without his realizing it, this small cottage had become a happy place. He felt at home here.

Everyone slept, including his mother. While he put away the groceries, he thought about this little family, picturing them as his own. After what they'd been through, he couldn't imagine life without them, but convincing Sarah would be a challenge. Back in the living room, his mother stirred from her sleep on the couch. She greeted him with a relaxed look of satisfaction.

"How's Sarah?"

"She looks terrible, but she's got her sense of humor, and the doctors say she's on the mend. They haven't given her a possible release date, but I'm sure it'll be in a few days. They want her hemoglobin back to normal before she comes home. She appreciates your coming to help with the children and so do I. Thank you, Mother."

Leaning over, he gave her an affectionate hug. As he stood, a sad conviction came over him—his mother wouldn't be with him always.

Although he loved his dad, his mother had never given up on him. No matter how far he drifted, she continued to pray for him. He regretted the years of resentment toward her for what he labeled interference. Now, he appreciated her challenging, convicting nudges.

"You mean my grandchildren?" She interrupted his thoughts with a hint of mischief. "They're great, and those babies are adorable. I forgot to ask what Sarah named them. We can't keep calling them the babies."

"She hasn't named them. She has some names in mind, but to her, names are important. They express a certain significance which often denotes meaning and purpose. She promised to come up with names after she prays about it. I hope that's soon because we must also register their births. Hospitals usually do that for new parents, but since we never made it there, we have to do it ourselves." He hoped Sarah might allow him to help select the names, but that looked more like one of his pipe dreams.

His mother raised an eyebrow and wrinkled her brow. "Alex, I'm worried that you're getting too close, too soon. I don't want to offend you, but I notice how you inserted yourself into Sarah's affairs without waiting for an invitation. You get these grand ideas and take off running, expecting others to follow your lead. I recognize Sarah as a woman of strong faith who also requires independence. I'm surprised someone like her would interest you. Don't get me wrong. I'm happy that you've found her, but I'm concerned about how fast this happened. Does she know how you feel, and does she feel the same?"

"Well, I haven't told her in words, but I've bent over backward the last few hours to express my intentions. If she can't read love and affection into that, she has her eyes closed." Alex didn't say it, but he feared Sarah's heart was closed instead of her eyes.

"Does it bother you that Sarah can't have more children?"

"At first I was disappointed, but it's as if her children are a part of me. I don't know what I would do should she reject me. It sounds crazy, but it's like God maneuvered this family of five into my life for me to love, protect, and enjoy. I know I haven't told you much about them, but I've spent most days with the boys since we met several weeks ago. As unbelievable as it sounds, I became acquainted with Sarah through her children. The boys brighten my dull life."

"I didn't realize that you felt your life dull, Alex. You always acted as though you had the perfect life sitting here on the beach by yourself."

"I guess I became so absorbed with writing and the characters within the pages of my books that I never took a realistic look at my own life or the real people surrounding me. Those two little boys opened my eyes and awakened a longing in me like I've never felt before—and their mother—I can't tell you how that woman makes me feel."

"I can see she's turned your head, but more than anything, I'm grateful that you recognize the need for God in your life. No matter how it came about, it's an answer to many prayers. As for the children, if you can accept Sarah's children as your own, then your father and I will love them. You know that, Alex, but I don't want you to get hurt.

"I'm certain of one thing. You have changed since you met Sarah and her family. You were good, kind, and thoughtful when circumstances called for it, but more often you appeared self-centered and arrogant, and as you suggested, ignored those around you. Now, you've put your entire life on hold for this family. I'm still a bit confused as to how this all came about, though I can see God's hand in it. Sarah still doesn't know how much she needs you, but if you'll be patient, she'll come around."

She stood and headed toward the kitchen, "Are you hungry? I'll fix you a snack before those baby girls demand our attention."

CHAPTER NINE

Instead of relaxing and resting to regain her strength, Sarah imagined every disastrous scenario. Were the babies fed on time? Did the formula agree with them? Were the boys feeling deserted? Did they miss her? Was the house a wreck? And to think, Alex's mother would see the mess. His housekeeper came in and out. Who knows how many others might show up? She went on and on, making herself sick with worry.

Sarah knew what the Bible said about anxiety, but her concerns overwhelmed any thought of "prayer and supplication" or "casting all your cares on him." She wouldn't rest until the doctor released her from the hospital and allowed her to return home where she belonged. Only then could she replace the strangers who cared for her children. Alex and his mother had been great, and she appreciated their involvement, but her family needed her, and she needed them.

Although they'd shared some intimate moments, Alex remained an acquaintance, and she wouldn't allow his romantic overtures to continue. She preferred the casual status of good neighbor. Oh, why deny it? She considered him far more than that, yet she dared not reveal her true feelings to him. She wasn't prepared for the kind of relationship he wanted. The quicker she removed him from her house, the easier to dispel the unwelcome feelings.

As if Alex wasn't enough, her mother posed yet another problem. Though Sarah had forgiven her, the woman seemed determined to compensate for the past. After a few hours of unneeded attention, Leslie was driving her crazy. Sarah couldn't relax until her doting mother gathered her purse and left.

At Sarah's insistence, Leslie returned to her nearby hotel to rest and refresh herself. With her daughter recovering so well, she felt confident the hospital would release her soon. How she longed to return to the island with her, but she cringed at the thought of revisiting the little cottage. The memories of Ben associated with that place were still so fresh. She couldn't imagine being there without him.

She'd never told Sarah, but a few months after her husband died, she'd tried to return. After driving all the way from Raleigh, she couldn't make herself cross the bridge. Fear paralyzed her until she pulled herself together enough to find her way home in defeat. The depression far outweighed her memories of the island.

Better if Sarah and the children came home with her. Although Leslie would be forced to endure a little noise and interruptions, the time had come to put her daughter's needs before her own. The plans came together in her mind, but convincing Sarah would be another matter.

By the time Leslie dressed to return to the hospital, she had resolved to be positive and not worry Sarah further. Unfortunately, the handsome neighbor gave them both reason for concern. When Alex came to the hospital after her arrival, his reaction to her questions surprised her. Sarah and the babies should've been admitted soon after the births. Instead of justifying himself, Alex acted like a whipped puppy. The arrogant writer had been replaced by a warm, tender, young man.

Of course, she felt confident in his care of the children and appreciated his involvement, but his stated intentions were a little over the top. Furthermore, she was surprised to hear that Grace Caine came all the way from Virginia. Did his mother assume a meaningful relationship between Sarah and Alex? Surely not. Tom hadn't even been gone a year. Her daughter wasn't ready for another commitment.

When Leslie became aware of her surroundings, she'd unconsciously pulled into visitor parking. Arriving on Sarah's floor, she saw her daughter walking the hall, free of tubes and wires.

"Look at you, Sarah. It's amazing how much you improved while I was gone."

"Thanks, Mom. I'm doing all I can to get home to my children. I appreciate Alex and his mother's help, but I miss my family, and I know those babies need their mother."

"Have the doctors mentioned when they might release you?"

"When I saw the surgeon today, he indicated that if I did well with the exercise and my numbers continued to rise, I'd be released soon. What do you think of that?"

Sarah seemed so excited, Leslie didn't want to bring up what she considered the obvious, so she waited until they returned to the room. "Would you consider coming to my house while you recover? I know you feel comfortable at the beach, but I'm not ready to return there. It's too hard for me. I hope you understand."

"I do understand, Mother, but uprooting the boys and packing the necessities even for a few weeks would be even more difficult. Before long, I'll be well enough to manage on my own, and I don't want you to feel responsible. Thank you for coming when I needed you. Just this morning, I realized it's time for me to take charge of my family. Until Tom died, I'd never been on my own. I would like to at least attempt a semblance of independence. I hope you can appreciate how I feel."

Leslie understood Sarah's desire to be alone with her children but dealing with two toddlers and two infants without assistance seemed impossible even for a healthy woman. Her daughter's stubborn streak kept her from facing reality. And how on earth would she dismiss her hovering neighbor?

"Sarah, I know Alex has been a tremendous help to you, but you can't keep depending on him. The more involved he becomes, the more difficult it'll be to release him. I don't think you realize how committed the man is, and I assure you, he's not just playing the role of a good neighbor. The way you describe him with the children, he reminds me of an over-zealous daddy goose. You'd think they were his own children. Do you think you could ever fall in love with him?"

"Mom, don't read so much into his involvement. He knows I appreciate him, but I've told him I'm not ready for a relationship. I admit, he makes me feel wanted and needed, but friendship is all I care to deal with right now."

Sarah knew she strayed slightly from the truth. Alex made her feel a great deal more. She felt loved, cherished, and beautiful when he came into the room. But she refused to acknowledge it.

"He claims to be praying and seeking God." She shrugged. "I'm just not sure about him. How did he transform so quickly from the playboy author portrayed by the media to this wonderful Christian man?"

"The more I hear about him, Sarah, the more I wonder if the media might be wrong about him. We haven't talked much, but he does seem sincere."

"He may be sincere, but we have nothing in common, and a relationship with him would only complicate my life further."

Sarah winced when she thought of how dissimilar they were. Alex wore the finest brands found at high-end department stores while Sarah searched for bargains at superstores. He rubbed shoulders with the rich and famous as she wiped the noses of sweet little boys. She cared deeply for him but had convinced herself she couldn't be the person he desired.

When her mother described him as a daddy goose, she remembered the time she and Tom had taken the boys to a park on the bay side of the island and observed the waterfowl with their families. Either the mother or father goose was alert and constantly watching over their goslings. The gander ruffled his feathers and charged in fury when he sensed a threat to his family. In contrast, the female mallard duck stood alone in protecting and caring for her little ones. Might Alex be God's provision? Surely, God wouldn't send someone along so soon?

"Well, if you're sure about staying alone, I'll plan to drive back to Raleigh the day of your release. When I feel strong enough to deal with the cottage memories, I'll come for a few days. It's been a while since I saw the boys, and I feel guilty. Do they ask about me?"

"Yes, all the time. The boys want you to visit so they can show you 'their beach.' Mom, you should see them. They play in the sand each morning and get so excited when Alex comes by with his dog. They love that dog. Alex taught them to throw the Frisbee and let Bailey catch it. He licks them from head to toe and leaves them rolling in the sand, laughing and playing. I'd get them their own dog if they were old enough to take care of him, but it's too much right now, and the house is too small for four children and a dog."

"You don't think it's going to upset the boys when you discharge Alex and Bailey?" Leslie asked the question with a raised eyebrow and a knowing look.

The idea of dealing with the fallout gave Sarah pause. "I don't know, Mom. I suppose he might still come by occasionally, but he can't be as involved as he is now. I'll have to fill in the gap as best I can. Perhaps I can set aside some time to play outside with them."

Sarah thought about what she said, knowing she'd be a poor substitute for Alex and Bailey. Oh, why couldn't circumstances be less complicated? That man strolled along the beach and turned their lives upside down.

"Mom, do you realize you still haven't seen the babies? Aren't you a little jealous that Grace Caine saw them before you?"

"Don't go there, Sarah. I absolutely hate it, okay. I've said it, and that's all I'm going to say on the subject." Sarah knew when to quit with her mother, but perhaps, a small seed had been planted.

After her mother left for the evening, Sarah sat in bed, longing for a few hours of uninterrupted rest. With the nurses routinely checking her temperature and blood pressure and the lab technician drawing blood, a deep sleep seemed impossible. She'd prefer waking to the cries of her babies instead of a parade of medical personnel. Since her thoughts returned to her children, she called to check on them.

"Well, how is our little mama tonight?"

"I'm missing my children. Are they okay?"

"And here I was thinking you might be missing me."

"I'm serious, Alex. Are they really doing okay? Are you sure they're getting enough to eat? They're not throwing up the formula, are they? I must get home as soon as possible before they forget they have a mother."

"The children are fine, Sarah. You'll never get out of that hospital if you continue allowing anxiety to control you. It's a known fact that stress and anxiety contribute to many illnesses."

"Just stop your psychological analysis right there. I merely called to check on my children."

"I'm sorry, Sarah. We all miss you. You are the anchor that holds us in place and keeps us on course. Nothing's the same without you. How's that for sounding poetic?"

"You sound exhausted, Alex. I bet you're not sleeping at all. Are they a lot of trouble?"

"They are, but you know, Sarah, I wouldn't want to be anywhere else. I love these children."

"Well, I'm coming home soon, and I hope you remember where you lived before you moved in and took over my home and family."

"Ouch, Sarah! That hurts. How do you manage to put me in my place no matter how comfortable I become elsewhere? Are you sure you're feeling better?"

"I'm tired, but I do feel better. Thank you, Alex."

Sarah hung up the telephone feeling so lonely and anxious she'd twisted the sheet into a tight cone before she realized it. The butterflies doing a dance in her stomach kept her from the rest she craved. She picked up her Bible from the bedside table. The verses of Psalm 25 became her prayer: "Turn to me and be gracious to me, for I am lonely and afflicted."

After the prayer, Sarah felt peaceful and fell asleep encouraged. But each time she awakened, a handsome face invaded her thoughts. Even over the telephone, he managed to reassure her. Alex proved to be God's answer to her anxious thoughts. No matter what she told her mother, he'd put his life on hold to care for her family, and she felt at peace knowing he was there. Would she ever be able to resist his charming presence?

CHAPTER TEN

While Sarah rested in her hospital room, Alex put David and Jonathan to bed at the cottage and then took over the care of the babies from his mother. Knowing Sarah wouldn't mind, he'd given Grace the guest bedroom on the ocean side and tried not to disturb her during the night. Sarah had been gone less than forty-eight hours, yet it felt like forever. He rubbed his irritated eyes and massaged his temples to relieve the pressure inside his head. Oh, for a few hours of continuous rest. How could such little creatures be so demanding?

Alex half dozed on the uncomfortable sofa when he heard the tiny sound of mewing. He jumped up and rushed to retrieve the baby before she disturbed her sister. In his haste, he failed to notice the unfinished construction project in his path until he landed in a heap on his backside. He bit back the scream along with the curse word and crawled over the multi-shaped blocks.

"Hush, sweet baby. Are you hungry?" When he picked her up and continued the one-sided conversation, she ceased crying and relaxed against his chest. Returning to the living room, he stepped around the building blocks while his aching back reminded him to talk to the boys about picking up their toys.

By the time he diapered, fed, and returned the first baby to the crib, her sister started her play for attention. The few occasions when the girls awakened at the same time pushed him to the limit. If he hadn't experienced it for himself, he'd never believe it possible to cuddle one baby while changing the diaper of the other. This baby business proved quite the stretch from creating literature. Mistakes wouldn't correct with the click of a mouse.

Surely Sarah had realized the need for help when she returned home. He'd hire a nanny for the babies, but he could imagine her protest in her syrupy southern drawl, "I want to take care of my own children, and I don't require anyone else in the house. Besides, I couldn't possibly afford to pay a nanny and no way would I accept charity from you, Alex." He lived in his big house on the beach with more money than he'd ever spend, and nothing would please him more than to help Sarah. Though she wouldn't admit it, he recognized her struggle to stay within budget. But her stubborn pride kept her from accepting help from anyone, especially him.

Alex survived another long night and anticipated visiting Sarah in the afternoon. After feeding the girls their early morning bottles, he left them in the care of his mother and took the boys for a walk. He vowed to enjoy the reprieve despite his sleep-deprived body or his concern over leaving his mother alone.

With the sun barely rising over the horizon, the three of them headed south toward his house to pick up Bailey. Their early morning trek became an adventure as they scanned the area for treasures left behind by the tide. The boys gave an excited yelp at each discovery and came running to share their find with him.

"Why do the seagulls follow us?" The gulls made cawing noises and dived up and down over their heads.

"I think it's 'cause they like the bread Mama sometimes lets us feed them. They must 'member us. Do you have some bread at your house we could give them?"

"You're probably right, David. I'll check the kitchen when we get there, but we'll have to find a secluded spot down the beach before we feed them.

"When I first moved here, I fed the birds every morning off the deck. I'd throw the bread high in the air and watch them dive for it. I enjoyed the entertainment until Miss Anna noticed the mess and chased them off with a broom."

Alex laughed with the boys as he related the scene. His feeding frenzies resulted in his house becoming a magnet for every bird in the area. He still remembered Anna's threat. "If you want me to remain as your housekeeper, I suggest you find another form of entertainment."

Initially, Alex struggled to keep up with Bailey and the boys, but as they continued the walk, the moist pure air cleared his mind and invigorated him. He stopped for a moment to enjoy the view of the sun still low on the horizon. The seascape looked unfamiliar to him as though seeing it for the first time. The combination of sky, ocean, and land merged into a picture of perfection. As if synchronized to music, the constant sound of the waves spoke of divine appointment. Warmth enveloped him as he sensed the same presence that filled the cottage before the babies were born. *God, are you responsible for all this?*

Alex shook his head. His teen and young adult years had been firmly planted in the theory of evolution. How had his entire belief system changed so quickly? A battle raged between his prior thinking and the reality of the past few days. Was God revealing himself in answer to his mother's prayers? The explicit response filled his mind with thoughts of love and gratitude for the world—thoughts he wouldn't have considered before meeting Sarah and her family.

Interrupting his quiet reflections, the boys came running, excited about something they'd found near the water. Jonathan carried an unusual conch shell while David displayed a glob of muck encrusted in mud and sediment. Their interest in even the smallest sea creatures amazed him.

"Let me see that, David. There might be a treasure buried beneath all that gook. You never know."

Alex rubbed with gentle movements until he discovered a perfect sand dollar hiding behind the debris. "What do you think, buddy?"

"It's great. I'm going to take it home and keep it in our room."

"I'll clean it up more when we get home and soak it in bleach. That should make it white as snow.

"You're just like Jesus! Mommy says when we're bad sin makes our hearts dirty, but when we're sorry, he washes us white as snow."

Alex stopped rubbing and stared at David. A powerful conviction attacked his insides and shook him to the core. With shaking hands, he pulled the child into a hug. "I wish I could be more like Jesus, David."

Alex released David and removed his sunglasses to wipe the perspiration from his brow. He took in a breath of salt air and exhaled in relief when Jonathan interrupted their conversation with a less serious request. "Can we feed the seagulls now, Mr. Alex?"

At first, the boys had called him "Mister," but they soon tacked on his name. The moniker worked for now, but he'd love for them to call him "Daddy." Though he felt like a father to them, reality reminded him of Sarah's reservations. He needed this family far more than they needed him, and he refused to allow discouragement to keep him from his pursuit.

"I think that's an excellent idea, Jonathan. Here's a bag of bread and crackers for each of you. Watch out for the bombs they might drop on your heads, though." Alex laughed at their shocked looks when the perceptive little boys realized what he said.

When Anna arrived in the afternoon and the boys were down for naps, Alex left for the hospital. On the way, he stopped at the drug store to pick up a box of dark chocolates. His head told him he was getting ahead of himself, but his heart didn't quite get the message.

Arriving at Sarah's room, Alex found her alone with her eyes closed. The color had returned to her cheeks, and she looked peaceful. He hadn't intended to wake her, but without even thinking, he moved to the bedside. When he brushed her hair back and placed his lips on her forehead, her eyes opened. "How's my Nanny?" She shifted to get a closer look at his face. "Alex, you look so tired. What's going on? How are the children? Are the babies eating okay?"

"Hey, hold on. I can't answer more than one question at a time. Yes, I'm a little tired from the night feedings, rising at the crack of dawn, and eating with an infant in my arms, but other than that, I'm fine. The babies are great, but they miss their mama. They eat constantly, especially at night. The boys are well but also miss you. We all miss you. So, what else do you want to know?"

Alex didn't want her to know how fragile he was—almost on the edge of a good cry and he rarely cried. If she knew how inept he considered himself and how empty the cottage felt without her, she would insist on coming home before she fully recovered. He wanted her well and strong before she came home. He couldn't endure another night like the one that landed her in the hospital.

Even with the overwhelming tiredness, the longing and desire he failed to hide tempted him to do and say things he shouldn't. Nothing would satisfy him more than to crawl into bed with her, hold her close, and sleep even for a few minutes. Knowing the effect Sarah had on him, sleep would be impossible, so what's the point in allowing his muddled mind to drift in that direction? In addition to an uninterrupted night's sleep, he could use a cold shower.

Even before Alex pushed back her hair and pressed his lips to her forehead, Sarah knew he was there. She ignored the romantic gesture and brushed it off. Although she loved the feelings he stirred, one day soon she'd have to confront him about these overt displays of affection. However, it would be cruel to do so while he exhausted himself caring for her little ones.

Alex brought a box of chocolates from behind his back, "Here you go, sweetheart. I think it's time for a little nourishment to make you sweeter."

Sarah politely thanked him but frowned at the term of endearment along with the hungry look he gave her that had nothing to do with chocolates. She hoped it expressed fatigue and nothing more, but she doubted it. With his thoughts and feelings so obvious, she could read him as well as one of his books.

"Alex, that's sweet, but I am *not* your 'sweetheart.' You've been extremely generous to help me through this crisis, but I hardly know you. Right now, you can be nothing more than a kind neighbor and a potential friend. If you can't accept that, you should return to your solitude and write about your character's sweetheart." So much for waiting until she got home, and he'd moved back down the beach.

"It's all right, Sarah. I'm willing to be your friend, for now, and I understand your reluctance to move into a new relationship, but I won't give up on you. I'll wait for as long as it takes to make you mine. Does that bother you?"

"Of course, it bothers me. You should be looking for a woman who can give you children and a wife with time to love and support you in your work. I'm a worn-out widow with a house full of children and more baggage than the average man should endure."

"Well, if you don't know by now, I'm not your average man. I have so little to offer that I feel bankrupt compared to you. I'm set in my ways and inflexible much of the time. Sometimes I retreat for days to complete a manuscript, and I've always been the nerd of all nerds. I'm not as handsome as the man in the picture on your dresser, and there's no way that I deserve a beautiful woman like you. But I do know that I'll love you and your children for the rest of my life. You are the only woman I have or would ever consider marrying. I'm not going away, Sarah."

Sarah adjusted the covers and looked everywhere but at the man who'd just rendered her speechless. When she finally looked up at him, she vacillated between anger and pleasure that a man such as Alex would care for her.

"Alex, I'm flattered, but I don't know what to say except that I'm not ready for this. I don't want you to be hurt or disappointed, but it's not that easy to pack away my former life and move on with another man. Tom and I had a wonderful marriage, and I can't dismiss it that easily. Please try to be my friend."

Alex frowned. "I will always be your friend, Sarah, but one day I plan to be much more. You'll see. Right now, I must return to my nanny position, as you so rightly pointed out. My mother wanted me to pick up a few items at the grocery store.

"Speaking of home, do you have any idea when you'll be released? Will your mother be coming home with you?"

"The doctor said if my hemoglobin continues to improve, I might be discharged as early as tomorrow. However, Mother won't be accompanying me. She offered to take me home with her for a few weeks. That was a big step and went a long way toward improving our relationship, but it's merely a start. We both need more time to heal. Besides, I couldn't begin to deal with packing for such a trip. How would I even get there?

"I know you think I'm incapable of managing alone, but I must at least try. This isn't the first set of twins I've nursed through infancy. The children are my responsibility, not yours, your mother's or my mother's. Please, say you understand."

Sarah watched Alex struggle for the right words, probably for the first time ever. "I see where you're coming from and your desire to manage on your own, but it hasn't been easy for me even with the assistance of Mother and Anna. Couldn't Anna at least come in the afternoons for a while to help with the house and laundry? And I refuse to leave until I see that you are well and strong enough to make it alone. Don't even suggest it."

Thoughts of comforting words and loving gestures disappeared as Sarah's anger flared. "You are the most stubborn individual I've ever met.

Didn't you hear a word I said? I'll manage fine without you or Anna. Who gave you the right to dominate my life, anyway?"

"Why God, of course. You said I was his gift to you and I'm taking my role seriously. Get used to it. Got to run. If you are released tomorrow, plan for after lunch. That's the best time for me to get away if you wish me to drive you home. Surely, you'll accept assistance this once? Do you think that would be acceptable to your new role as independent housewife and mother?"

Sarah wanted to throw the box of chocolates at him, hard, while the even-tempered Alex acted as if they discussed the weather. It infuriated her to admit it, but he was right. She wouldn't be able to drive for a few weeks and based on the last conversations with her mother, there wasn't another soul she could call. Why did she have to be so dependent on this overpowering man?

"Yes, thank you. That's very kind of you, but don't become too comfortable with being the answer to all my problems."

Sarah sensed Alex's frustration as he started for the door. He sighed and returned to stand before her. With an intense look, he paused for a moment before bending over to kiss her—on the cheek this time. She frowned as she realized the proximity to her mouth. Her plan involved easing him out of her life, not drawing him closer. Despite his domineering ways, she loved his visits and adored his attention. She wondered how she'd manage without him, but she had no choice. Alex made himself too comfortable in her family, and if she wasn't careful, in her heart.

CHAPTER ELEVEN

Alex hoped his loving gestures disguised his hurt, but the pretense was gone as soon as he left Sarah's room. He rehearsed her rejection as he rushed wildly through the grocery store and tossed items haphazardly into the cart. The steering wheel took the brunt of his anger on his return to the cottage. When he saw his mother, he had yet to cool down and needed to lash out at someone.

"How can she be so ungrateful? Here I am putting my whole life on hold to take care of her and the children, and she's trying to blow me off. We'll see how she manages without me."

His mother left him to stew while she put away the groceries. Conviction soon replaced his fury as he realized the anger hurt only himself and in turn caused pain for his exhausted mother. Alex tried to be careful with her, but he saw the worry lines on her face and realized he was responsible.

Being with Sarah's little ones allowed him a glimpse of the concern parents have for their children. He gained a greater appreciation for his mother who often expressed her fear that he might end up hurt. Of all the problems he might experience, neither he nor his mother was prepared for his obsession with a woman with a ready-made family.

The next day when Alex picked up Sarah from the hospital, she huddled against the passenger door with her body turned away from him. She thwarted all his attempts to engage her in conversation. Most of the time she refused to look at him. When she did turn his way, her distant look had him worried. He prayed she wouldn't succumb to postpartum depression. She certainly didn't need anything else.

"Are you feeling all right, Sarah? You seem unusually quiet. You're on the way home to see your children, for goodness sake. Can you not act a little excited?"

"I'm sorry, Alex, but I need some quiet time. Is that okay? You gave me a lot to think about yesterday. Please let me be for a while. I know you don't mean to, but your strong personality overwhelms me. Sometimes I feel as if I'm being run over by a steamroller."

"I'm sorry, too, Sarah—I can't help the way I feel about you or my desire to be a part of your life. What will happen when we get home? I know you don't want me to stay at your house, but I would worry so much if you were alone. I cannot repress this desire to help you and the children. Please, for my sake, allow me to stay at least tonight. I won't interfere, but I'll be there in case you need me. Also, I've been taking the boys for a walk on the beach each morning. They'd be disappointed if you forbade it."

"It's okay, Alex, if you stay tonight—but only tonight. For now, you and the boys may continue your walks. I realize how much they love and enjoy you."

For the first time that day, Sarah looked directly at him—through narrowed eyes. "You're a devious person, you know, trying to secure my affections through my children."

Alex chuckled at the amusing reprimand while raising folded hands upward. *Thank you that she'd allow me to spend time with her boys.* In his heart, he believed that God had put Sarah in his life for a purpose. Meeting those rambunctious boys on the beach couldn't have been mere coincidence. Though it seemed complicated, he loved this woman and her children. *God, help her not to resent my attention.*

By the time they pulled into the driveway, Sarah acted more like herself. She pulled down the mirror and checked her appearance before releasing her seatbelt.

"Look, Sarah. You have a fan club waiting on the front stoop."

The boys rushed to greet their mother with "gentle" hugs as they'd been coached. They ushered her inside to see their sisters who were asleep in their crib. Sarah kissed each one while checking them over and remarking as to how they'd grown.

After the boys went down for naps, his mother planned to retire to his house for a few days before returning to Northern Virginia. She'd been a lifesaver for Alex, but the ordeal hadn't been easy for her. It grieved him to see her concern for his unhappiness. He often overheard the distress and tears in her voice when she talked to his dad each evening. The time had come for her to return to the comfort and peace of her home.

Before leaving the cottage, Grace went into the bedroom to visit with Sarah. They whispered so they wouldn't wake the babies, but Alex still overheard most of the conversation.

"Mrs. Caine, thank you for coming to help with the children. What a blessing you've been to us. I felt relieved knowing you were here with Alex."

"Call me, Grace, Sarah. You're no longer that little girl I used to see playing on the beach. As for helping, it's been a pleasure to be with my son and your children. Seeing him focused on something besides a book brought joy to this mother's heart. Do you know how long I've prayed for him to return to the Lord?

"At the age of fourteen, Alex rejected God. Teenage boys should be joking with their friends, teasing girls, and playing video games, not making life-changing decisions to deny their faith. You owe me no thanks—I should be thanking you and your children. It was after he met your family that he began to change. He loves you, you know."

"Oh, Mrs. Caine, er, Grace, I think I'm just another project or research for his next novel. You'll forgive me, but I almost hope that's the case. I've lost both my father and my husband within the last two years, and I'm not ready for another man in my life. As much as I admire and care for Alex, there's no way he can be anything more than a friend and good neighbor. Neither of us wants him hurt, but I must accept the responsibility for my family."

"I understand, Sarah, and I realize you need time to come down out of this whirlwind. You're still grieving for both those good men. My husband and I have known your parents and socialized with them over the years, but I find it ironic that you and Alex never met, though I believe you played with my daughter, Jana.

"After our children grew up, we stopped coming to the island and had lost touch with your parents until Alex bought his house here. When we did visit, we often met them for lunch or dinner. After your father's diagnosis, your mother telephoned and asked for prayer. I called a few times after your dad passed away, but Leslie sounded so withdrawn. She didn't want to hear from a mere acquaintance. I'm sorry that life has dealt her such a heavy blow and now, here you are facing a similar loss.

"May I pray with you, Sarah? Only God can fill the emptiness that Alex desires to fill. God has promised to be a father to the fatherless and a husband to the widow. Just remember, though, God allows good people in our lives to walk with us and help us carry the load. Please be open to what he might have for you in the future."

Alex didn't hear her response, but he suspected Sarah of crying. His mother prayed so quietly he couldn't understand the words. A few minutes later, she joined him in the living room. Embarrassed at hearing himself sniff, he rubbed his face against the throw pillow he'd been squeezing against his chest. How could he continue without hope regarding a relationship? His mother seemed to think that with God, Sarah would be fine, but what about his need of Sarah?

He saw concern in his mother's eyes. "I guess you heard some of our conversation. I thought you'd gone back to the kitchen. Please forgive me for talking behind your back. You know I love you and care about what happens. More than anything, I don't want you to be hurt. Surely you see that Sarah isn't ready for the love you want to give her and the children. She requires time and space to come to her own conclusions. Love her from afar, Alex, but love God more. Let me pray for you, darling."

Alex tensed when his weeping mother put her head near his heart and hugged him. She prayed under her breath for him to seek a relationship with God instead of desiring to be with Sarah. Though he appreciated the admonishment to put God first, at this point, he didn't see that happening. His reluctant Sarah stood front and center, and no way could anyone or anything take her place.

After the boys were in bed for the evening, Alex came into Sarah's bedroom to check on his patients one last time before retiring to the couch. He stumbled over to the bed and sat down briefly to talk with her about the busy day while she swaddled the babies in their blankets. In the middle of a sentence, he suddenly felt so tired he couldn't sit up. "If I only rest for a minute ..."

Sarah turned to look at Alex when he stopped talking mid-sentence. *What in the world?* There he lay on his side, making himself comfortable in her bed, quietly snoring. Though she wanted to hit him with a pillow, tender feelings stirred within her as she considered his exhaustion. *What am I going to do with the infuriating man?*

Dare she try to wake him? She decided to slip off his shoes, cover him, and let him rest. For a second, she was tempted to climb in on the other side. He wouldn't even realize it, she rationalized but nixed the troublesome idea. Her boys were her first concern, and the examples she set would stay with them for the rest of their lives. She would sleep on the couch where Alex had slept the last few nights.

Her next thought pricked her conscious when she realized that if she could hear the babies from the living room, Alex probably had heard her conversation with his mother. Sarah prayed he wasn't in the living room when she bared her feelings about him. In his fragile state, that would've been terrible for him to hear. As she looked again at the person she'd come to admire, she growled aloud at her own frustration. *Why do relationships have to be so difficult?* Although she ached at the thought of hurting him, she saw no other solution.

During the night, Sarah tiptoed in and tended the infants without disturbing the "big baby" in her bed. Each time she came into the room, Alex slept on. She couldn't get over how he made himself at home, not merely in her house, but in her bed. Would he ever wake up?

When the boys awakened early the next morning, they raced past her on the couch, searching for Alex. She quickly intercepted them and shooed them to the living room.

"He's sleeping in your bed?" Jonathan pointed out the obvious. "Does that mean he's our daddy now?"

Sarah nearly choked on her son's misplaced observation. "What on earth would make you think that, Jonathan? Mr. Alex fell asleep while we were talking, and since he's so tired, I let him have my bed. I slept on the couch."

"Oh!" Jonathan's shoulders slumped. "Can we wake him up? It's time to go for a walk and get Bailey."

"I think we better let him sleep. He worked hard to take care of you and your sisters. We should let him rest awhile. Since it's a beautiful day outside, why don't you two play a little before breakfast? Maybe by then, Mr. Alex will wake up, and you can take a walk. Stay near the porch today, though. I won't be able to watch you every minute."

As it turned out, Alex missed his walk with Jonathan and David and continued sleeping through breakfast. The boys were disappointed, and she caught them making more noise than usual, hoping to rouse their playmate. No matter how much they tried, he slept on.

A little after eleven o'clock when she tiptoed in to pick up one of the babies, he turned and looked at her. He blinked a couple of times, looked down at himself and sat up in bed. After his eyes roamed around the room, his gaze returned to her only a moment before he lowered his head sheepishly. She watched in amazement as a satisfied grin swept over his face, and sleepy eyes met hers. She felt herself melting under the look Alex gave her. Warmth spread throughout her body, and her lonely heart pounded in her chest. Sarah grimaced at her weakness and quickly came to her senses. She chose to ignore the feelings his bedhead and sleepy look stirred within her. Sarah wouldn't allow this kind, caring individual to sidetrack her. The quicker she got him out of her bedroom, the better off they'd both be. With that resolved, Sarah attempted to lighten the mood.

"Well, good morning, sleepy head. You must've been exhausted to sleep so soundly. You slept through everything. How did you ever wake up to feed the babies when I was away? You should've gone on home and slept in your bed instead of kicking me out of mine. So much for being available to help." Sarah knew she laid the teasing on a bit thick, but his confused look was too tempting. His cuteness almost had her yielding to his charms.

Alex squinted at the clock, rubbed his fingers through his hair, and straightened his shirt. "Is it really eleven o'clock? I can't believe I slept all that time. Guess I was making up for lost sleep over the past few days. With sole responsibility for the babies at night, I rarely closed my eyes for fear I wouldn't hear them when they cried. What a relief to relax and leave them in the care of their mother. It's hard to imagine falling asleep so suddenly. I'm so sorry, Sarah. You're right, I should've gone home. Although, I probably would've stayed awake half the night with worry. Please forgive me for taking your bed and not being available. I guess it's a little presumptuous to ask if you slept with me. Wouldn't that be a hoot? Sleeping with a beautiful woman and not even realizing it."

"You know I slept on the couch, silly man, but I think this indicates you should return to your home and resume a normal life. Perhaps you will enjoy some uninterrupted sleep for a change. Don't you think it's about time you continued work on your novel?"

Although Alex disliked her suggestion, he knew she was right. "Well, if you're going to kick me out, I guess it's time to go. I still want to spend time with the boys every morning and come by to see the babies. You can't take them away from me cold turkey because you don't want me around."

"It's not that I don't want you around, Alex. We've discussed my need for independence before. You're welcome to come by, but please, as a guest. Can you handle that kind of withdrawal after having the run of the house and being in charge the last few days?"

"I think so, but you know I require a bit of encouragement."

Alex had become comfortable fulfilling the husband role in this family, and he had trouble relinquishing it. Awakening to Sarah's beauty and charm stirred feelings in him that made him long to pull her to him and never let go. He wanted her in every way, and he couldn't walk out the door without some assurance that he hadn't dreamed the last few days. He had greeted her with chaste kisses filled with affection, cuddled the children closer than ever, and taken his role more seriously than anything in his life.

He moved toward her. "Kiss me, Sarah."

"What? Are you out of your mind? Absolutely not. You can't be serious. Knowing how I feel, why would you ask me such a thing? Haven't you heard anything I said to you?" Sarah backed away. *Was he wrong in thinking that she returned his affection?*

"I'm more than serious, Sarah. I've never been kissed by a woman, and I want your kisses to be my first and my last. If you won't do it out of love, reward me as a thank you. That's all I need."

Alex wasn't surprised by Sarah's response. He hated to beg, but a desperate man takes desperate measures. He had to know where he stood with the perplexing woman.

"I'm having a little trouble believing that you've never been kissed. Those celebrity magazines couldn't have gotten it that wrong. You've dated beautiful models and actresses. How could you want someone like me?"

"Believe me, Sarah, you outshine any other woman. I'm not playing with you. The past week has been the highlight of my whole life. I've waited a long time to feel what I do with you. Please let me express my love."

Alex saw the look of resignation as Sarah gradually acquiesced. "This is probably not a good idea, and I know I'll regret it, but I'll do my best to give you a nice sisterly kiss. I suppose you deserve that as appreciation for saving my life."

"No way, Sarah, I've had more than my share of air kisses and pecks on the check. I want the real thing. Can't you at least pretend a little affection toward me?" He wasn't letting her get away with a peck, and he hoped she knew it. His heart pounded, and beads of sweat broke out on his forehead. If he could entice her to respond to him, perhaps she'd discover the love she tried so hard to hide, and there would be hope for their future.

"Oh, all right. You sound so pathetic. Go for it."

Sarah's plan to give him a peck, quick and benign, went rapidly awry. When his lips touched hers, she unconsciously leaned into his embrace and wrapped her arms around him. Her knees grew weak. She clung to him. He held her and kept the romantic gesture going much longer than either of them planned. Not sisterly, and far from inexperienced.

At the height of her pleasure, she abruptly came to her senses. *What am I doing? I can't let this happen.* She pushed him away.

"Alex, that was far from sisterly. You cannot do that to me. I won't allow it. Go home, right now. You're too much of a temptation. You toy with my emotions, and I don't appreciate it. And another thing, you lied to me. You must think I am the most gullible woman on the planet if you think I believe that was your first kiss. Just go."

Alex looked at her with so much love and desire that her resolve weakened under the waves of pleasure attacking her body. She had missed the romance of marriage, and his kiss brought back feelings she'd almost forgotten. Her deceitful heart wanted him and longed for him. With a slight move on her part, those desires would be fulfilled. Thankfully, common sense burst her dreamy bubble and brought her back to reality. She couldn't allow this attraction to continue but dismissing him didn't seem to help.

"I'm not your brother, Sarah. I love you, and I'll never forget how you made me feel. You were responding with love, but I know you won't admit it. We'd be so good together. Thanks for that bit of encouragement, though. Regardless of what you think, if you don't count the times I've kissed you in my dreams, that was my first real kiss. In all my dreams, however, none ever felt like that, and though you gave reluctantly, it gave me hope. See you soon."

Alex felt pleased with himself as he turned to walk out the door. He ran out to the beach and gave a victory leap into the swift wind. "She loves me," he yelled at the waves. As his emotions calmed, he couldn't stop rehearsing the warmth and love of Sarah's embrace. It was his first real kiss whether Sarah believed him or not. Her passionate response made him long for more, and he wouldn't be satisfied until he had all of her. Alex wanted forever. It mattered not that she came with a house full of children. To him, the children were icing on the cake—sweet.

CHAPTER TWELVE

The following day, Alex headed north to pick up Jonathan and David. He waved to Sarah while the boys romped with Bailey. When they reached the beach, his steps matched those of the boys as they bounced along—sometimes playing tag with the waves and often stopping to gather unique shells. He never felt better.

"Guess what, Mr. Alex?"

Alex laughed as Jonathan skipped backward before him, bouncing with excitement. "Tell me."

"Mama says you don't have to help her with the babies. We're gonna make a giant sand castle after breakfast, and you can help. Right, David?"

Now that he'd been released from house duty, the boys expected a full-time playmate. Alex caught up with Jonathan, pulled him under his arm and gave him a head rub. "We'll see."

When they returned from walking on the beach, Alex ignored Sarah's request that he play the role of a guest. Not bothering to knock, he entered through the back door and followed the boys into the kitchen. He pulled out a chair at the table, made himself comfortable and started talking as if continuing a conversation from a few hours before. After all, he'd been there almost a week and felt quite at home in the cottage.

"Sarah, do you realize that we haven't named the babies? We must do that and get their births registered. I'm not sure how much time the state allows you on this, but it surely can't be delayed much longer. What do you think? Do you have any ideas about names? Seems to me you've had more than enough time to pray about it."

When Sarah turned from the sink, he saw trouble written all over her face. Her normally pleasant countenance turned red with anger. His offer to help register the babies couldn't have triggered the kind of fury her demeanor suggested. Perhaps, that bit of passion the day before had her in a tiff.

"There is no 'we,' Mr. Caine. And what gives you the right to walk into my house without knocking, sit down, and interfere in my life. I tell you, I won't have it. You've overstepped your bounds. You did it yesterday with that passionate kiss, and you've done it again today. Just get out. Get out of my house and get out of my life."

Between the two of them, Alex didn't know who showed more surprise—the livid woman or her victim. As soon as the words came out of Sarah's mouth, he saw a look of utter horror cross her face. But recanting didn't seem to be an option. Instead of letting her see the hurt she inflicted, he chose to respond in kind.

"I don't deserve this, Sarah. Call me if you need me."

When Alex jumped from his seat at the table and turned over the chair with his abrupt departure, Sarah burst into tears. From her view at the kitchen window, she watched him walk dejectedly toward his home. Although he tried to cover his feelings with the angry exit, Sarah didn't miss the unshed tears and that initial look of hurt and rejection. Thankfully, the boys had gone into the bathroom after their walk and hadn't heard the venom coming from their mother's mouth. That wasn't proper behavior for anyone much less a mother of two impressionable boys. Yet, she had to put some distance between herself and the infuriating man, and her cruelty seemed to work. Perhaps Alex would finally realize what a basket case she was and forget he ever knew her.

The real challenge would be to forget him. When everything was right between the two of them, she never felt happier or more at peace. Even now, her traitorous heart wanted to run after him and beg forgiveness, but there was no choice. She had to let him go.

Sarah refused to take all the blame. Trying to reason with Alex or set boundaries hadn't worked. Regardless, she shouldn't allow anger to motivate her. What if her actions drove him away when he'd just begun seeking God? But what more could she do? She regretted that Alex would have to be hurt until he saw reason, and she had time to cool off. As the boys returned to the room, Sarah managed to erase her tears and hide her misery.

"Where's Mr. Alex?" David asked. "He said he'd stay and help you with breakfast. He wanted to see our sisters. He wouldn't leave without saying goodbye."

The boys ran into the living room, then out to the porch searching for their friend. "Boys, come back inside for breakfast. Mr. Alex had to go. I'm sure he'll come to see you soon, but we no longer require his help, and he has other important work he needs to do. Let me check your hands before you set the table."

Distracting them had worked in the past, but now, they'd have none of it. Jonathan acted out with an almost belligerent attitude as he pleaded their case. "But he promised to help us with a sand castle after breakfast. I bet you were mean to him. We do need him. He's like our daddy, and he loves us."

"You had a wonderful daddy, Jonathan, and you don't need a replacement. Alex can be your friend. Maybe he'll come by tomorrow and help with the sand castle. I didn't tell him he couldn't come to see you."

Sarah's explanation sounded shallow and unconvincing—even to her. Yet she couldn't tell her sons about the disagreement. With her self-esteem near extinction, she didn't need them defending Alex against her. Sarah should have disciplined Jonathan for talking back, but what could she say? She recognized the truth, even coming from a child. Regardless, she refused to change her mind.

With Alex anywhere near her, he incited emotions that she didn't want to feel. The chemistry between them wasn't just strong—it sizzled. Those unwanted feelings threatened to erase all memories of her husband and the passion they shared, and she could no longer tolerate them. Raising her family came first, and nothing nor no one should distract her.

If she were honest with herself, she feared falling in love again. First, her father died, and then her husband. She couldn't handle the pain of another abandonment. Sure, it'd be nice to have someone beside her to help carry the heavy load, but must that someone walk a dozen steps ahead? Was she destined to always live in some man's shadow?

When she put the breakfast on the table for the boys, the old fears crept forward attempting to overpower her. She forced herself to look up. God was the only one who hadn't left her. Though at times, it seemed as if she'd left him, especially when she allowed anger to control her. She'd been home alone for only one night, and everything seemed to be falling apart.

As Alex walked home, he prayed and cried. He shook with grief and disappointment. He hadn't felt this alone and rejected since he'd attempted to publish his first manuscript. Not even that rejection compared to Sarah's.

He made his way to the study where he paced the floor, vacillating between anger and deep-seated hurt. How could a woman wreak such havoc on an ordinary man? Not only had she lured him with her beauty, but she'd moved in for the kill with her acid tongue. He couldn't stand her when she acted so ruthless, but now that he had tasted her sweetness, he didn't know how he would survive without her.

As he perused the overloaded bookcases, his vision landed on the gift his mother had given him when he completed confirmation classes. He removed the leather-bound book from the upper shelf and traced his name engraved on the front cover. Like a thirsty man longing for a cup of water, he searched for something to fill the vacancy left by Sarah. As he flipped the thin pages, his eyes landed on Jeremiah twenty-nine. Reading from the beginning, he stopped at the thirteenth verse. "You will seek me and find me, when you search for me with all your heart." As soon as he read the passage, he remembered his mother's prayer urging him to seek God.

Thinking he might find something more suitable, he turned to Matthew and discovered a similar message: "But seek first His kingdom and His righteousness, and all these things will be added to you." The answer appeared in bright red letters, Jesus's own words telling him to put his relationship with God above all. The truth hit him hard. While longing for Sarah, his soul ached for something greater.

For a long time, Alex meditated on the thoughts and Scriptures running through his mind and then fell to his knees and prayed, *God, I surrender. Though I desire Sarah, I want to know you more. I don't want to continue without your presence in my life. Please help me relinquish my obsession with this woman and look solely to you. Your will be done.*

It turned out to be a prayer of surrender. His desires and the emptiness he felt inside could be filled by none other than the One who had restlessly pursued him for the past fourteen years.

Alex walked south the next few days to avoid Sarah and the boys. Though he missed them, he ached at the thought of being unwelcome in a place he felt so at home. He mourned the loss as though a dear friend had died.

When he returned from his walk on Friday, the boys were standing on the beach near his house. As they ran up to him in tears, he feared another crisis with Sarah or the babies. He pulled them into his arms. When their distress turned into a reprimand, his fears were put to rest.

Jonathan spoke first. "Why didn't you come help us build the sand castle? You promised."

"And you left without saying goodbye," added David. "We need you. Mommy doesn't do things like you do. We like it better when you're there."

Holding them as tightly as possible, he kissed their heads and murmured comforting endearments as he silently prayed for wisdom and the right words. *Lord, I don't want to hurt them.*

"Your mother and I felt it would be better if I gave her time to adjust to the new babies and see how she does without my help. You are big brothers, and she knows she can count on you."

"But she said you could come by to see us," David sniffed. "We miss you."

"I know, and I miss you too, but would you do something for me? Please play without me the way you did before we met. I'll check to see how you're doing, but I can't be with you every day. You know that I write stories, and I've neglected my job for the past few weeks. Who knows, I might write a book for you one day. How would you like that?"

That seemed to satisfy them as they gave him excited, affirmative nods. "How about I walk you home now? Maybe you could show me what you've done to build your sand castle. Okay?"

When they were almost at Sarah's cottage, Alex heard her frantic call long before he saw her. "Your mom's worried about you. You must never go out on the beach without an adult and without your mother's permission. It's too dangerous. Do you promise?"

They nodded and ran toward their mother. Alex merely waved at Sarah and turned toward home feeling like a rejected intruder. With his heart still so fragile, he couldn't take another confrontation with Sarah. Even seeing her from a distance made him feel as if an invisible force hit him in the chest. He'd have to trust the boys to tell her the truth and take the blame for their disobedience. Though it wasn't his problem, he longed to be included.

Despite the empty feeling, he went to his study and started outlining a new novel. The plot developed at such a pace he knew God directed his thoughts. Inspiration seemed to jump from his mind onto the pages. In the past, he considered his books a clean read, but looking at them with renewed scrutiny, he realized they were written from the world's perspective. Since God provided the talent and insight for this new book, he'd honor him with the content.

While working, he decided to search for classical or elevator-type music. Instead of turning on the stereo, he flipped the dial and searched radio frequencies. Almost immediately, he landed on a soothing melody with Christian lyrics. Though he'd heard of contemporary Christian bands, he hadn't bothered to listen.

This song spoke so much into his current situation that he recognized the whisper from God through the anointed words. When the song finished, he checked for it on YouTube and continued to listen. Tears clouded his eyes as the message of the John Waller song, "While I'm Waiting," motivated him to serve others, worship God, and walk in obedience while waiting for the answer to his prayers. *Was he willing to wait and trust God with Sarah?*

Until Alex saw her out on the beach this morning searching for the boys, he thought he'd replaced his obsession over Sarah with faith and dependence on Christ. But his reaction told a different story. His heart palpitated within his chest, and perspiration beaded his forehead as he watched her with her children. He continued to long and grieve for something beyond his reach. Laying aside his work, he knelt beside his desk and asked God to take away the aching desire. *If Sarah is your will for me, God, please give me patience to wait for her, even if it takes a lifetime.*

Somehow the song built his faith and gave him hope that Sarah required time—time for God to modify him into a man worthy of such a woman. Since God answered his frantic prayer the day the babies were born, a gradual transformation had occurred. But, as his mother pointed out, he often acted self-centered and independent, wanting his way. How would he ever become an acceptable husband and father with such a domineering personality? Even Sarah called him a steamroller. Surrendering his stubborn will wouldn't come easy.

Although Alex hadn't attended church for several years, he jumped out of bed Sunday morning anxious to visit the little Community Church on Shell Island. Church attendance seemed to be expected of Christians and certainly couldn't hurt. Opening the side door leading to the doggy run, anticipation built for what he planned to do. Bailey ran directly to his leash and nearly pulled it off its hook.

"Not this morning, boy. I'm going to church!"

As he coaxed Bailey into his kennel, Alex didn't let the dog's sad eyes and pitiful whine deter him from his mission. After an abbreviated shower, he pulled on a pair of black jeans along with a collarless shirt and a light-weight suit coat. Before heading for the garage level, he rushed up the stairs to find his Bible. His wayward thoughts turned to Sarah and his avoidance of her the day before. Surely, she wouldn't be there to mess up his morning. *Would she?* He dismissed the idea with a flick of his wrist and punched the down button on the elevator.

When he'd parked the car and stepped out into the brisk wind, he shivered and wished he'd worn a heavier jacket. The weather seemed cold for mid-November. Viewing the storm clouds over the ocean, he rubbed his arms and dashed for the ornate doors that graced the beautiful, old church.

Words of the opening hymn, "Great Is Thy Faithfulness," greeted Alex as he slipped into a back pew. Several years had passed since he'd heard the song, but with the occasional help of the hymnal, he managed to follow along. In his prodigal wanderings, he'd never considered what stirring messages the hymns conveyed—he felt almost as if he was hearing them for the first time.

The light shining through the stained-glass window at the front of the church drew his attention to the image of Jesus carrying a lamb in his arms. "The Good Shepherd" read the caption. He remembered reading something similar in one of the gospels and made a mental note to revisit the story. Seeing himself as that little lamb, he felt God's presence enveloping him with love. He had come home.

Alex returned his attention to the words of the song and closed his eyes to reflect on the beauty of the music. When the song ended, he sat down and looked toward the front where the pastor was greeting the congregation. That's when he saw her.

The peace left him so quickly he sympathized with a lonely piece of driftwood bobbing on the tide. His heart beat erratically. His body tensed. Beads of sweat broke out on his forehead. There sat Sarah and her little charges—all four of them—on about the third pew from the front intruding on his worship. A couple of women cuddled the girls. The boys, one on each side of her, were quiet and still for a change. How could she look so confident and efficient?

Well, his "Miss Independence" coped well, seemingly. She wouldn't let him help her but allowed perfect strangers to hold his babies. He should be the one snuggling them—not strangers. How could she look so beautiful and rested with the responsibility of taking care of four little ones all by herself? She didn't seem to miss him in the least.

He pondered leaving until the words of the song he heard on the radio came to mind. Sarah hadn't disturbed his worship. He'd allowed his emotions to control him. How many times must he relinquish the dear woman? Convicted again, of unbelief, disappointment, jealousy, anger, and sarcasm, he prayed a silent prayer of repentance. He should've been proud of her for handling the situation so well.

A few more minutes and additional worship songs were required for his heart to settle enough to focus on the sermon. Alex hadn't come expecting an intellectual dissertation or inspiration, but not far into the homily, he was pleasantly surprised. The pastor, an apparent student of the Bible, quoted verse after verse that spoke to him. The man seemed to know the Author of the Book well.

Pastor Mark Abbott took his text from Hebrews and proceeded to describe a life of faith. His casual delivery moved from Bible characters who had lived by faith to examples from history and finally to even present-day illustrations. He praised their perseverance through trials and their faith that sustained them during persecution.

"I challenge you, dear friends, to adhere to the apostle Paul when he said in Romans 10:17 "So faith comes from hearing, and hearing by the word of Christ." If you really want to increase your faith, read the Bible and hear the stories of God's intervention in the lives of his people throughout the ages. Study the Scriptures over the following weeks and expect an increase in your faith as you live it out in the world."

The pastor's closing prayer petitioned God to direct the steps of each person that they might have the greatest impact on those around them. Inspired by the challenge, Alex determined to practice his new-found faith in every way, beginning with Sarah.

Alex planned to sneak out during the closing prayer to avoid a run-in with Sarah. Moved by the service, however, he forgot his original intention. He could have made a quick exit from the rear pew, but a new resolve to surrender to God's timeline kept him from rushing past the minister and his wife as they greeted parishioners. The man introduced himself as Pastor Mark and invited Alex to meet him for lunch the following Tuesday.

Alex hesitated, citing a busy schedule, but something stopped him from rejecting the invitation. Although the man looked old enough to be his father, he felt an extraordinary connection. The minister struck Alex as having a wealth of experience and wisdom that would benefit any new Christian. When they'd finalized their plans, Alex hurried toward the exit.

He had almost gotten to his SUV when the piercing sound of his name stopped him. Jonathan and David raced toward him. He grabbed them up in his arms and held them tight. How he'd missed them. He would always think of them as his boys, and he regretted not seeing them more often. Only his pride and wounded spirit kept him from seeking out Sarah and giving equal time to the baby girls.

"Wow! You guys are getting so big. Before long I won't be able to lift you both at the same time." Alex gave them another hug, tickled them, and let them down.

"I'm so proud of your behavior in church, not a peep out of you. And your baby sisters were good, too."

"You should've been with us. We could've scrunched together or sat on your lap."

"Well, I'm sorry, but I didn't see you until I was seated. You see I came a little late."

"Mama says you shouldn't be late for church. It's improlight!"

Alex laughed unable to restrain his enjoyment of these two munchkins. "The word is impolite, Jonathan. As you know, Mama's always right, so I'll try to do better next time. I'm glad you came to say hello, but I've got to run, guys. Maybe I'll drop by with Bailey in the morning for a few minutes. You two be good and help Mommy with the babies."

Alex turned them toward Sarah and sent them off with a quick pat on their behinds. Praying they wouldn't feel neglected, he watched as they dragged their feet and looked back several times before reaching their mother. Sarah glanced at him as she stood talking with some of the church families. He turned away before she could see the longing in his face. *God give me strength.* He would meet with the pastor on Tuesday as planned, but he didn't think he could endure another Sunday at the church. His heart resisted further abuse. Is this what it felt like to be love-sick? If it was, Alex required miraculous healing.

On Monday, he spent time on the beach with the boys, but only saw Sarah and the babies from a distance. It almost felt like a divorce except he couldn't file for joint custody or contribute to their livelihood. She'd made it perfectly clear that she didn't want him in their lives, and he'd have to accept that for now, but hopefully not forever.

CHAPTER THIRTEEN

With some uncertainty, Alex looked forward to the meeting with Pastor Mark on Tuesday. From observing the man during the service, he felt sure he could trust him and maybe even help him sort out the complicated situation. Perhaps he merely required a place to vent his frustrations. Instead of talking over lunch as originally planned, Alex asked to meet at the pastor's office where he'd have the privacy to bare his soul.

A small sign near the church entrance directed him toward the stairs. No receptionist greeted him in the outer office. Alex knocked on the door labeled Pastor's Study and entered at the invitation. Meeting new people had never been a problem for him, yet as he greeted the minister, he felt nervous and anxious. Pastor Mark stood, reached across his desk, and shook hands with Alex.

"Let's sit here—" he gestured toward two comfortable chairs near an open window—"and enjoy the fresh air."

Alex relaxed.

"I'm so glad you came, Mr. Caine. Good to see you in church on Sunday. I remember when your parents used to come in the summer, but I don't recall ever seeing you. It's not every day we have the honor of a published writer in our congregation. I hope my invitation to meet with you didn't come across as celebrity treatment."

Alex smiled but didn't admit to thinking something similar. "From the moment you entered the sanctuary on Sunday, I felt God directing me toward you. Forgive me if that sounds presumptuous, but I've learned over the years to heed those little nudges. I trust we allowed you the freedom to worship in peace. Most people recognized you, however, and even Sarah Stuart's boys were quite excited to see you. I hadn't realized the connection."

The pastor's reference to Alex's writing didn't embarrass him. The exuberant greeting from the boys was harder to explain. Most of the residents on the island knew of his books and chose to ignore the celebrity status in favor of respecting his privacy. They treated him like any other resident, and if his place of refuge should be compromised, he suspected they'd shield him from unwanted intrusions. However, no one could miss the enthusiastic greeting from David and Jonathan aimed at the hermit writer who rarely came out of seclusion. Those boys meant so much to him but trying to explain his feelings presented a problem. Alex struggled to understand the mysterious connection himself. He couldn't imagine what others might think.

"Well, authors must acknowledge their Maker and the Source of their gift as much or maybe more so than other professions. Although it's taken me a while, I'm glad that I came to realize the responsibility we have for our readers. And yes, I do know Sarah and the children. That's one of the reasons I'm here. As convenient and enjoyable as your church is, I don't think I'll return."

Pastor Mark frowned. "Did something offend you, Mr. Caine?"

"Please call me Alex. No, nothing like that at all. Quite the contrary. The worship was wonderful, and your sermon seemed to speak directly to me, but it's Sarah. You see I didn't expect her to return to church so soon. She's gone through a lot and circumstances threw us together at a time she really needed someone." Alex hesitated, embarrassed at the truth, but felt compelled to continue.

"I don't quite know how to say this, but along with helping her, I fell in love and can easily see myself stepping into the role of her husband and father to her children."

The pastor arched his eyebrows and gave him a quizzical look as Alex continued his quick synopsis regarding Sarah and her family. "I'm sure you're aware that she lost her husband a few months back, and she's not ready to move on with her life. Although I understand her position, when she's near, my heart aches for her. Meeting this young family caused me to change so much, but at the same time, completely disrupted my life. In fact, my return to God happened shortly after meeting her family. For my peace of mind, I must give her some space, at least for a while."

"I see." The pastor thought for a few seconds as Alex's dilemma settled in his mind. "I've known of you for a while, Alex, through your parents and your books. Your writing is exceptional, by the way."

"Thank you. I didn't know ministers had time in their busy schedules to read fiction."

"Well, I consider it part of my job to read what my parishioners read. How can I caution them about the 'evils' of the world, if I don't know what's going on out there? Besides, a minister must relax sometime. What better way than with an enjoyable book?

"So, you love Sarah. As wonderful as you appear to be, Alex, I can't make her fall in love with you, so what else can I do for you?"

Alex felt a little put out that the man dismissed his feelings toward Sarah so quickly. Besides, no one would convince him that she didn't love him. Did the man think he'd be satisfied with a few compliments on his writing? The pastor had a lot to learn if he thought Alex that gullible.

Just as he considered walking out on the man, Pastor Mark continued. "I know you think I'm giving you the brush off regarding Sarah, but I think there's a greater need here, and I'd like us to get to the real issue. Might we begin with prayer?"

As the pastor bowed his head and allowed a few minutes of silence, Alex's frustration dissolved. In its place, Alex sensed a peace and love that could only be attributed to God. After what seemed like an eternity, the pastor cleared his throat and prayed.

"Dear Father, we come to you humbly as your children, knowing that you love and care for us. Enlighten us, as we share together and turn our hearts toward you. We don't have the answers, but you are the one who made us, and you know our anxious thoughts. Provide us with wisdom and grace to seek your will in all that we do. Help us to see the plan you have for Alex, Sarah, and those dear children. In Jesus's name. Amen.

"Now, Alex, let's start at the beginning or where you think the beginning might be."

"The beginning, let's see. Well, up until a couple of months ago, I would've described my life as perfect. Nothing interfered with my well-organized, creative, and satisfactory existence. I lived in virtual seclusion. I had no enemies except maybe a few paparazzi, and I needed nothing—especially a God I believed fictitious.

"At the age of fourteen, I decided God was merely a myth and my head overflowed with my own stories. I didn't make this decision lightly but studied the Bible extensively before reaching my conclusion. Thus, I rejected the Christian faith as a waste of valuable time, refusing even to attend church with my parents and younger sister. I had no real friends, but lots of acquaintances. Most people considered me a nerd or a bookworm.

"After college graduation, I saw my parents and sister on special occasions like birthdays and major holidays. To avoid the crowds and guard my privacy, I moved to the island about five years ago. Most of my creative ideas came early in the morning as I walked on the beach with my golden retriever, Bailey. I led a peaceful and fulfilled life until the neighbor up the beach turned my life upside down. Although you say you can't help me with Sarah, I can't relay my problem without referring to her and her family."

"It's okay, Alex, say what's on your heart."

Alex told the pastor how he met Sarah, fell in love for the first time in his life, played with her twin boys, and delivered her twin girls. Before he'd even realized it, the family had worked their way into his life so completely he felt as if he belonged. He talked about how he sensed God's answer to his prayers during the delivery and when Sarah was rushed to the hospital. Sarah's fears and rejection hurt not merely his ego, he explained, but also his heart. He considered the possibility that she would never be his. Then he shared the emotions he experienced as he turned toward God and God's response with the Scriptures and song.

"I came to this island to avoid crowds, and each time I cross that bridge, I expect no interruptions to my solitary life. I've never entertained here or expected to receive invitations from others. Of all the places I could've gone, I somehow ended up at an overcrowded little cottage, feeding babies, changing diapers, doing laundry, and wiping up spills you don't want to think about. In the middle of all that chaos, I found myself suddenly surrounded by an incredible sense of peace—a peace that makes you feel at home even in an awkward situation. Not only did the place feel right, I knew that something bigger than Alex Caine had brought me there. At that moment, I recognized the reality of God—a God who desired I acknowledge him. Fourteen years of defensive walls came tumbling down in the chaos surrounding Sarah Stuart and her family.

"You've heard the expression, 'My life passed before me?' Similarly, I saw how God had pursued me throughout my life. Little interferences that I had discounted or chosen to ignore, I now recognize as divine intervention. Without a doubt, my mother's prayers kept God on the job."

The pastor had listened up to that point without interruptions. His eyes grew wide when Alex described the births and caring for the babies, even the fact that his mother had come to his rescue from Northern Virginia when Sarah's mother couldn't bring herself to go to the cottage.

"Wow! You've had a busy two months. I get tired just listening to you. I have three boys and have yet to deliver the first baby much less be responsible 24-7 for the well-being of four young children. No wonder you feel close to this family."

Pastor paused a minute and then continued, "I'm not making light of your situation, but I want you to know that I believe as you do that God brought Sarah into your life. Are you familiar with the classic poem, *The Hound of Heaven* by Francis Thompson?"

"Yes, I've seen it. I believe my mother included it in a birthday present or two over the years. She not only prayed, but she had a subtle way of sneaking in her religious propaganda that I'm just now beginning to appreciate. As I recall, my first impression of the poem had me dismissing it as complicated and of little importance."

"That poem is about God's pursuit of man. Without a doubt, God's hound pursued you a long time before he treed you at that little cottage by the sea. When we belong to him, he won't let us go until we acknowledge him and his lordship over our lives. As you described that moment of transformation, I couldn't help but think how accurately you explained what happens when a person finally understands the truth. God has his hand on you, my friend.

"As for Sarah, she requires time to settle her heart regarding her late husband. Losing her spouse feels as if a limb was severed from her body. Under God, the celebration of marriage mysteriously binds the couple together in love and commitment. That pledge unites them until they are parted by death. When death comes prematurely and especially without warning, the remaining spouse tends to be thrown for a loop. Coming to grips with that kind of severance takes time and space to heal. Her life abruptly turned upside down after a short marriage. As you allow her time, Alex, God will give you the grace to continue waiting. Finding John

Waller's song on the radio couldn't have been a mere coincidence. God's character speaks of hope and encouragement toward his children. You can be assured that while you wait, God will be at work in both of you.

"I am a little concerned, however, that you would drop out of church or even find a place to worship on the mainland. Seeing Sarah might be hard, but she must recognize you as a man of God who takes his faith seriously. Your attendance at church will be good for all of you, especially the boys. If you don't come, they might feel that you're rejecting them or, perhaps, turning your back on God. That's the last thing you want them to think. Also, you've succeeded in retaining a certain amount of understanding and privacy among the year-round residents. I'm not sure what you'd find at a mainland church."

Alex shifted in his chair and rested his elbows on his knees. "I see your point. No matter what I decide, there'll be consequences. All my life up until I met Sarah, I had no desire to be with a woman. People assume because I'm a celebrity that I'm also a party animal. The entertainment magazines often print an occasional out-of-context picture to justify their point and sell their products. The truth is I wouldn't know how to go about a sexual encounter, but thinking of Sarah makes me want an intimate relationship with her. I desire her, yes, but it goes way beyond that. It's like the bond we formed over those few days has been severed. I ache when I think about her not returning my love. Avoiding her is my way of protecting my heart. But if you think it best, I'll endure the torture of seeing her at church, knowing that she's not now and may never be mine."

"Even though I haven't experienced anything similar, I do know a little about fatherhood and believe me, it's not easy. My children are young adults, one just spreading his wings, and my twin boys are about your age. Although the older boys are somewhat settled, I find they require my prayers now more than ever. It's a big responsibility you're taking on, Alex. You'll need an extra dose of God's grace. Speaking of God's grace, let's pray again before you have to leave."

Pastor Mark prayed asking God to give Alex patience while waiting for God to show him what to do next.

When he finished praying, he looked at Alex with a grin, "You know James says that trouble in our lives builds patience. I hope I haven't prayed more difficulties for you."

"I don't know if I could take anymore right now." Alex stood, not wanting to monopolize more of the pastor's time.

"Thank you so much for meeting here with me. It helped to verbalize my feelings and share with someone who would listen. I feel like a load's been lifted from my chest. Without prayer and Bible study, I think I'd have lost my mind. I felt so empty until I allowed God to fill the void. I'll try to be here on Sunday. Pray for God to give me the grace and the desire to seek him rather than obsessing over something I can't have."

"I wouldn't call it obsessing. God promised to give us the desires of our hearts, but he does want us to seek him first.

"One more thing before you go, Alex. I remember you saying you wouldn't know how to go about a sexual encounter. Of course, I recommend you wait until marriage, but if marriage does occur, I suggest you read the Song of Solomon. God's Word even deals with our relationships with the opposite sex. Paul admonished us to love our wives as Christ loved the Church. Solomon's writings are an allegory of the love Christ has for the Church, but it's also a lesson in physical intimacy between a man and a woman. Get your heart in the right place, and those romantic experiences will come naturally. If Solomon doesn't inspire you, I don't know who will."

Alex laughed. "I never even thought about getting married until I met Sarah. Now I can think of little else. I sincerely hope I will soon require the wise king's advice."

Before Alex climbed the stairs to leave, the two men promised to meet weekly for further discussion and accountability. The pastor's willingness to see Alex on a regular basis increased his confidence. Despite the age difference, the two men seemed to understand one another. As he made his way to his SUV, Alex felt encouraged when he realized that he'd probably made a guy friend for the first time in his life.

CHAPTER FOURTEEN

Sarah had never felt so welcomed as she did the first Sunday she returned to Community Church. Although it had been years since she'd attended with her parents, she felt like she'd come home. She remembered, even at an early age, how much she enjoyed the sincere, quiet worship. Being here now, warmed her heart and strengthened her spirit.

Many of the year-round residents greeted her. They recalled her parents, and some even remembered Sarah as a child. Of course, two sets of twins were a novelty leading to many offers of assistance. A few of the women were about her age, and after a brief encounter, she recognized them as kindred spirits. Not long into the conversation, they made plans to get together during the week. Susan Lane had a little girl, Mollie, about the age of her boys. Her husband, Sam, worked as a marine biologist for the state of North Carolina. Since his job required travel, Susan was delighted with the prospect of someone available for mutual support.

Her new friend offered to watch the children on occasion. Sarah returned the gesture by offering to take care of Mollie. One more child would hardly make a difference. Considering the ratio of four to one, it seemed a good deal for her, but maybe not the best for Susan. The young mother assured her she would have no problem managing five little ones. They planned a play date for the following week where the two mothers might become acquainted. It felt good to once again have the support of the body of Christ.

Sarah had no idea Alex attended the service until the boys spotted him and went screaming toward him as he attempted to leave. She presumed he came to worship rather than to check up on her. Her resolve to bury him in the back of her mind would be thwarted if she was forced to see him every Sunday. Even in his absence, his sad, handsome face resurfaced, reminding her of how much he cared and how easily she could fall for him. Even her children loved him, especially the boys. They considered Alex their best friend.

Sarah would have stopped the boys and avoided embarrassing him if she'd realized where they were heading. But they disappeared before she could respond. Even from a distance, she saw the love he held for her children as he lifted them and swung them around. Alex had given so much of himself to her family. Not only did he love them, but he also had probably saved her life and the lives of her babies. It grieved her to see his pained look as he sent the boys back to her.

Sarah had no complaints as far as his character, but she had been concerned about his lack of a relationship with God. Of course, he prayed under pressure, but she hadn't heard any real confession of faith. With his sudden interest in church, maybe he had changed. Was God becoming real to him? She wanted that for his sake, if not her own. Ever since the conversation with his mother, she'd been praying for him to renew his faith.

When her new friends noticed the disturbance caused by Alex and her boys, their questioning looks left her a bit embarrassed as she tried to hide the longing she felt for him. Standing there on the church lawn wouldn't have been the time to discuss her relationship or lack of a relationship with the famous Alex. But if she wanted to cultivate friendships with these women, she'd eventually have to be honest with them. She breathed a sigh of relief when the unpredictable man sent the boys back to her, started his car, and drove away.

As she left for home, she continued to mull over Alex and her boys. When they had been disobedient a few days before and walked down the beach to his house, it took all Sarah's composure not to blame him for their poor behavior, but she knew that wasn't the case. The boys missed him. She regretted having to punish them, but they had to learn the importance of adult supervision when out on the beach. Never had she been so afraid. She imagined every possible danger, and if something had happened, it would've been her own fault.

When she asked them why they thought it permissible to be out there without her, Jonathan looked around as if searching for the right answer. "But Mr. Alex was with us. He always takes us for walks on the beach."

Knowing that didn't sound quite right, she looked at David for a more honest answer. As he had listened to his brother's lie, his expression told all. The child couldn't get away with anything. "David, is that what happened?"

David studied his toe as he scratched a line in the sand. Sarah saw his struggle—he didn't want to get his twin into trouble, but neither could he agree to the lie his brother told so easily. Instilling traits of honesty and integrity into the children became overwhelming at times, especially when the responsibility fell to her alone.

"Jonathan, are you certain that's the way it happened?" Jonathan looked unsure of himself as he observed his brother's reaction. She saw him weighing the consequences in his mind, trying to choose the easiest way out.

Finally, after considerable thought, her sweet firstborn hung his head, "I'm sorry," he whispered. After a moment of contrition, he quickly regained his courage and proceeded to make his point. "But we were safe. We had to see Mr. Alex. He told us not to go out on the beach alone, too, but we had to see him. It's been a long time since he came by. We thought he was mad with us or something happened to him. You said he would come see us."

"You know you were disobedient, Jonathan. It doesn't matter why you went without permission, and I'm disappointed that you didn't tell the whole truth at the beginning. That's the same as a lie. If you had asked permission, do you think I'd have allowed you to take off like that? Of course not. You both will be punished for disobedience and you, Jonathan, must know you cannot lie. What do you think your punishment should be?"

"Please don't spank us. We won't do it again. Mr. Alex doesn't want us to. He promised to come by to see us soon. Could you do something besides spanking?" Sarah didn't recall ever using corporal punishment on the boys, but she had threatened enough to make them fearful of the idea. Thankfully, they were both easy to discipline, even her strong-willed Jonathan.

"Okay, here's what's going to happen. If you're certain that you've learned your lesson, I'll find verses in the Bible about disobeying and lying. Tomorrow morning instead of playing outside, we'll be studying those Scriptures together. How does that sound?"

The boys rather liked the idea until they realized they would be losing their outside play time. "When will we get to play in the sand again? It'll be winter, and then it'll be too cold and what if Mr. Alex comes by and we aren't there? What will he think? He will miss us."

"Mr. Alex will probably remember that you should be punished for your disobedience. We'll only take a couple of your mornings away from the beach."

The boys thought they could probably handle that. Sarah continued, "But I'm telling you right now, if you ever pull a stunt like that again, you will be severely punished. You frightened me when I didn't know where you were, and that's not right. I can't be leaving your sisters to go searching for you on the beach. Do you understand?"

In the long run, the study turned into an enjoyable learning experience. Sarah searched the concordance and read the verses from their children's Bible. They talked about what it meant to obey and to tell the truth and what the rewards were for doing the right thing. They also talked about the consequences of disobedience and lying. Sarah tried to keep it on a level they'd understand with illustrations familiar to their preschool minds. The boys asked questions and came up with their own examples. It proved so fruitful, they agreed to make it a habit. Of course, the time would be changed to right after breakfast "in case Mr. Alex comes by."

Unfortunately, they looked for Alex every morning and came to the breakfast table with their heads drooping and complaining about his absence. She didn't know whether to be upset with her nemesis for not coming or herself for sending him away.

Sarah missed him more than she ever imagined possible. How quickly Alex had moved into her heart, made himself at home, and become irreplaceable not merely in her heart, but in her home. She barely coped with all the responsibilities and even considered asking him for help. But she feared he would reject her after the way she treated him. She refused to take the risk. Besides, she was already heavily in debt to the generous man.

On Monday, the boys were out early looking up and down the beach. They insisted that when they saw Alex at church, he had promised to stop by. Sarah sat on the porch nursing the babies within easy supervision of the boys. Their disappearance the week before frightened her so much she feared letting them out of her sight. The weather seemed unseasonably warm compared to the chilly wind that caused them to bundle up the day before. There would be few mornings left for Jonathan and David to enjoy the outdoors.

Just when she thought they would again be disappointed, Bailey appeared out of nowhere jumping, licking, and romping with her happy children. Sarah's concern quickly turned to delight as she watched their reaction to the exuberant dog. She understood wanting something so much that it hurt. She wanted Bailey's master, but that wouldn't be happening for a long time, if ever. Tom had been gone a little over eight months, but she wouldn't forget those four wonderful years with a loving husband who fathered her four children. She wanted to honor his memory for the sake of their children and his parents. Why couldn't Alex be satisfied with friendship and why couldn't she?

Alex soon came into view, greeting the boys with hugs and high fives, almost as excited as his dog. When Bailey settled down, the boys recruited Alex to help construct a sand castle. It reminded her of the visits before the babies were born. He sat in the sand with crossed legs, constantly talking and encouraging them. Occasionally, he'd scold Bailey for stepping on their artwork. They played about thirty or forty minutes before Alex said goodbye, and the man and his dog continued their walk.

As he started to leave, she saw him looking toward the porch with the saddest expression she'd ever seen, even his body language spoke of discouragement. She had to stop herself from calling out.

If he would only focus on something besides her family. Alex lived a lifestyle totally out of her league, filled with hundreds of beautiful women. One special woman could make him forget his obsession with her. Thinking of him with another woman brought pain deep in her chest. Her heart was torn between longing for him and her desire to move on with her life and demonstrate her independence. But while she was making up her mind, she didn't want anyone else to have him, either. No wonder Alex felt rejected. How long would he continue to wait for her to get her act together?

Sarah's busy life became even busier as she carved out time for her new church friends, played and studied with the boys, and cared for her babies. Her house looked a mess compared to how Alex had kept it. The clean house and laundry and full cupboards had been a shocking surprise upon her return from the hospital. Of course, he'd had help from Anna and his mother, but regardless, he managed to make it look easy. She wallowed in self-pity, feeling lonely, tired, and extremely inadequate.

Keeping their clothes clean and preparing meals took much of her time. The disposable diapers were expensive, but the addition of cloth diapers to the mounds of laundry would be impossible. At least she didn't have to buy formula. Come to think of it, she still owed Alex for the purchases he made while she recovered in the hospital. No point in mentioning it though. He would refuse to let her reimburse him, and if she insisted, she would cause him further pain.

When she took the time to pray about the babies' names, Sarah decided on Elizabeth Anne and Hannah Grace. Elizabeth, the mother of John the Baptist, and Hannah, the mother of Samuel, were both strong women of faith and two of her favorite Bible characters. She wanted her girls to have that same strength of character, exhibiting courage and grace. Anne was her mother's middle name, and for some reason, she chose to honor Alex's mother when she gave Hannah the middle name of Grace. Tom's mother would be pleased that she named Elizabeth after her.

CHAPTER FIFTEEN

The brisk days turned into weeks, and before Sarah knew it, the babies were over a month old. Her mother invited her to bring the children to Raleigh for Thanksgiving and stay through the weekend. Leslie still hadn't seen the girls, and Sarah heard the longing in her mother's voice. "I can't wait to get my hands on those baby girls, and it seems like forever since I've seen the boys. Oh, Sarah, it will be so wonderful to spend time with you and the children."

With the holiday a few weeks away, Sarah planned to shop for Christmas gifts while they were in an area with a selection of stores. Her mother looked forward to watching the children. What she couldn't accomplish plowing through the Black Friday sales, she'd order over the internet there. Her tight budget didn't allow the monthly expense of Wi-Fi at home. Sarah ached at the thought of Thanksgiving and Christmas without Tom. Every season brought new reasons to miss him. She never realized how much he contributed, not only to the budget but also in the small ways she'd taken for granted. Finding the right Christmas tree and patiently stringing the lights had been one of his favorite activities—even when the boys insisted on helping. And he never complained about using his day off to watch the boys. Sarah sighed and wiped away the stray tear that found its way down her cheek.

Shame filled her heart when Sarah remembered how she whined and complained when she became pregnant only a few weeks after their marriage. Motherhood was thrust upon her without the first class in childcare. Her degree in teaching hung on the wall of the den as a stark reminder. She saw herself as a failure on so many fronts. Though the idea of fatherhood took Tom by surprise, he soon adjusted to the new reality and became an encouraging rock for his weepy, disgruntled wife. How she longed for another chance to express her appreciation and love.

This long, lonely, difficult year would culminate in February with the anniversary of his death. The boys were too young to remember, but it would be a distressing day for Sarah as she relived the day in detail. She often felt tempted to blame God for cheating them out of the life that could've been. But his goodness and blessings far outweighed the sorrow. Sarah refused to become like her mother who grieved the death of her spouse as intensely now as she did the day he took his last breath.

Packing and preparing for the trip to Raleigh hadn't been easy, but Sarah finally left shortly after lunch. A few miles down the road, quietness descended on the car as sleep claimed the children. Sarah turned her thoughts toward God and used the time for praise and worship. She would never be alone with him by her side. Surprisingly, the time flew, and before she knew it, the boys were waking up with the usual question, "Are we there yet?"

"We'll be at Grandma's house in about thirty minutes," Sarah whispered. "Please don't wake your sisters. If you do, I'll have to stop and feed them, and that will make us even later." The boys complied, occupying their time with the drawing materials she'd thrown in the car at the last minute.

When Sarah pulled into the driveway of her childhood home, her mother came running out of the house with her hands framing her face. The car had barely stopped before she opened the doors of the van to get her first look at her granddaughters. Sarah watched as the dear woman held her hand over her heart and her face lit up with sheer joy. This long overdue visit with her mother looked promising.

Leslie felt relieved when she saw Sarah's car. For the last hour, she'd been checking at the window every few minutes. When she saw those beautiful, blue-eyed baby girls, her heart raced with anticipation, and she couldn't stop the flow of tears. How could she have deprived herself of such pleasure? She could hardly wait to hold them and feel that maternal love that so readily extends to grandchildren. The boys seemed so much older since their last visit. Guilt assailed her as she thought of all she'd missed.

"Why are you crying, Grandma?" Jonathan hugged her.

"I'm just happy to see you. These are tears of joy. You've grown so much, and now you are big brothers."

The boys danced around her, both talking at once and proudly showing her their artwork. Leslie found David's drawing quite interesting, though slightly embarrassing for her daughter. The sensitive boy had drawn a family with a mother, a father, two boys, two girls and a dog. The stick figures had big smiley faces. When she asked him to describe the people in his drawing, without the least hesitation, he proclaimed the man to be "Mr. Alex."

"That's a wonderful picture, David, but you left me out."

"It's okay, Grandma, 'cause this is at the beach, and we just see you here."

Realizing the truth in his words, Leslie's heart ached. She'd made considerable progress toward resuming some normalcy, but David's admonishment made her more determined than ever. Why would anyone want to keep punishing themselves or their family?

After spending those few days at the hospital with Sarah, Leslie had come home resolved to reclaim her life. She first repented of her anger toward God for taking her companion and toward Ben for leaving her. When the anger disappeared, she dared to return to church and reconnect with some of her friends, especially her friend Barbara. They had grown up together and shared everything—both good and bad. It didn't take long to realize that the friends who became prayer partners over the years were the ones who'd be there for her no matter what. When Leslie apologized for rejecting them and refusing their comfort and support, those dear women didn't hesitate to forgive and reinstate her into their fellowship.

Returning to church without Ben had been the hardest thing ever, but after several attempts, she finally made it into the sanctuary. When Barbara saw her standing frozen at the entryway and unable to move forward, she rushed to intercede. Her friend enveloped her with love, whispering words of encouragement and comfort as she led her to a pew occupied by her own family. Surrounded by the beautiful praise and worship, Leslie relaxed and turned her thoughts toward God. Tears surfaced as she cried over her loss. Looking upward, God's healing presence flowed through her, turning her sorrow into joy and lifting her depressed, heavy spirit. God's promise of peace had been renewed.

Thanksgiving would be special with Sarah and the children. Almost like old times, except for the absence of Ben and Tom. She could wallow in the sorrows and regrets of the past, but she chose to be thankful for the blessings right before her eyes. Leslie hadn't felt this happy and contented since her husband had died. All this time she'd deprived herself of the children because she cowardly refused to return to the cottage. Now she couldn't get enough of them.

At six weeks, the baby girls responded to her voice when she sang and talked to them. Her heart filled with praise. She remembered the verse she read in Job, "The Lord gave and the Lord has taken away; Blessed be the Name of the Lord." Although the babies couldn't replace their father or grandfather, they were another of the many blessings to remind her of God's faithfulness.

Sarah had arrived early to avoid holiday traffic and help her mother prepare the Thanksgiving feast. The list of dishes expanded by the hour. Leslie wondered how her small family would ever consume such a meal. The lengthy menu included the traditional southern fare with turkey, dressing with gravy, mashed potatoes, sweet potato soufflé, green beans, fresh cranberry sauce and fruit ambrosia. In addition to pumpkin pie, they had apple pie and chocolate mousse, made especially for the boys. The food tasted delicious, and she didn't know when she'd enjoyed herself more. Even the boys ate well.

The excessive meal gave Leslie an idea for the following year. She'd check with the church and find a family or individual who might be alone at Thanksgiving. Instead of continuing her inward focus, she and Sarah would reach out to others who might also be hurting.

Before dessert, they continued the tradition that Ben initiated when they were first married. Each person at the table expressed what they were most grateful for during the year. Sarah gave thanks with tears brimming her eyes, "I'm most thankful for you, Mom, and this time we have together. Also, for the safe delivery of the babies. And for my boys and the wonderful father God gave them. We only had him a brief time, but we will always remember his love and care. Thank you, God."

Leslie thanked God for her daughter and grandchildren. "Thank you also for my dear friends that I've finally welcomed back into my life and for you, dear heavenly Father, who never left me, even when I rejected you."

Jonathan prayed next. "Thank You, dear Jesus, for my mommy, my grandma, and David and the babies, even though they're a lot of trouble."

David sat quietly for a few moments, then almost whispered, "Thank You for our friend, Mr. Alex. He likes to play with us, and we miss him. I wish he was here. Help him have a good Thanksgiving, too."

Leslie noticed the tears clouding Sarah's eyes when David finished praying.

While the children napped, Sarah and her mother cleaned the kitchen and put away the leftovers. As they tackled the mound of dirty dishes, they talked about her mother's recent healing. Sarah couldn't get over the difference since they were together at the hospital. With the stimulating conversation, the untidy mess soon disappeared, and the dishwasher was left to finish the job. After admiring their cooperative efforts, her mother suggested they have a cup of tea in the sunroom.

"That sounds like a pleasant way to relax after kitchen duty," replied Sarah. "Everything tasted delicious, but I ate more than any woman should consume."

"Well, you could stand a few extra pounds. I've never seen you so thin. You are feeling better though, aren't you?"

"I'm much better, thank you. I find it almost impossible to gain weight while I'm nursing, and by the time the girls are weaned and walking, they'll keep me in shape trying to keep up with them."

They laughed together in understanding as they contemplated the days to come. Sarah looked over at her mother and silently thanked God for restoring their relationship. "Thank you, Mom, for this time together. It means so much to me. I've missed our closeness, and I realize I'm partially responsible for the friction between us. I don't think I fully understood your grief until I lost Tom. I now see how difficult it was for you. Please forgive me."

Leslie shook her head in disagreement. "No, Sarah. I'm to blame more than anyone. Those few days with you made me realize I'd become so consumed with my own grief that I failed to see the pain of loss in my daughter. I'm embarrassed to admit it, but at times I felt jealous of the relationship you had with your father. Please forgive me for not being there for you when he died."

"But Mom, you were, and you were there when Tom was killed. I couldn't have survived that terrible loss without you. When you arrived, you gave me the courage and support to accomplish the overwhelming tasks. Also, you brought love and encouragement when I landed in the hospital."

"Well, let's just say that we've both made mistakes. I need you now, and I know you need me. Let me help you carry the load."

They hugged again and agreed to be more sensitive in the future. When they were comfortably seated with their cups of tea in the quiet and warmth of the lovely room, Leslie hesitated a moment before asking, "What did you think of David's Thanksgiving prayer?"

"He had the courage to say what I wish I'd said. Mother, that man sacrificed so much for us. I know he loves me, but I can't commit to him while Tom remains so significant in our family. Also, I hate the thought of muddling my husband's memory with another man, even one as wonderful and dear as Alex. I know it doesn't make sense, but I must be in love with two men at the same time. Is that even possible?"

"It's complicated and confusing. I realize you need more time, but please don't reject him forever. I want to see you happy, and I believe Alex came into your life for a reason. I'll be praying as you sort it out and come to terms with your loss. Those boys really love him, especially David. He seems to need an adult male role model more than Jonathan. Please don't be offended, but may I speak frankly?"

Sarah nodded. Leslie continued, "Part of your problem might stem from the fear of abandonment. You've had two wonderful men, your dad and then Tom, but for some reason, they were both taken from you. Your loss has been great, Sarah, but don't be afraid. You'll know when it's time to open your heart again."

"Thank you, Mother. Keep praying for me. The idea of trusting anyone right now, much less a man, is more than I can handle. I appreciate your honesty, though, and your prayers."

Sarah gave her mother another hug, then changed the subject. "Are you sure you'll be okay with the children while I Christmas shop? They can be a handful, but I really must do this while I have your help."

"We'll be fine, Sarah. I'm getting to know the babies. If it becomes too much, my friend, Barbara, promised to come over. She wants to see the children anyway. If Grace Caine could do it, I should think I can manage. I'm still amazed she would come all the way from Northern Virginia. When I get the nerve to swallow my pride, I plan to call and thank her.

"Sarah, I want to apologize for not allowing you to live here when you were forced to move. I'm not going to make excuses, but I want you to forgive me and consider staying now. This is a big house, and it feels so right full of happy chatter and sweet gurgling babies."

"Mother, you don't know what this means for you to offer. I love this house and feel comfortable here, but we've grown accustomed to the island. It's become home for us, and Jonathan and David love the beach. We've made dear friends within our church and community—friends who will pray with us and offer their support. Although it's hard at times, I enjoy the independence I'm experiencing for the first time in my life. Can you understand that, Mother?"

"I'm disappointed, Sarah, but yes, I understand. However, the cottage is quite small and not built for full-time residency. It might work fine for now, but when the girls start walking, you must make other arrangements. Just know that the invitation remains open for you and my grandchildren. Thank you for coming this week, Sarah, and I fully expect you to return for Christmas. Why don't you leave the gifts here? I'll even wrap them for you. What do you say?"

Sarah thought about the offer, but something caused her to hesitate. "Thank you, Mother, but would you consider joining us at the cottage? I know it won't be easy, but please think about it. It would mean so much to the children and to me."

For a moment, fear swept over her mother's face, but just as suddenly, it was replaced with a bold, determined look. "Sarah, I won't promise you now, but I'll pray about it and do my best. If I can't manage though, you will come back here, won't you?"

Sarah sat beside her mother on the love seat. She hugged her and silently prayed for the fragile woman who gave her birth. "Of course, Mother, I wouldn't think of having Christmas without you. I love you and enjoy the time we have together."

CHAPTER SIXTEEN

Miserable seemed to be the only word to describe Alex. The boys told him they were going to their grandma's house for Thanksgiving. In their excitement, they wanted to know if he might come with them. It would be a long week without them. Perhaps the arrival of his parents and sister would keep his mind off his neighbor and her four children.

On Tuesday before the holiday, his sister, Jana, showed up a day earlier than planned. He saw her tears through the security camera and thought the worst. Coupled with the fact that she'd scheduled extra time from work, Alex's concern escalated. Jana rarely let anything interfere with her job, but there she stood waiting for the elevator. They say, "Misery loves company," and it looked as though his sister brought her share to join him. Alex took the elevator down to greet her, setting aside his wretchedness for the moment.

"What brings you here more than a day early, my dear sister? Did you wish to spend additional time with your big brother?" He laughed, hoping to lighten her mood. She stormed past him looking more miserable than he'd ever seen her.

"What's wrong, Jana?"

"He fired me! That's what's wrong. One minute, Paul tells me what an asset I am to the company, and the next he insists he can't stand to be near me. And I have no idea what I've done to deserve this. It's not fair. I've won awards for his company. I've worked my butt off for that man. Now that the company is booming, he sends me packing. What's wrong with me?"

Jana drenched his shirt with tears as Alex held her in his arms. Though they'd never been particularly close, he loved his little sister and hated to see her hurt. They'd both lived sheltered lives with few disappointments, but he suspected reality had also arrived for Jana.

"Jana, there's got to be more to this. I thought you and Paul were friends. You talked several times about your relationship and even spending time together outside the office. It's hard to believe he would fire you without a reasonable explanation."

His next thought took even him by surprise. "Is it possible that you're in love with him, Jana?"

"He means a lot to me, I know that, and yes, I could see myself falling for him. I thought he cared for me, too, though he never indicated that we were anything more than friends. At times when we were alone, he seemed nervous and uncomfortable. I respected his professionalism. But firing me? Does that sound like something a person in love would do? Who does he think he is?"

"He was your boss, Jana, and he has the right to fire you, but I can't believe he didn't give you an explanation. From your past descriptions, I had a favorable opinion of the man. What exactly did he say to you?"

"He called me into his office yesterday morning and said, 'I can't take this anymore, Jana. Please clean out your office. We can no longer work together. Forgive me, but you've got to go.' I was so shocked I didn't know what to say. I finally found the courage to question him. 'What are you saying, Paul? This job is my life; you can't fire me. And don't you dare blame it on the economy. I see the figures more often than you.' He shook his head and said, 'Just go. I can't deal with this one more day.' Alex, what am I going to do? That job means everything to me. It's all I know."

Alex continued to hug Jana and rub her shoulders. "I don't know, Jana. I'm the last person to give you advice regarding your job or relationships, but it does sound as if your boss might need time to reconsider his rash decision. Why don't you stay here at the beach for a while and see how it goes? In the meantime, I'll pray God's will for both your lives."

Jana pulled away from Alex, frowning. "Since when do you pray to anybody, Alex, much less God? Mother told me something about you making changes in your life and that you met a neighbor or somebody. I don't remember the details. She usually calls while I'm at work, and I confess, I barely listen. I occasionally reply so she thinks I'm interested. What more can I say? I'm an ungrateful daughter. When did all this momentous change take place?"

"Since I realized that God is the one person who could fill the empty hole in my heart. I met a woman, Jana. An amazing, beautiful woman who talks to God as if he's in the same room with her. She prays about everything. I wasn't near her long before I fell in love. Unfortunately, she's not in love with me, or if she is, she won't admit it. Our relationship is on hold for now, but she made me realize how much I've missed by living here alone, focusing only on my work.

"Ever since she rejected me, I've been miserable. I had to find some way to overcome my longing for her. Oh, I still want her, but it's easier now that I've decided to trust God. I read a quote recently from St. Augustine that I can relate to. He wrote, 'Thou has made us for thyself, O God, and our hearts are restless until they find their rest in Thee.' Now, my desire is to abide in him and let him be my rest."

Alex picked up Jana's suitcase. "Let's go upstairs. Anna arrived just before you. I'll ask her to make us a sandwich. While we eat, I'll tell you about the disruptive whirlwind that blew in early last month. You won't believe all that's happened."

Over lunch, Alex shared his complicated journey and how God dealt with him through the stress and rejection. Jana's eyes grew large, and a mischievous grin spread across her face at his uncharacteristic involvement in his neighbor's problems.

"Will I be permitted to meet this goddess and her little imps?"

"I'm afraid not, Jana. She and the children are in Raleigh with her mother for Thanksgiving. If you stay long enough, you might join the boys and me for a walk on the beach or meet the family at church. Other than that, we rarely see each other. I ache when we cross paths and see how well she manages without me. She is an incredible woman. But, life goes on, and for her, it seems to be going quite well.

"As far as Paul goes, my only advice is what Mother gave me. Seek God's kingdom first, and the Sarah's and Paul's will be added if they are in God's perfect plan for you."

Jana laughed. "I don't think that was a direct quote, but I get the gist. I know I've neglected God lately. I used to be so faithful with my quiet times and prayer, but now I tend to rush off to work without even a moment of meditation. Perhaps God allowed me to lose my job as a way of slowing me down and putting me back on track. Thanks for the advice and the invitation to linger. I can't think of a better place to sort out my life. I don't know how long I'll stay, but you may be tired of me before I pack my bags to leave."

"Never, dear sis. It'll be fun. Quite frankly, I've been a bit bored since Sarah gave me the boot. When I'm with her and the children, life seems full and exciting, never a dull moment. I hadn't gone into a grocery store in over five years until I met Sarah. Now I go to engage in conversation. So much for my desire for peace and quiet.

"Right now, I need to get busy. I've neglected my writing since becoming so obsessed with Sarah. Make yourself at home. You know where to find your room if you want to rest. Knowing Anna, it's all fresh and ready for you. We'll take a walk later if that's okay. I intend to spend as much time with you as possible."

When Jana left to find her room, Alex concealed himself in his office and spent the first few minutes in prayer. Revisiting the conversation with Jana, he realized how distant he and his sister had become. His preference for solitude and the few years separating their births meant they'd never really been friends. He did remember being jealous and aggravated when she was born and trying to ignore the unwanted disruption. Perhaps they'd have more in common as adults.

Alex prayed for Jana as she faced some of the same battles that he'd experienced—anger, rejection, and disappointment in others. He prayed that she would seek God instead of stewing over her irrational boss. As his thoughts turned to Paul, he felt a strong urge to pray for him. He didn't know what had prompted the sudden change in her boss's behavior, but Alex was confident that God would work it out.

A couple hours later, Jana joined Alex on the deck where he'd gone to relax following his writing session. He watched as she plopped into the recliner near him. She closed her eyes and took in a deep breath. She seemed so calm, he wondered if she'd heard from Paul. Was that a Bible she held?

"Well?"

"Alex, I had the most amazing quiet time. When I first closed the door to my room, I ranted and raved at Paul until I cried myself into an exhausted sleep. After my power nap, I felt refreshed and began to view the circumstances with clearer vision. I moved to the window seat and turned my thoughts toward God. Almost immediately, he convicted me of my anger. God reminded me of Paul's past devotion and kindness and how comfortable I feel when we're together. I consider him my best friend. The last year was indescribable. We even attended church together. Although we enjoyed a close relationship, he never indicated anything more than friendship, nor did he even once give me any reason to think that I displeased him.

"When I finally asked God's forgiveness and forgave Paul in my heart, I found a Bible I must have left behind last year. Some of the verses in the Psalms encouraged me. Listen to this from Psalm 138. "The Lord will work out his plans for my life—for your faithful love, O Lord, endures forever. Don't abandon me, for you made me."

Alex couldn't believe how quickly God had answered his prayers for Jana. Tears of gratitude trickled down her cheeks. He wouldn't be surprised to hear that God was dealing with Paul at the same time.

"Alex, can't you see God was present, even when we neglected him? Coming back to this island was the best thing I could've done. There's something about the sea that turns my focus heavenward."

When Alex and Jana's parents arrived on Wednesday, Alex saw their surprise at finding Jana already in residence. Mother patiently listened to his sister's version of the problem, and with her motherly wisdom, attempted to put things in perspective. Although Alex knew the hurt hadn't completely disappeared, Jana managed to control her emotions and accept the love and understanding offered by her family. Their mother dealt gently with his sister, reminding her, as she did him, to seek God.

"Yes, I know, Mother. Alex gave me the lecture. Jobs come and go, but God is always with us. My quiet times overlooking the ocean are good reminders of his presence and what my priorities should be. Instead of letting this ruin our holiday weekend, I've decided to trust God and wait for his answer. This will be a great Thanksgiving with the three people I love most in the world."

With Anna's assistance and a little help from Alex and his dad, his mother and Jana prepared an abundant feast. Following instructions from his mother, the men prepared the sixteen-pound turkey for baking, and after much discussion regarding food poisoning, they decided against stuffing it. The women entertained Alex and his dad by quoting recipes they found on the internet and often referred to Google to settle their differences. No computer search competed with Anna's expertise. Her wisdom baffled them all.

Most of the dishes were traditional, but the cooks tried to add something new each year, which resulted in a groaning buffet. Jana contributed a spicy Thai dish that made a hit despite the contrast with the classic favorites. Mother added a new cake to the menu. Alex wondered where to put a slice of cake amid a variety of pies with ice cream and real whipped cream topping?

With the food finally prepared, Anna left with a few dishes to add to her family's meal while Alex and his family settled their hearts for his dad's prayer—a prayer that turned out to be both thanksgiving and petitioning. After words of thanks, he added, "God, please be with our children. They are both seeking you, and I am thankful, but something is missing. The mate you gave me over thirty years ago has been the joy of my life, and I want them to experience this kind of love. It will be a gift from you when they find the spouses you've chosen for them. We pray for the man who is to win the heart of my little girl and for the woman you've prepared for Alex. Be with them wherever they are. Draw them into a strong relationship with you so they will be worthy mates for our children. We pray all this in the name of your Son, Jesus. Amen."

When his father finished the blessing, he reached over and kissed his wife on the lips. "In case I haven't mentioned it today, Grace, you are the love of my life. Thank you for putting up with me all these years and for giving me two fine children."

Alex looked at his sister who smiled back at him a bit misty-eyed. Her reaction reflected his as the food waited on the server behind them— the hot food on warming trays and the cold chilled on ice. Though holiday meals were never rushed at the Caine household, something about this family gathering seemed different. A spiritual connection existed that hadn't been there before. He wondered how he could have been present on each occasion without noticing it.

While the women filled their plates, Alex leaned over to his dad. "Thank you for your thoughtful prayer. I've probably never told you, but I appreciate the way you treat Mom, making her feel so loved and cherished. Someday I want that same kind of marriage."

His dad hugged him. "That was a kind thing to say about your old man. I do try to make your mother feel special."

After a brief pause, his father continued, "I'm proud of you, son. You've accomplished a lot for a young man, but I want you to know that when your mother told me that you'd returned to your faith, I felt so blessed. Wait for him, Alex. God's timing might not be the same as yours, but he's more than enough. He knows what you need and when you need it."

His father's spiritual admonition took him by surprise. Hadn't his mother always been the more religious one? When did his father become this serious man of faith? And why hadn't he noticed it before? It embarrassed him to think of the way he'd neglected his parents. He often existed in some self-centered state without a thought of them or anyone else. *I need a lot of work, God. Please don't give up on me.*

Their mealtime conversations ranged from church activities and neighbors to sports and politics. Alex told them about his friendship with Pastor Mark and how the man was mentoring him in his current disappointments and trials.

Listening to their exchanges, he realized how different they were from past table discussions. His change of heart toward religion had freed his family from avoiding certain subjects. They still carried on spirited debates over politics and the latest trends, but the debates sounded less heated. Listening to and respecting the other person seemed more important than being right.

In the middle of a lively discussion over the current conflict in the Middle East, the doorbell rang. Alex first thought of Sarah, but then remembered that she'd still be in Raleigh. He turned the intercom on and asked, "May I help you?"

They heard someone clear their throat, then a long silence and finally a hesitant voice. "I'm Paul Bryant. I hope I'm not disturbing your Thanksgiving meal, but I need to speak with Jana Caine. Is she there?"

Alex turned toward Jana. Her surprised look quickly transformed into an enormous grin. "Come on up, Paul. You're in time for dessert." He pushed the button to send the elevator to the lower floor before Jana had time to react. Too late, he saw her disappointment that he hadn't given her time to hop on. She paced by the elevator door in nervous anticipation.

When the door opened, there stood Paul in a wrinkled suit, sweat pouring from his face and an expression of miserable defeat. With his sad look focused on Jana, he hurried from the elevator and stood before her with outstretched arms. "I have been miserable, Jana. I thought if I weren't forced to see you every day, my life would return to normal. But it turned out worse than ever. I can't live another day like this. The truth is, I love you. I have for a long time. You dominate my thoughts, day and night. I can't work. Please put me out of my misery. Tell me you care, and that you need me as much as I need you."

"You fired me. Is that any way to treat someone who loves you?"

Jana didn't seem to remember any of the drama from Monday as she rushed into his open arms. The crowded foyer didn't prevent her from kissing the ruffled man, touching his face, crying and laughing at the same time. All those pent-up emotions of the last several months burst forth into hysterical joy.

"Marry me, Jana. It's the only solution to this exhausting problem. You can no longer be my assistant. I can't have you working so close without holding you in my arms. Please, I love you."

Despite the highly awkward scene playing out before them, Alex and his parents patiently waited to greet their guest. Jana and Paul seemed oblivious to their audience as they looked into each other's eyes and exchanged passionate kisses between bouts of laughter. Alex stood with his arms crossed amazed at how suddenly a situation could change. Why was he denied a similarly swift answer regarding Sarah?

Reluctant to interrupt, Jana's father cleared his throat, "Well, I'm not sure what this means, but perhaps you could introduce us to your friend, Jana."

His sister turned toward her family with an embarrassed grin. She pulled Paul to her side and introduced him. "This is my boss … or former boss, it appears—Paul Bryant. He loves me. He came here to ask me to marry him."

Alex couldn't help but tease her. "Well, after that little PDA I should think so, but I'm still slightly confused. I thought you described him as the mean old boss who fired you without a reasonable explanation and sent you here a day early in tears."

Jana grinned sheepishly. "One and the same, Alex, and I expect a full explanation from Mr. Bryant before the day is over." She addressed her last remark to Paul who stood beaming with a look of unadulterated love. Alex wondered if he ever looked at Sarah with such love and admiration.

"Getting engaged is exhausting. I'm ready for dessert."

"We might be ready for dessert, Jana, but I have a feeling Paul might appreciate some turkey and dressing. The food is still out—I'll get you a place setting. What would you like to drink?"

Although they had never met Paul, Alex's parents welcomed him as a member of the family. That was no surprise considering Jana had been singing his praises for the last couple of years. Alex watched as Paul relaxed in his seat next to Jana. The family discussed work, Alex's writing, the island and surrounding area. Later, talk turned to wedding plans. Everyone but the groom thought a June wedding would work best. Paul insisted he couldn't possibly wait that long, but with some reasoning from the mother of the bride, he reneged.

When they finally exhausted their discussion, Paul and Jana left for a romantic stroll on the beach. Alex helped his mother with the cleanup and then sat down with his parents to rehearse the most unusual Thanksgiving ever. They all agreed that God had orchestrated the day, from beginning to end.

Just when Alex thought he'd unselfishly dismissed his desires, his mother chose to remind him. "Alex, does it bother you that your younger sister has found her mate and is moving on with her life before you?"

"Last year, I could've cared less, but now, it's a different story. I'm trying not to be jealous, Mother, but I do want what she and Paul have. Is it wrong to experience that kind of longing?"

"Of course not, son," his father interjected. "We all have desires often put in our hearts by God, and it's natural to want a wife and family."

"Are you thinking of Sarah?" His mother looked concerned. He would love to pretend all was well, but that would be far from the truth. Sarah seemed much farther away than a couple of hours west in Raleigh.

"I can't help but think of Sarah, especially when I see how happy Paul has made Jana. Thank you for your concerns, but it's not an easy fix. Pray for me."

Alex, desiring time alone, went out to the deck to wallow in his misery. The weather was beautiful for late November and watching the waves and smelling the salt air the perfect antidote to his disappointment. Not long into his solitude, Paul joined him.

"Alex, since we're to be brothers, I wanted to get to know you better and explain why I fired Jana on Monday morning. Your sister is something else. She strolled into my office about two years ago, with her perfect figure and high heels clicking on the marble. As we worked together for a few months, I couldn't help but fall in love with her. The problem soon escalated into her being too much of a temptation. I loved her to distraction and couldn't keep my wandering mind on advertising and promotions when I would rather have been making out with my executive assistant."

Alex laughed at Paul's description of his sister. "I understand your problem, but why didn't you ask her to marry you instead of firing her?"

"Jana is such a perfect, competent young woman I didn't feel like I measured up. Quite frankly, I feared her rejection or even an accusation of sexual misconduct. I know it doesn't make sense to you, but when you're as insecure around women as I am, you'd have a reason for apprehension."

Alex almost laughed out loud when he thought of his own insecurities. "I understand, but you certainly seemed to give her mixed signals when you awarded her performance and then, without warning, fired her. She arrived here an emotional wreck Tuesday afternoon. The only way I knew to console her was to point her to God."

"I know, and I'm sorry. There is no question that she proved invaluable to the company, but I'd rather have her in my home than in my office. I really love her, Alex.

"When I left New York to come here I didn't know how it would turn out or even if Jana would speak to me after the way I treated her. I knew I had to overcome my fears and try to win her affections. I'm so blessed, Alex, to know that God is giving me the desire of my heart, a beautiful woman who returns my love and agrees to love me forever. By the way, Jana told me about your friend, Sarah. I'll be praying for God to work out your relationship as well."

After a few more minutes of discussing his bond with Jana, Paul left to find his bride-to-be. Alex understood why the man ran a successful business. His energy level was exhausting. Laughing to himself, he mulled over the one-sided dialogue with his future brother-in-law. Paul had expressed a desire for the two men to get to know one another, but their conversation turned into one-sided proclamation of the man's love for Jana. Well, there'd be other opportunities to become acquainted.

Alex thought about what the couple had gone through—loving each other, but afraid to express their emotions, trying to settle for friendship when their hearts longed for so much more. Theirs was a double dose of unrequited love. On the surface, his situation with Sarah appeared similar, but he feared Sarah didn't return his love. His uncontrollable fear competed with his hope that God would also give him the desires of his heart.

Since Paul had to drive back to New York the next day, the family worked out last-minute details for planning the wedding. Jana would stay with her parents in Northern Virginia. On weekends when Paul could get away, he'd come to Northern Virginia, or she would go to her condo in New York so they could spend some time together.

With her hands on her hips, Jana frowned at Paul. "It just occurred to me that you've asked me to marry you before we ever went on a formal date. That's a bit like getting the cart before the horse. Don't you think?"

"I know, honey. Forgive me. Not only was I highly unromantic, but I showed up without an engagement ring. When I left Manhattan, I hadn't slept for two nights, not to mention one confusing, unproductive day squeezed between. I doubted you'd even accept my proposal. If you hadn't agreed to marry me, I don't know what I would've done. As far as dating, each time you walked into my office became a date as far as I was concerned."

The family enjoyed the banter between the two of them as they thought of all the preparations to be accomplished in a few short months. Alex squelched his sigh as he longed to be the one planning a wedding with Sarah. All this talk of love and happiness caused an ache so deep—almost more than he could take.

CHAPTER SEVENTEEN

Alex's parents and Jana stayed on through the weekend and attended church with him on Sunday. They searched for an empty pew in the sanctuary crowded with holiday visitors. The hymns spoke of tradition and anticipation as the liturgy moved into the Advent season. Most of the resident parishioners remembered Alex's family, and several asked about Sarah and the children, expecting him to have the answer.

When his family left on Monday, Alex thought about Jana's drama of the past few days. He felt as though he'd taken a roller coaster ride, but this time without Sarah and the children. The happiness he felt for Jana and Paul disappeared with their departure. The house felt lonely and empty. His castle groaned for a family of its own.

Alex's attitude regressed until he found himself in the throes of a serious pity party. Fortunately, no one saw him in such a funk. Even Anna had taken the day off. When he thought he could take no more of the dreary stillness, the words of John Waller's song, "While I'm Waiting," came back to him, reminding him to focus on God. His Bible was open to Psalm 42 where he had underlined verse five: "Why are you in despair, O my soul? And why have you become disturbed within me? Hope in God, for I shall again praise him for the help of His presence." Rather than feeling forsaken, he'd pray for patience to endure the long wait.

While the circumstances appeared hopeless at times, he still believed that Sarah would be his. She and the children rarely left his thoughts or prayers. Despite the disruptions accompanying them, he wandered around the empty house feeling unsettled and lost without them.

If he truly believed God answered prayer, sitting and feeling sorry for himself indicated nothing but the opposite. He'd rather occupy himself with something positive. Remodeling some of his guest rooms bordered on the extreme, but at least, it showed faith. When God willed that he should be with Sarah, his house would be ready for his new family. Excitement replaced his weariness as he walked from room to room visualizing a bedroom for the boys, a nursery for the babies, and a playroom for all four. He chose to keep the project a secret. That probably expressed the opposite of faith, but he couldn't take the possible ridicule or speculation.

He put in a call to Jean Edwards, a professional who had decorated his home when he first moved to the island. Jean came out the next week, and together they developed a plan. When the workers arrived the following week, he retreated to the beach or out on the deck to avoid the construction noise. In a couple of weeks, his bachelor pad had been transformed into a mother's dream and a happy place for her children.

Christmas presented yet another problem for Alex. He wanted to buy the children something special, but the gifts had to meet Sarah's approval. Expensive items would be out of the question. He chose new sand toys with a promise of playtime on the beach when the weather warmed. Since they shared his love for the ocean, and he wanted them to discover the pleasures he'd found in reading, he threw in a couple of books about sea life. For the girls, he settled on soft dollies—perfect for infants.

If he had his way, Sarah would receive an engagement ring, but he could anticipate her reaction. Instead, he ordered a bouquet of red roses and a basket of fruit. The gifts would be delivered the week before Christmas. Call him a coward, but his heart ached too much to give them in person. He barely survived watching from a distance on Sundays.

On unseasonably warm days, he walked with the boys, but those times were now rare. When he did get out, they waited for him. Following their walk, he returned them to the cottage and remained only until their mother opened the door and ushered them safely inside. The fact that Sarah trusted him that much with the boys gave him a measure of satisfaction.

Christmas came and went with no response from Sarah. At least she didn't return the gifts. When he'd lost all hope of hearing from her, he received a note in the mail which read:

> Alex, you made the boys so happy when they received your gifts, especially the note promising to play with them in the spring.

> Since the babies now notice everything, they showed considerable interest in the sweet baby dolls. When they're older, I'm certain they'll cherish them. I know you meant well, but I would rather you hadn't given me anything. I didn't get you a gift, which is ironic since I owe you so much, and now I owe you a Christmas gift. What do you give a guy who has everything? However, the roses were beautiful, and we all enjoyed the fruit. Thank you for being your usual thoughtful self.
>
> Fondly, Sarah.

Alex wanted to scream loud enough for her to hear him. "I don't have everything, Sarah. I don't have you, and you'd be the perfect gift for me." Why did he ever think he could send those gifts and not feel hurt? He'd escape this miserable place if he thought it would help, but the kind of grief he carried wouldn't be left behind.

As he paced the floor, grieving the emptiness of both his home and his heart, a verse from Psalm 46 came to mind: "Be still, and know that I am God." He stopped and took in the peace that had so quickly replaced the feeling of abandonment. Alex fell on his face and cried out his fears, regrets, and disappointments to the One who would understand. *God, please give me the grace to continue this miserable waiting.*

Later, after he came to terms with the card from Sarah, he reflected on his Christian journey and his early rejection of God. Recalling his awkward adolescent years, Alex hit on an idea to encourage her boys to remain steadfast in their faith. His mind worked overtime as he considered the kinds of stories that might interest preteen boys. Action, adventure, battles, and mystery came to mind. The ideas arrived faster than his fingers could type. God seemed to dictate the story—he merely the scribe. Within two weeks, he finished the first volume and sent the manuscript off to his publisher.

Expecting his overdue adult fiction, the editor and publicist, along with his literary agent, were surprised when the new manuscript arrived in a completely different genre. After he promised another best seller within the month, their vision expanded to see the potential of an altogether new market. Alex recognized the look of dollar signs dancing before their eyes as they perused his youth series. When he released the book for publication, he prayed for God to bless his efforts and use them for his purpose.

In March, Alex received an unexpected invitation to the boys' birthday party. He smiled when he imagined their mother's reaction. 'Mommy, we have to invite Mr. Alex. He's our best friend." Regardless of who initiated the invitation, it made his day. His adrenalin pumped in anticipation of spending time with his favorite family.

Once more, he had to come up with both an appealing and acceptable gift. After searching the internet, he decided on a Lego model for each, appropriate for their age level. He ordered an airplane for David and a rocket for Jonathan, knowing they'd share and help each other with the assembly. Perhaps, after attending the party for the boys, Sarah would let him help the boys put them together. Being in her presence would be difficult. He'd endure it to spend time with the children. Their brief greetings on Sunday morning only increased his desire to see more of them. Coming from him, Sarah would probably view the "inside" toys as manipulation. He shook his head in frustration. *Why must I scrutinize every move to avoid offending the sensitive woman?*

Sarah wanted everything to be special for the boys' fourth birthday. But the babies were restless, and she was exhausted and sleep deprived. Although the girls were a little young for teething, something had them upset. Perhaps they were reacting to her unresolved feelings. The party would be small with a couple of families from church—and Alex.

Sarah tried to ignore the boys when they insisted he come. The man intimidated her to the point that she dreaded party time. It's true she'd missed him, even longed for him, but she couldn't think about him now. Tom's parents were coming to the island the following week, and she preferred not to welcome them with another man in tow. They deserved to see the love that remained for their only child instead of her moving on and leaving his memory behind.

Without extra funds for preschool, the boys' only friends were from church. Between the crowded cottage and her reduced energy level, a small party would be all she could manage anyway. The children would've been satisfied with just Alex, but the thought of them alone in the same room tied her stomach in knots. In addition to needing the parents to help supervise, Sarah welcomed a few friendly faces to serve as a buffer. Not that she didn't trust Alex. She worried about her own reaction.

The plan for the party came together despite her apprehensions. When she heard the weather forecast, Sarah relaxed for the first time in days. The afternoon temperatures would be warm enough for the children to play outside and even eat at the picnic table on the deck. Clean-up would be easy.

Her mother had managed to conquer her fears to celebrate Christmas with them on the island. Now she seemed excited to return for the party. When Leslie arrived early and assumed responsibility for the babies, Sarah relaxed. The girls were near the crawling stage and no longer content to be confined to their play yard. The extra pair of hands freed Sarah to finish last-minute preparations and set out the prizes for the games.

Later, she'd grill hot dogs—another in a long list of reasons to miss Tom. Feeling herself slipping into despair, Sarah rejected the temptation to feel sorry for herself and focused on the celebration. Perhaps she might talk one of the dads into taking over the grilling. After the meal, the boys could open their presents, and they'd wrap up the party with birthday cake and ice cream.

At one minute before three o'clock, Sarah heard a knock on the back door. The boys ran screaming to welcome their friend. Alex still used the back door, but at least he knocked. He must have learned his lesson. She cringed with embarrassment when she remembered the hurt she'd inflicted on him. Their conflict seemed trivial now, and she wished for the courage to swallow her pride and run to him like her boys.

Alex's concern that day had been over naming the girls, and she'd never told him her final decision. Since the boys still referred to them as the babies, she doubted he learned their names from them. Perhaps after the party, they might attempt a conversation without a disagreement.

The boys were all over Alex, but Sarah noticed as he held his face against David's forehead. "You feeling okay, buddy?" Her neighbor's worried expression prompted her to take a closer look herself. Fear seized her as she recognized an extremely pale child. He'd complained of being tired the day before but still managed to keep up with his brother. Now, she realized something must be wrong. Not wanting to disrupt the party, Sarah prayed her son would have the strength to enjoy his birthday and that Alex would wait until later to mention his concerns. The boys deserved a fun day with their friends without distractions.

Tomorrow, she'd be forced to find a doctor, which she should have done long before. The babies were five months old and had yet to receive a well-baby check. Every day she saw how important two parents were to the welfare of growing children. That excuse might satisfy some, but she should have been more observant.

The party went well, although Sarah worried about David and continued to chastise herself. If she hadn't bothered to be concerned, Alex's close observation was enough to convince her. He never seemed to take his eyes off the child, and when the early evening temperature dropped, he went inside to find light jackets or sweaters for all the children. For a person who'd never been a father, he showed unusual perception. Sarah wondered if he still claimed her children as his own. He seemed to by the way he interacted with them.

With the last present opened and mere crumbs left from the birthday cake, her friends gathered their children and headed toward home. Sarah watched Alex from the kitchen window as he returned the grill to the storage shed and directed the boys to pick up the stray trash from the outside picnic area. Displaying the confidence of a homeowner, he returned the garbage cans to the side of the house and surveyed the area before bringing the boys inside.

"Sarah, you did a fantastic job with the party. Thank you for inviting me." He didn't give her a chance to respond before turning his attention back to the boys. "Why don't you guys take your showers, and I'll come in a few minutes to help you get ready for bed?"

"You won't leave without saying goodbye?"

"I wouldn't think of it, buddy."

Sarah covered her mouth as she watched Alex slip back into the comfortable role of parenting her children. She decided to ignore his presumptuous attitude and be grateful for his attention to detail.

"Sarah, I know you have to prepare the babies for bed, but when you've finished, I need to talk with you."

Sarah also wanted to talk to Alex, but she feared what he might have to say. She didn't want to get into another discussion regarding their future. That look of hurt and longing Alex gave her after such conversations took its toll on her fragile heart.

"Sure, I'll meet you in the living room."

Alex headed for the boys' bedroom while she excused herself to feed the babies. Her mother had the girls in their pajamas and stayed with her to talk while she nursed them. "The party went well considering what all you had to do. I should have come a couple days earlier."

"You were a tremendous help, Mom. I'm not sure I could have managed without you. Was it hard to come back? I know it wasn't easy when you came for Christmas."

"I appreciate your concern, Sarah. Crossing that bridge at Christmas was difficult. I left the island, however, with a renewed appreciation for the peace at the cottage. Rather than feeling paralyzed by fear, I allowed myself to remember the good times, and it freed me to share them with you. We helped each other."

Sarah admired her mother's courage and determination. She had changed so much in the last few months. Sarah hoped she could cope with her fears in the same way.

They exchanged knowing looks during a moment of quiet when they overheard a conversation between Alex, Jonathan, and David. Alex kept a steady dialogue going while encouraging the boys to brush their teeth and get into their pajamas, much like old times. "Did you enjoy your birthday? Tell me your favorite part?"

Each boy vied to answer first. One responded, "The games." The other said, "The presents." Then the first said, "Our friends." She recognized the last response as coming from David, "The best thing was you, Mr. Alex."

"Well, that's nice of you to say, David. Thank you for inviting me. How are you feeling, buddy? You look a bit tired."

"I feel a little tired, but we had so much fun. I wish we had a birthday every week. Right, Jonathan?"

"I don't think we'll suggest that to your mother. You two need to get in bed. Give me a hug, and I'll send Mama to hear your prayers."

By that time, Sarah had the babies asleep and knew she could no longer avoid the overdue conversation with Alex. She met him in the hall coming out of the boys' room. "I believe the boys are ready for you to hear their prayers, Sarah. Are you free after you tuck them in?"

"That will be fine, Alex. There's something I need to tell you, as well."

As Sarah entered the boy's room, she noticed her mother speaking with Alex—probably thanking him for his involvement with the party. Leslie usually retired early to relax and read in bed before going to sleep. Although her mother would've preferred a longer visit, she had an appointment scheduled for the following afternoon in Raleigh. She planned to leave early the next morning.

When Sarah re-entered the living room, Alex sat on the couch cradling a cup of coffee—concern written on his face. He pointed to the cup he'd placed on the coffee table for her. She took it but chose a nearby chair.

"I'll get right to the point, Sarah. I'm worried about David. His coloring isn't good, and he barely kept up with the other children today. Also, he looked as if he was in pain. Have you noticed him being more tired than usual?"

"I think I saw it more today, and I've decided to take them all for checkups tomorrow. Susan gave me the name of a good pediatrician who also treats Mollie. It helps that you noticed though. Thank you for bringing it to my attention."

"Would you let me know the doctor's opinion, especially about David?"

"Of course. I appreciate your concern. I'm glad you came for the boys' birthday. Also, thanks for helping with the party and getting them ready for bed. You didn't have to do that, you know."

"I know, but I enjoyed being with them again. I love those boys, and I've missed them. The girls look well. I can't believe how much they've grown. At the party, I heard people calling them Elizabeth and Hannah, so I suppose you settled on names. Nice names. I'm pleased."

Sarah stood when Alex got up to leave. "I think you'll be even more pleased when you hear Hannah's middle name. I named her Grace after your mother, and Elizabeth is Anne after my mother. What do you think?"

Alex moved toward Sarah. She stepped back, distrustful of the blissful look trained on her. "Oh, Sarah. What a thoughtful, loving thing to do. Does this mean there's still hope for us?"

"Well, there's always hope, Alex. But nothing's changed between us. You remain a dear friend and neighbor, and I need more time to deal with all that's happened. Please, don't pressure me. I appreciate the fact that you've given me space and time to find some closure to a wonderful marriage. Forgive me for not being ready to move forward."

Alex backed away, shaking his head in frustration, "Don't do this to me, Sarah. This is the very reason I've stayed away from you. My heart can't take the constant rejections. You named one of the babies after my mother.

For goodness sake, Sarah, what am I supposed to think? Just call me after you take David to see the doctor."

Alex stomped out of the house with one thought in mind. I never plan to go near that woman again. He couldn't decide if he was angrier with himself or Sarah. She had a knack for doing or saying something to get his hopes up then dropping him like a hot potato. Never again would he put himself in the position for her to cause him such pain. All these years he'd refrained from allowing anyone outside his family to come that close. This blatant example proved the rightness of his decision.

Alex shook his head as conviction came over him. The woman drove him crazy. One minute he'd turned her over to God, willing to let her go, while the next, she made him furious when she refused to agree with his plans, his desires, his wants. Alex hung his head in shame. His mother had been right when she accused him of selfishness. *God, please forgive me for taking my eyes off you.*

CHAPTER EIGHTEEN

Sarah's mouth dropped open, stunned at Alex's angry exit. *What is the man's problem? Out of appreciation, I name one of the babies for his mother, and he's ready to move in.* Sarah's complaints stopped the moment she sat on the couch and felt the warmth of his body. She remembered his participation in the party and how he comfortably moved through the house as if he belonged here.

Replaying the conversation in her head, Sarah couldn't shake her regret. She didn't mean to give him false hope, but he had the uncanny ability to see past the surface into those hidden places she wasn't ready to reveal. She did love him, but if she expressed her true feelings, he'd insist on the kind of commitment she wasn't ready to give. Would she ever be able to move ahead with her life, or would fear continue to keep her from the love and security of such a wonderful man?

Tired of brooding, Sarah returned to the bedroom to check on her boys. When she kissed David's cheek, he felt warm to her lips and seemed restless. A temperature check with the ear thermometer indicated a slight elevation, but not enough to disturb him for medication. She breathed a healing prayer over him and returned to her room. Despite her exhaustion, sleep refused to overtake her troubled mind. Her thoughts rambled between worry for David and confusion over Alex.

After checking the clock yet again, Sarah finally drifted into a fitful sleep. Moments later, she awakened from a nightmare filled with piercing screams. The frightened cries of her son had her bolting from the bed as she heard the unmistakable sounds of vomiting. Her concerns escalated when she pulled David into her arms. He shook violently and felt hot to her touch. She picked him up from the foul-smelling covers and carried him into the kitchen. The soothing presence of his mother calmed him enough to sip ginger ale and swallow the dose of liquid fever reducer.

The soiled linens could wait until morning. She brought David to her bed and pulled his fevered body close to hers. Sarah whispered prayers and encouraging words over her son as he drifted into a fidgety sleep. Her body would protest a second sleepless night, but the weight of responsibility kept her awake. She had to find out what made her child sick.

Sarah's mother rose early and planned to leave right after breakfast. Still treading carefully with her mother, Sarah didn't mention her concerns. David looked pale, but he teased his brother and tried to talk Grandma into staying. More than likely, he suffered from a nasty virus, but a quick trip to the doctor would relieve her worries.

After her mother left, she called the number for the pediatrician. The doctor's office had one opening at ten thirty, which initiated a mad rush to arrive on time. Sarah hated to be late for anything. She frantically threw on a pair of slacks and a wrinkled top she found in the clean laundry hamper and rushed the children out the door. Sleep-deprived and exhausted, Sarah checked in with the receptionist at 10:35.

When she'd completed the endless paperwork, her attention returned to David who looked as if he might faint at any moment. She prayed under her breath for a quick diagnosis and over-the-counter treatment. After a brief lull, an attractive young woman came out to greet them. Sarah shrank in embarrassment when she compared her rumpled appearance to the classy woman.

"It's nice to meet you, Mrs. Stuart. I'm Dr. Scott. While you were hospitalized a few months ago, I assisted Mr. Caine with instructions for the babies. How is that good-looking fellow, by the way?"

"He's fine. He attended the boys' birthday party yesterday, and he's mentioned several times his appreciation for all you did. Thank you."

"You're quite welcome. Mr. Caine certainly impressed me with his concern and care for your children. He seems comfortable with your family."

"Yes, he is, but I'm here about David."

The doctor smiled when Sarah changed the subject. Sarah disliked discussing her relationship with Alex, especially with a perfect stranger. Of course, Alex was wonderful, but it embarrassed her to hear a constant rendition of his many attributes.

Since the girls were asleep in their stroller, Dr. Scott arranged for one of the nurses to watch them and Jonathan in the well-baby area. When Sarah felt certain the three children would be supervised, she picked up David and followed the doctor back to an exam room. They briefly conversed as she undressed her son and prepared him for the exam.

"So, David, your mother tells me that you're not feeling well." Dr. Scott continued talking to him as she looked in his ears, nose, and throat and listened to his heart. She checked his temperature, then looked at Sarah with concern.

When she pressed on his right side, David cried out, "You're hurting me!"

"I'm sorry, David, but I need to figure out what's making you sick. Can you tell me exactly where it hurts?"

As David pointed to his lower right side, the doctor addressed Sarah. "Has he been nauseated?"

"He threw up during the night, but I blamed it on the junk food he ate at the party. After he drank a bit of ginger ale, he seemed better and slept the rest of the night. Do you think it's something serious?"

The doctor's worried look gave Sarah reason to question her casual handling of the situation. Her usual tendency to lean toward the positive had worked with minor problems and prevented many unnecessary trips to the doctor. But this time, she didn't know. Had she erred by not being more concerned? Had Alex turned out to be a better parent?

Dr. Scott interrupted her. "I'm not positive, but if I had to guess, I would say he has an infected appendix. His fever is up to 104.8, he's lethargic, and he's hurting in the approximate area. However, appendicitis doesn't usually attack a child this young. I can't be certain without sending him to the hospital for a sonogram. Is there someone available to pick up the other children?"

What was happening to her family? For a moment, Sarah was unable to respond, feeling as if she'd hit a brick wall with no way around and no means of scaling it. She took a deep breath and leaned against the examination table to steady her weak legs. When David looked at her with such trust and confidence, Sarah knew she wouldn't have to face this alone. She'd look to God with that same assurance.

"I'll find someone."

Sarah grabbed her purse and headed for the door. The doctor stopped her with one final comment. "We'll keep David here for blood work. They might redo it at the hospital, but I'd like to have an initial analysis to eliminate some of the possibilities."

Sarah's self-confidence faded as her mind raced. She needed someone to help her. She couldn't leave her son here alone, crying in fear at the mention of blood work. She had to find a responsible person to watch the other children.

First, she telephoned Susan. No answer. Then a second friend. Same response. Her only other option was Alex. Why did she continue to fear her mother's rejection? If she'd told her about David, she'd have gladly stayed. Now, she'd be forced to rely on the one person she went to great lengths to avoid.

Alex had been sitting at his desk and staring out at the ocean all morning. He attempted to write but seemed unable to do anything but pray for David. The boy had acted so unlike himself yesterday. Alex couldn't believe that Sarah hadn't noticed.

When he heard the phone and saw the name on the caller ID, he answered on the first ring. "Sarah, what did the doctor say?"

"She doesn't know for certain, but Dr. Scott thinks it might be appendicitis. She's sending him to the hospital for a sonogram and further tests. I'm looking for someone to pick up the other three children from the doctor's office. Do you think you might help? I know you're busy, and I hate to keep bothering you, but there's no one else."

Alex heard the reluctance in her voice, but at least she had dared to ask. Relieved to know the other three children would be in his care during yet another crisis, he said, "You know I will. I'm glad you went to Dr. Scott. Remember how she helped me when you were in the hospital? She seems competent. Don't worry. I'll take care of the children. I'll be right there."

"Thanks, Alex."

As Alex backed the car out of the garage, he realized he had no idea where he was going. Before he reached the street, he redialed her number. "Sarah, I'm sorry to bother you, but could you give me the address?"

Alex heard Sarah fumbling for the information, followed by a loud sigh. "Alex, you don't have car seats. How will you get them home?"

"It's okay, Sarah. I'll transfer David's seat to my SUV for you to drive while I use your van. Will that work for you?"

"I guess so. Why must life be filled with these unbearable complications and why do they keep happening to us?"

Alex figured he probably knew the answer, but he wouldn't go there in the middle of the crisis. "God is with us, Sarah, and he loves David. Let's pray and trust him."

Sarah hesitated a moment as if she didn't know what to say. He hated the uncomfortable silence, but wishing things were different wouldn't help them through this latest ordeal.

"Thanks, Alex. I'll see you in a few minutes."

When Alex arrived at the medical offices, he rushed inside to find Sarah and retrieve her keys. The nurses directed him to the exam room where he found Sarah caressing David's hair and speaking softly to him. When his buddy saw him, he cried and reached for him. "Daddy, I got appicitus."

Alex hesitated briefly and looked around in confusion at David's familial greeting. Sarah gasped as she turned in surprise toward her son. Alex ignored her and picked up David, while he mumbled to himself, "Out of the mouth of babes." Father-like concern swept over Alex. He felt the heat coming from the child's lethargic frame and noticed how pale he was.

"I'm so sorry you don't feel well, David. Do you know that Dr. Scott helped me with the babies when I didn't know how to feed them? I know she's going to take care of you. These problems happen to the best of us. I had to have my appendix out when I was a little older than you."

"You did? Did it hurt?"

"You'll be sound asleep the whole time, and when you wake up, it'll all be over. Mama will take you to the hospital, and you'll feel better. When the weather gets warmer, we'll be out on the beach building castles in the sand."

"Can you pray? I'm so scared, and my stomach hurts."

"I know you're afraid, but remember your namesake, David, in the Bible. There were times when he felt afraid, but he trusted God to give him the courage to face the dreadful things that happened to him. Let's pray. 'Thank you, God, for reminding us of how you helped King David. Could you please help our David as he goes to the hospital? Give him courage and comfort. Please help the doctors to make him well and strong again so we can play together on the beach. We pray this in Jesus' name. Amen.'"

David continued to cling to Alex, "Will you go with me?"

"I have to take care of Jonathan and the babies, David. Mama will go with you so she can kiss away your booboos. Mommies are better at that. You'll need her, buddy."

"I want Mama and you. I got to have a mommy and a daddy when I go to the hospital."

Alex didn't know how to respond to the child longing for his father. At a loss, he turned toward the mother. "Help me out here, Sarah."

"David, Mr. Alex must take your brother and sisters home first and find someone to watch them before he comes to the hospital." Sarah's answer surprised him, but she could see her son was upset.

"Would that be okay with you, buddy?"

"I guess, but don't take too long. They might do something I don't want, and you can stop them."

"I'll do my best, but you have to promise me that you'll be brave and do what Mama and the nurses and doctors tell you. Do you promise?"

David nodded and reluctantly let Alex put him down. As he left the room, he reassured the boy, "While I'm gone, your mama will make sure everything is okay."

Retrieving the keys from Sarah, he ran to her van, got one of the booster seats and then ran back to his SUV. He groaned in irritation as he examined a tangle of straps that defied logic. After several unsuccessful attempts to install the complicated seat, he slammed the car door and chastised himself for not paying attention before yanking it out of the van. Since he'd already taken so much time, he drove the SUV to the entrance and rushed inside to find Sarah. He found her at the check-out desk.

"Where's David?"

"He's still back in the exam room. Could you get him for me? As you probably observed, he prefers your comfort to mine." Sarah sounded defeated, afraid, and slightly miffed.

"Don't take him too seriously, Sarah. He's traumatized now, and I'm just someone different. I'll settle him in his car seat if you don't mind securing it first. I'm afraid I failed the class on installation."

A knowing smirk spread across Sarah's face as he left to find David. When Alex came back carrying the boy, Sarah followed him toward the exit. "The babies and Jonathan are in the well-children's waiting room. You can return for them after we leave. Is that okay?"

"You don't have to worry about the other children, Sarah. I'll take care of them," Alex replied as he opened the car door and stood back for her to install the car seat. Alex scratched his head in disbelief when she reached for David and helped him into the perfectly secured seat.

"I'm a big boy, Daddy. I can do it myself even when I'm sick."

"Yes, David. You are a big boy, and I'm proud of you. I'll see you in a little while. I love you, buddy."

"I love you the most!"

As Alex gave Sarah a quick hug, he felt her body shaking. He held her a moment longer before helping her into the driver's seat of his car. "Please try not to worry, Sarah. I believe this is but a slight bump in the road, and David will be fine. Were you serious when you said I could find someone to watch the children and return to the hospital?"

The woman, who seconds ago had seemed to melt into his embrace, now glared at him. "With reluctance, yes. I don't lie to my children, *Daddy!*"

Alex recoiled. Sarah's anger subsided a bit, and she began ticking off a to-do list for Alex. "Call Susan Lane first. I couldn't get her earlier, but she may be home by now. If she has a cell phone, I don't have the number. Her home number is on a pad by the telephone. If you can't find anyone, it'll probably be all right. David will be out for a while, depending on what time they prep him for surgery. If it works out for you to come, it might be best to arrive before they give him the anesthetic. We'd better go."

Alex wrote Susan's number on his hand and went back inside to find the children. The girls were awake and enjoying the attention from Dr. Scott's nursing staff. Alex hugged Jonathan, "How are you doing, buddy? I know you're worried about David, but I believe he's going to be fine."

"Well, if it isn't Mr. Caine." Dr. Scott said as she came toward him with her outstretched hand. He gave her hand a firm shake while she continued in a teasing manner. "I see you're still playing Mr. Mom to Sarah's children. I suppose additional advice from me won't be necessary since you're quite the expert by now. Thank you for coming to her rescue."

"Yes, involvement in Sarah's family has become a habit, but you know I love them all. Offering help to a neighbor should be easy, but in this case ... I don't think I'll go there. You're needed at the hospital, and I have to settle the other three at home, but I may see you later."

Alex gave Jonathan the diaper bag and asked him to hold the door while he pushed the double stroller through. What should have been a simple task turned into a wrestling match similar to the impossible car seat. He looked around the area and observed an audience of amused onlookers. He scowled at them as he made a final attempt paired with a bit of manipulation. Success for him, but by then, Hannah and Elizabeth were in tears.

"Jonathan. Did you happen to notice the last time your mother fed the babies?"

"We were still at home, I think."

Alex concluded from their wails that it'd probably been a while. Their upset mother undoubtedly thought of little but getting David to the hospital.

Jonathan put the diaper bag on the front seat and buckled himself into his car seat, while Alex struggled to get Hannah out of the stroller. Nothing he did released the multiple straps holding the screaming baby. Jonathan's shouted instructions only added to Alex's frustration.

"You have to push the little button, Mr. Alex."

Alex pushed every button he could see. Finally, he found the last one and freed the squalling child. She shook with a few more sobs until she realized he held her. His kisses and soothing words comforted her. While Elizabeth continued to scream, Alex put Hannah in her car seat—wrestling again with the myriad of straps and clasps required to hold an infant secure. Once again, Jonathan gave unsolicited advice.

Repetition proved to be an excellent teacher. He released Elizabeth from the stroller and secured her in the car seat almost as if he'd done it dozens of times before. Where was his audience when he didn't look like a chump? Alex gave equal time for snuggles before installing the baby in her seat. When both girls realized they no longer had his attention, the chaotic cries resumed.

"Can't you shut them up, Mr. Alex? They're hurting my ears." Jonathan held his hands over his ears, shouting above the noise and creating more bedlam.

Meanwhile, Alex frantically worked to close the complicated stroller. He tried everything, including Jonathan's suggestions. Finally, he opened the rear of the van and forced the stroller inside, half open. At least he'd save time on the other end, provided he could retrieve the contraption from the limited cargo space.

Alex climbed behind the wheel and sat there for a minute listening to the babies' cries. He wanted to cry right along with them. With the worry over David and Sarah, his heavy heart ached and felt too large for his chest. All soothing reassurances he'd murmured to the babies hadn't eased his fears.

More advice came from Jonathan, shouting above the racket, "If you just start the car, they'll be quiet."

"Why didn't you say so sooner, Jonathan? Thanks for the suggestion." As soon as Alex turned the switch, the only sound he heard came from the quiet car engine.

"That's amazing, Jonathan. Best advice I've heard all day. You deserve a reward for that bit of magic. We'll have to think of something fun to do when your brother recovers. Let's go home."

Alex entertained his charges with one of his favorites. "The Itsy, Bitsy, Spider, went up the water spout." He watched through the rearview mirror as Jonathan joined in the song and exaggerated the motions. The babies listened, kicking their legs in excitement.

When they pulled into the driveway, Alex sent Jonathan inside to search for formula while he unbuckled the girls. Holding Elizabeth in one arm, he somehow managed to free her sister and carry them both into the house. At five months, two squirming girls were a challenge.

Jonathan found enough formula in the pantry for one feeding. Alex would have to make a trip to the store when he did find someone to watch them. As he picked up the phone to call Susan, he remembered Anna would arrive soon and could pick up the formula on her way.

Since the girls demanded immediate attention, Alex situated himself on the couch with a baby on each side and held a bottle to each mouth. Not the best arrangement, still it proved successful and was the only solution that came to mind. Alex recruited Jonathan to hold the bottles in place while he dialed the phone. He placed the first call to Anna who agreed to stop for the formula and additional diapers. Anna offered to watch the children if he failed to find someone else.

When he called Susan, she'd returned early from a shopping trip with a sick child of her own. Not wanting to expose the children to a stomach virus, Alex opted for Anna. He liked Susan, but Anna had more experience with Sarah's children.

With the phone calls over and decisions made, Alex relaxed with the babies asleep in his arms, until he remembered he hadn't changed their diapers. With Jonathan's assistance, he took one at a time to the changing table and was relieved when they slept through his awkward efforts. The poor babies had worn themselves out.

After the clean babies slept soundly in their beds, he made Jonathan a peanut butter and jelly sandwich. Although it'd been years since he had a PB&J with a glass of milk, it looked so good, he made another for himself. The comfort food hit the spot under the circumstances.

"Jonathan, I appreciate your help today with your sisters. I wasn't kidding when I said we'd do something special when your brother recovers. You and David must help me decide. How's your sandwich?"

"Good, but Mommy doesn't make it like this. She puts jelly on one side and the peanut butter on the other. You put it all on one side. That way we didn't get as much jelly."

"What a good suggestion. Next time I'll take your advice and make it like Mommy does. Thanks, Jonathan. You are a wealth of information. Now, I want you to finish your milk and prepare for your nap. Miss Anna will be here soon to stay with you and your sisters while I check on your brother at the hospital. When you wake up, you can help her with the babies until I come back. Is that a deal?"

Jonathan didn't much like the idea of Alex leaving, but since he planned to visit his brother, he reluctantly agreed.

CHAPTER NINETEEN

Alex saw the pain and misery on Sarah's face the moment he came through the double doors. She inched toward him looking uncertain of her reception. Surely, she knew how he felt. Pulling her into his arms, he held her in a tight embrace while her tears dampened his shoulder.

Alex kissed near her ear and whispered, "Sarah, don't be afraid. We must trust God. What have they found out so far?"

Sarah looked confused as she struggled to answer, "I was so upset, I don't remember much of what they told me. The doctor did say something about the blood tests and the sonogram indicating acute appendicitis. I'm waiting to talk with the surgeon and Dr. Scott."

At the mention of her name, the doctor appeared in the doorway. "Well, Mr. Caine, I see you're once again the answer to Sarah's prayers. When do you find time to write those page-turning novels? I'm glad you're here, though. David has been telling us how much he needs his daddy. It took us a while, but soon we realized he spoke of you."

Alex ignored the doctor's amusement, feeling certain she took the welfare of her patients seriously and would show special concern for one so young destined for surgery.

"What's happening, Dr. Scott?" Alex asked as he moved Sarah to his side.

"The tests all show that the appendix is inflamed and must be removed as soon as possible. David's temperature is elevated, and he's thrown up several times. I would like for the two of you to go in and try to calm him before the anesthesiologist arrives. We've given him an IV to stop the nausea, but it's important that he relax. He needs your reassurance."

"Show us the way." Alex couldn't help but take charge, touching Sarah's back gently and escorting her down the hall. Being here with Sarah and her son seemed as natural as breathing.

"Dr. Murphy asked me to tell you that he'll see you as soon as the surgery is over. After we administer the anesthesia, you may wait in a room down the hall." Dr. Scott continued to talk as she led them toward David.

When Alex saw his little man scrunched in a tight fetal position with his face wet with tears, his heart grieved for the frightened child. He left Sarah and moved toward David's bedside. Sarah's children had awakened an unexplained parental longing in him that seemed uncharacteristic for a confirmed bachelor.

David reached for him, but the IV lines prevented Alex from holding him. "It's going to be all right, David. Jesus is right here with us, and he'll take care of you. There's a doctor with a big name coming in a few minutes to put you to sleep. You'll have a nice, peaceful rest and you know what? Since Jonathan is taking his nap right now, you can pretend to be home with your twin brother. When you wake up, the operation will be over. You might be a little sore for a few days, but soon you'll feel better than ever."

"You promise?"

"I promise. Hey, I forgot to tell you. Jonathan and I are planning something special for you when you get well. But you must help us decide what fun thing we should do. Perhaps you'll dream about it while you're sleeping. Now give me a big hug so Mama can have her turn. Mommy hugs and kisses are the best, especially coming from *your* mommy."

Alex gave David a reassuring hug and stepped back to make room for Sarah. The boy relaxed with his mother and had almost forgotten about the dreaded surgery until the anesthesiologist arrived. When he looked up and saw the bearded stranger, he started to cry.

Alex returned to his side. "Remember David, you're going to be brave and courageous like the shepherd boy. Before you count to one hundred, it will be all over, and you'll wake up with a smile on your face."

"But I can't count that far," David protested. They all laughed as the doctor prepared to put the child to sleep.

Alex led Sarah to the surgical waiting room and hoped to continue the comfortable rapport they achieved earlier. When he reached for her, she quickly moved to the far corner of the room. He ignored her cold attitude, walked through the wall she'd erected, and pulled her into his arms.

Instead of resistance as he expected, Sarah molded her warm body against his. Her arms moved around his waist and pulled him even closer. Alex couldn't breathe. His heart picked up speed. All the months of longing hit him at once. His arms tightened around her as he kissed her hair and rubbed her back. Embracing her seemed so perfect—as if they were made for each other. With his lips gradually moving toward her neck, he felt himself responding to her softness against him. With another of her delicious kisses only inches away, his conscience rudely interrupted. *What am I doing?* Sarah didn't belong to him, and it would be wrong to take advantage of her vulnerability. The distressed mother needed his comfort, nothing more. He gently took her shoulders and looked at her tear-streaked face.

"Let's pray, Sarah."

Alex rested in the quiet presence of the Holy Spirit for a moment, then petitioned God for David's protection during the surgery and recovery. He prayed against fear and doubt and asked for peace and faith instead. As he thanked God for hearing their prayers, Sarah again relaxed against him.

Alex breathed a calming prayer and offered to go for coffee—anything to put some space between his erotic thinking and the tempting woman. During the walk to the cafeteria, he telephoned their pastor and filled him in on David's condition. Pastor Mark said he'd be there soon. In the meantime, he promised to contact the emergency prayer tree. Alex wasn't sure what the term meant but assumed it would alert people to pray.

When he returned to the waiting room, Sarah paced the floor, obviously praying with each step. "I'm glad you're here with me, Alex. I don't think I could've dealt with this alone. I feel so helpless and distraught. Who did you find to watch the other children? Are they all right?

"My dear, dependable Anna is taking care of them. I fed them the formula Jonathan found in the pantry, and Anna stopped at the store for more before coming to relieve me. The woman is a jewel. I don't know where I'd be without her. Did I tell you she prayed for me long before I acknowledged God?"

"Well, I'm glad you have her, Alex, and I appreciate how she came to our rescue. Do you really think David is going to be all right?"

"I know you're worried, Sarah, but you aren't alone in this. I talked to Pastor Mark who promised to get the whole church praying. Besides, David has more faith than most adults. He'll be fine. Come, sit down, and have some coffee. I also picked up a couple boxes of milk. I bet you haven't had anything to eat all day, and that's not good when you're nursing."

Sarah furrowed her brow and gave him a slight smile but didn't comment. He wondered what she thought of his overly affectionate actions earlier. No way could she have missed it. *God, give me the strength to put Sarah's needs above my sexual desires.* Alex knew he had to be strong for her, even amid his own worry. She looked fragile enough to break at any moment. As he watched her sip the milk, he prayed for strength and courage as together they waited for word about David.

Sarah looked at Alex who sat with his elbows on his knees, and his head bowed in prayer. She admired him for the man of faith he'd become in a few short months. When he raised his head and looked at her, Sarah's curiosity compelled her to ask him about the sudden transformation.

"Thank you, Alex, for reminding me to trust God. My faith seems adequate when everything's going well, but under pressure, I tend to panic. How did you so abruptly transform into this serious man of faith?"

"The day I met your boys on the beach, something happened to me. My successful, contented life suddenly looked dull and empty. I'm not certain you're aware of it, but your boys are great evangelists. They intrigued me with the way they brought spiritual matters into every conversation. At first, I resented you for brainwashing them, but my resentment soon turned to admiration when I acknowledged their behavior. As I listened to their stories, the Bible came alive and made sense for the first time. Sometimes they made me uncomfortable, and some of their remarks challenged me. After you forced me to deliver the twins, I became aware of the reality of God's creative work.

"Then, when you rejected me, the emptiness and loneliness moved me to rethink much of my prior decisions about Christianity. I went through a powerful time of soul searching that culminated in my seeking a personal relationship with God. Oh, I struggle with discouragement and doubt, but more and more my faith moves me from the lowest valley to the highest mountaintop. I'm slowly learning that God uses those difficult places to pull me back to him. Through studying the Bible and prayer, I've found a friend who loves me as I am but challenges me to change. No matter the future, I know he'll be with me. Does that help you understand?"

"Yes." Sarah thought about her own situation. "I know God is also using this time in my life. Sometimes I get so caught up in being a mommy and facing the new experiences of widowhood that I forget to settle my mind and heart and focus on him."

Their coffees had grown cold while they'd talked. Now, they sat in comfortable silence, waiting for word that David's surgery was finished. Sarah closed her eyes and tried to get comfortable on the plastic couch. She felt the tension leave her neck and shoulders. Slowly, a sense of oneness and peace came over her as she admitted to herself she'd come to love and trust this good man.

As the minutes dragged by, with no sign of a doctor, a fresh batch of fear and doubt assaulted Sarah. The loving thoughts from moments before were replaced with guilt and self-loathing. She moaned inwardly, remembering how she cried on Alex's shoulder. How quickly the touch from an appealing man had erased her worry and concern for her son. She acted like some love-deprived fool, hungry for attention. When Alex abruptly pulled away, she felt cheated of the sensual kisses she craved. Her confidence dissolved into a pitiful, needy mother, depending on the strength of a man she should never consider.

Even the children saw him as the go-to guy in times of distress. Before the surgery, they'd been in the room but a few minutes before David acted like a different child, completely calm and captivated with his hero. Which brought up another problem—she didn't know what to do about her son calling him Daddy. She heard the moniker for the first time when Alex arrived at the doctor's office. While David's use of the term embarrassed her, it seemed to provide no small amount of speculation and entertainment for others.

Perhaps David feared Alex would leave him like his dad. How long would she be able to resist the man's advances when her children made a compelling case in his favor? Although it threatened her new-found independence, his take-charge, positive attitude seemed to be exactly what she needed for the present crisis.

Sarah's jumbled thoughts were soon interrupted when Pastor Mark rushed into the room. After greeting them and getting an update on

David, he read a few encouraging verses from the Bible and then prayed for her son. When he finished, he distracted them by discussing an array of subjects ranging from Alex's books to Sarah's adjustment to living on the island. Amid the lively conversation, Sarah watched Alex interact with their pastor. She noticed an unusual connection between the two men and was surprised to learn they had become close friends while she and Alex went to great lengths to avoid one another.

Their discussion ceased when the doctor appeared. As Sarah stood, he approached with outstretched hand. "Mrs. Stuart? I'm Dr. Murphy, the surgeon who removed your son's appendix. He did well during the surgery, but we were momentarily alarmed when he experienced a slight reaction to the anesthesia. He seems fine now and should return to full consciousness soon. It might help if you were with him. Also, I understand he wants his 'daddy,' er, ... Mr. Caine."

The doctor chuckled. Sarah wanted to crawl under the couch. The hospital gossip seemed to be moving full speed at her expense. For once, she was thankful for the Privacy Act; otherwise, they'd have the paparazzi chasing them. She felt even more embarrassed and a little angry when she looked up and saw a smile spreading across Pastor Mark's face. How much had Alex told him about their relationship?

Alex saw Sarah's face flush and hurried to explain. "We're not married, Dr. Murphy, but David thinks of me as his daddy. You see his birth father died last year in Iraq, and the family still grieves his loss. I'm merely playing the role to pacify a sick little boy. Thank you for allowing me to see David with Sarah."

Alex took Sarah's hand and followed the doctor back to recovery. As soon as they arrived, Sarah broke away and ran to her son. Smoothing his hair and checking him over, she whispered in his ear as he made a gradual return to consciousness. Alex moved to the other side of the bed so he could watch Sarah. His heart ached for this woman who'd been through so much.

David's eyes fluttered open. He looked at Sarah. "Where's Daddy?"

Alex moved near the bed. "I'm right here, David. How are you feeling?"

"I'm okay, but guess what I want to do when I get well?"

Alex laughed as he saw abnormal excitement bubbling from a child who moments ago was undergoing surgery. "Well, I have no idea, but it looks as though you've had an enjoyable time dreaming about it. What do you have in mind, buddy?"

"I want us to go to Disney World," David replied putting a dramatic emphasis on the words.

"David, you know that's a big request and expensive. You shouldn't expect that kind of gift from Mr. Alex."

Alex had about all he could stand of Sarah's penny-pinching. She could be as frugal as she wished with her money, but when it came to his, he'd choose generosity. "Well, Mrs. Stuart, the deal the boys and I made didn't concern cost or how big the request."

Alex then turned to David with a conspiratorial wink, "Not to worry, David. We'll talk her into it."

His mother's objections failed to diminish David's enthusiasm. "Do you think we could see Mickey Mouse and Donald Duck? I love those cartoons."

"It so happens that they're my favorites as well. We'll make sure to see them when we go to Disney World. But the most important thing now is for you to get well."

Sarah seemed ready to protest when Alex crossed his arms, frowned dramatically, and shook his head at her. He leaned across the bed and murmured for her ears only, "Keep your worries to yourself, Mama. This gift is for David."

In a few minutes, the nurse came into the room to check the patient and give Sarah information about his recovery. They expected him to experience some pain as the anesthetic wore off, but overall, the nurse felt encouraged by his progress.

Late in the afternoon, Sarah wondered aloud. "What about Anna? When does she need to leave? Or do you have someone else coming to stay with the children, Alex?"

He ran his hand through his hair. "No, there's no relief on the way. Why don't you go home, Sarah? I'll stay here with David tonight.

"Alex, I can't expect you to do that." She paused, then groaned. "Of course, I can't expect you to take care of three other children either. Why didn't I ask Mother to stay a few days? I never stop to think of the consequences. I keep plowing ahead, trying to manage on my own. You'd think I would've figured it out by now. It's frustrating that I'm forced to take advantage of you again."

Alex let her vent for a few minutes and then responded with his usual calm. "I know you want to be here with David, but he seems to be recovering nicely, and it would be easier for me to take care of him while you go home to Jonathan and the babies. Get someone to watch them in the morning for a couple of hours while you return to the hospital. I'll take over at home later. Please, don't worry about me. Being with you and the children makes me happy."

Sarah hesitated, then asked David, "Is it okay with you for Mommy to go home while Mr. Alex stays here with you?"

"Could he? That would be great! We could have a sleepover and talk more about Disney World."

Sarah rolled her eyes at Alex. He knew it wouldn't be long before he received a private reprimand. Ignoring him for the moment, she kissed David.

"I love you, David, and I'm thankful God is healing you. Be good for Mr. Alex now."

"Mama, he's Daddy. I told you that."

Sarah caught Alex grinning. He attempted to conjure up a repentant look to erase the pleasure, but it fell far short of genuine, and he didn't know how to rectify the situation.

"That you did. Just be good and get well. I'll see you both in the morning."

Even when miffed at him, Sarah's insecurity didn't escape his notice as she gave him a curt wave from the door. "You be good, too, Duh-add-dy," stretching out the despised word.

When Sarah left, Alex and David played a counting game the nurse pulled from a drawer. Numbers came easy for the boy. A short while later, a new nurse, Kelly, entered with ginger ale to see how well her patient tolerated liquids. At six o'clock, she piqued David's interest when she came through the door with enticing red gelatin. The squiggly substance even looked good to Alex, who didn't remember a meal since breakfast. One cup of cold coffee left much to be desired.

A few minutes later, Kelly returned with a tray for Alex. "I thought you might be a little hungry, Mr. Caine. Since David isn't eating solids, you may have his dinner."

"Is that okay with you, David?"

"I like my Jell-O. Do you want some?"

"Why thank you, David, but I guess I'll have to eat this yucky chicken and rice and veggies." David grinned at Alex's funny response as he inspected the supposedly offensive food.

"Be nice, Mr. Caine. I'll check on you two in a few minutes." After the nurse left the room, Alex ate the surprisingly tasty meal, then resumed playing the game.

On the nurse's next visit, she had an ice pop for each of them. "Which do you want David, red or orange."

"Which do you like best, Daddy?"

"Oh, I like them both. How about you?"

"Me, too. I'll have the red, and you can have the orange."

With that settled, they enjoyed their icy treat and continued their game mingled with conversation about what they'd see at Disney World and which rides they thought Jonathan would like best.

"The babies are too little. What will we do with them?"

"I don't know yet, but we'll make sure they have fun, too."

When Alex considered the logistics involved in a trip with young children, he realized it would be more complicated than he first imagined. Despite the considerable planning, he wouldn't disappoint the boys.

A while later, the nurse checked David's vitals and started removing the needle from his arm.

"What're you doing? That hurts!" David pulled his arm away while Alex rushed forward to calm the upset boy and help. Kelly continued to work despite the protest from her patient.

"You're doing so well, David, I'm freeing you, so you can sleep better. How does that sound?"

"I guess, but Daddy can still stay with me, can't he?"

"Of course, see the chair over there? It reclines back so he'll be comfortable. I'm going to bring you more ginger ale, but you should try to go to sleep. You need lots of rest to get well after an operation."

"We'll be ready for bed soon. Right, buddy?"

"I'm a little sleepy, but you won't leave me? Promise?" David yawned.

"I promise. I'll be right here in the room when you wake up, and your mama will be back first thing in the morning. Let me help you brush your teeth and go to the bathroom. When you're ready, I'll tell you a story, and we'll say our prayers."

Before the story ended, David's eyes were drooping. Alex skipped a few details to finish. After he said a quick prayer, he planted a kiss on the boy's forehead and retired to the uncomfortable recliner.

Just when Alex felt himself drifting off, the nurse came in and turned on the light to check on her patient. No apology, she merely did her job. David didn't stir.

After much tossing and turning, exhaustion claimed Alex, and he drifted into a mild slumber. A brief time later, the sound of crying slowly woke him. He unfolded himself from the awkward chair and rushed to check on his little man. "What's the matter, David?"

"It hurts. Could you hold me?" Alex picked the boy up and held him close while he pressed the call button. The nurse came after a few minutes with liquid pain medication, discerning the problem before he asked. David took the medication without protest but wouldn't let Alex put him back in bed.

"It's okay, David. I'll be nearby. Will that be all right?"

David snuggled toward Alex and refused to release him from the tight hold. He had no choice but to climb on the bed with him. Under his breath, he prayed for the little boy to relax and return to a restful sleep. It didn't take long for the prayers and medication to work. As Alex continued to hold him, he marveled at the love he felt for Sarah's children. If someone had told him six months ago he'd be spending the night in the hospital with a child not his own and trying to figure out how he could spend the rest of his life with said child, his three siblings, and their widowed mother, he would have laughed them out of the room. Even in his imagination, he could not have devised such a story. But here he was—sharing a hospital bed with a four-year-old who just had an appendectomy. Adjusting his position, he felt himself drifting into restful sleep.

When she arrived the next morning, Sarah found them cuddled together—a picture of peaceful contentment.

CHAPTER TWENTY

Alex woke stiff and aching from the awkward position he'd slept in. Turning his head to remove the cricks from his neck, he saw Sarah standing in the doorway. The woman had the unmistakable look of love. Her eyes, glistening with desire, captured him in an intense gaze. Despair, once again, gave way to hope. Before he made another fool of himself, he looked away and checked his emotions. Some lessons were hard to learn, but through numerous disappointments, he'd learned this one well. If she wanted him, she'd have to make the first move.

David stirred as his mother made her way to the bed. He rewarded her with a loud, wet kiss as Alex untangled himself from the sheets and proceeded toward the restroom. When he returned, Sarah sat on the bed examining David and grilling him about his night.

"I feel better. Can we go home now? I want to tell Jonathan about our trip to Disney World."

"We have to wait for the doctor to come by before we leave, but the nurse said you did so well that she feels certain you'll go home today. So, you planned your trip, huh? Must I ask if the trip includes your mother?"

"We wouldn't go without you and the babies. Would we, Daddy?"

"Of course not. We'd be lonely without them. It'll take some time to work it out, but we'll plan to go soon. Right, David?"

He grinned as he gave Alex a high five. "Do you need to use the restroom, David? I bet you can make it by yourself this morning."

With that, the boy jumped up and went toward the bathroom. Alex rushed to his side when David moaned.

"You'll have to move a little slower for a few days, buddy, until your incision heals."

"You won't leave me, will you?"

"No, your mother and I will be right here waiting for you. But you need to take it easy until your tummy has time to heal."

When David left, Sarah turned toward him with her hands on her hips and itching for a fight. What happened to that look of longing?

"You are in so much trouble, Alex Caine, making promises before running them by me, letting my son call you Daddy, and stealing my children's affections. What am I going to do with you?"

"You know the answer to that question, Sarah, and it's very simple."

The doctor came in and interrupted them. Sarah whispered between her teeth, "This conversation is not over, Mr. Caine."

She then turned to the doctor with a generous smile, "Good morning, Dr. Murphy."

"Am I interrupting something, Mrs. Stuart?"

When Sarah hesitated a moment too long, Alex answered for her. "Not at all, sir. Merely a technicality that concerns Mrs. Stuart. She'll figure it out, I'm convinced."

"I'm sure she will. Now, where is my patient?" At the doctor's question, David came into the room and jumped up on the bed, again forgetting his sore spot.

"Hello, David. How do you feel this morning?" The doctor looked at the tiny incisions made by the laparoscopic surgery, checked vital signs and stomach activity.

"Great, but I want to go home? Can I?"

"We'll see. Let me check you out."

It didn't take long before the doctor signed the discharge papers and the nurse came with instructions for David's recovery at home. While the nurse talked with Sarah, Alex helped David into the clean clothes she brought from home and encouraged him to eat a breakfast of vanilla pudding and a banana and drink some apple juice. The scant meal didn't look that appealing to him, but the boy devoured it with gusto. When he finished his meal, the nurse helped him into a wheelchair.

"Are you ready for a ride, young man?"

"Really? This is great! Can Daddy push me?"

"I think Daddy should bring the car for us," Sarah interrupted. David looked disappointed but understood.

"I'll see you out front, buddy."

When Alex left to get the car, Sarah made a quick trip to the business office. She cringed at the thought of the hospital bill. Most expenses should be covered, but even the co-pay would deplete her checking account. She felt relieved when the clerk only needed a signature for her son's discharge. They would bill her later for anything not covered by insurance.

Sarah finished the paperwork and met David and the nurse outside the hospital entrance. When Alex didn't come right away, she remembered the key to his SUV still warmed her pocket. Could he be searching for the van she left at home?

A few minutes later he pulled the SUV under the entryway. As he emerged from his vehicle, Sarah met him on the run. "I'm sorry, Alex. I forgot to give your key back. Thank goodness, you had a spare."

"Where's your van, Sarah?"

"It's at home. I received a call this morning from the nurse who said David would probably be released this morning. I asked Susan's husband to drive me so we could ride home together. Susan's with the children."

Alex buckled David into his car seat and helped Sarah in beside him. "I want Daddy to sit back here with me."

The sympathetic look Alex gave her didn't help. She hid the trickle of tears behind the scratched sunglasses she found in the bottom of her purse. As they exchanged places, Alex handed her the keys and hugged her. "It'll be all right, Sarah. We fellows need some downtime to talk on the way home. Do you mind?"

She didn't even bother to answer. Her first reaction was hurt that David would want to be with someone other than his mother. She didn't know why that upset her now. Her son had preferred Alex from the moment he'd known he had to undergo surgery. At the party, even the baby girls warmed up to him as if he visited every day. The man had captured the affection of her children, and there was nothing she could do about it. Truthfully, she didn't know how she'd cope without him. How had she become so dependent upon the man in such a brief time? Instead of being offended, Sarah should feel relieved that her boys had someone of Alex's integrity and character in their lives.

At the same time, he had taken up residence in her heart, but she refused to acknowledge it openly. She required time to sort through the last few disappointing months and adjust to life as a widow. Sarah only wanted her son well again, running and playing on the beach. She paused as she resisted the vivid scene of Jonathan and David playing with Alex and Bailey. So much for getting rid of him, even in her thoughts.

The next few days proved both difficult and enjoyable. Although David recovered from the surgery, the soreness from his incision, along with the cold north wind, kept the boys inside. Despite Sarah's uneasiness, Alex often came to entertain the children. The Lego sets he'd given the boys for their birthday brought hours of focused pleasure. They stayed busy creating spaceships and airplanes. He'd known exactly what would engage their active minds, and he seemed delighted along with them.

Sarah loved to watch Alex with the baby girls. He laughed and talked to them as if they understood every word. The picture much more resembled a proud papa adoring his children than a visiting neighbor. Sarah couldn't believe it when the sound of "Da da," came from Hannah's lips as the baby squealed and patted his checks.

The wide grin on Alex's face was priceless. "That's right, Hannah. You and your sister are my sweet girls. Just don't tell Mommy."

Alex smirked at Sarah and gave the baby a gentle toss. His laughter was contagious. She grudgingly admitted that things felt complete when Alex was around. The longer he intruded into their lives, the more difficult it would be to dislodge him.

When Alex wasn't with her and the children, he worked on getting his book to the publishers. She knew he made less progress than he would've liked, but when she suggested that he was neglecting his work, he told her the children were more important. Besides, he insisted, "Your family inspires me."

Alex's attention to the children gave her a chance to grocery shop and run quick errands. Though he probably never cleaned his own house, she often returned to a clean house and a load of laundry in the washer. No matter how much she objected, he'd minimize the gesture and brush off her concerns. At the hospital, Alex had expressed his love and compassion with affectionate hugs and mild kisses. But since coming home, he hadn't touched her. Not once had he treated her like anything other than a dear friend.

Sarah's feelings were a jumble of confusion as she vacillated between longing for something more and feeling comfortable with the hands-off treatment. Whatever might happen in the future, she'd decided against encouraging a relationship until after Tom's parents left town.

CHAPTER TWENTY-ONE

About a week after David's surgery, Sarah's in-laws arrived for a short visit. Although she encouraged them to stay in her mother's room at the cottage, they insisted on checking into a nearby hotel. They were concerned about increasing the workload for Sarah. She enjoyed Tom's parents and would have gladly made space for them.

Alex invited the Stuarts to use one of his guest rooms, but Sarah refused. "I want you to make yourself scarce when Mom and Dad Stuart are visiting. I don't want them to get the wrong idea about us."

"I'm not sure what it is you want to keep from them, but I won't come around unless summoned."

Unfortunately, she failed to fill her boys in on that slight detail. Not long into the visit, David wondered aloud why Mr. Alex hadn't come by. Sarah breathed a sigh of relief that he refrained from calling him daddy.

"Who's Alex?" Tom's parents inquired.

"Oh, he's a friend who lives down the beach." Sarah hurried to minimize Alex's role.

"You mean that enormous house on the beach?" Tom's mother loved architecture and never failed to notice the larger homes. She seemed especially impressed by the one dominating a rather large piece of oceanfront next door.

Sarah tried to act disinterested as she brushed it off and thought she had changed the subject. "Yes, that's the one. Why don't you show your grandparents the Lego models you've been constructing?"

As the boys rushed excitedly toward the models, she realized her mistake. Of course, the display included Alex's role in both the purchase and the workmanship. Which led to enthusiastic gestures as they described playing on the beach with their friend and his dog. When David mentioned the man staying the night with him at the hospital, Sarah wanted to put a muzzle on his sweet little mouth. Her failure to mention someone who'd spent so much time with their family, rendered her mute while the boys spewed an abundance of embarrassing information.

"Our daddy's in heaven, but Alex is our daddy down here."

"And he's going to take us to Disney World."

If possible, Sarah would've climbed under the carpet. Her face turned a million shades of red as she freed her tongue and tried to contain the damage.

"Mr. Caine has helped us through a few stressful situations since we moved here. In fact, he saved my life after the babies were born. Don't you remember my writing to you about their births and then my landing in the hospital?"

"Yes, but your description of him sounded more like an elderly gentleman, not a prospective daddy." Tom's father seemed amused at the disparity between the boys' excited description and Sarah's obvious discomfort.

Time to come clean. "To be honest, he would like for there to be more, but I'm not ready for another relationship. Your son meant the world to me, and I can't imagine replacing him. I do admit that if I were looking for a husband, Alex would be perfect. He loves us and is always available when we need him."

"What does this Alex do that he can drop everything to come to your rescue at a moment's notice?"

Colonel Stuart's concern prompted Sarah to defend Alex. Did he consider him a beach bum who took advantage of her family? "He's a writer, but I don't think he's published anything since meeting us. We've kept him busy with one crisis after another."

"What's his full name? Maybe we've read one of his books," Mrs. Stuart continued the questioning.

"Alex writes historical fiction. To protect his privacy, he publishes under the pen name of Stephen Jacobs. I'm certain you've heard of him."

"Are you kidding? He's one of our favorite writers. When might we meet him?" The woman was insistent and wouldn't let it go.

"If you want to meet him, he often drops by early mornings with his dog to play with the boys. I'll give him a call later."

The anticipation of a visit from the celebrity seemed to satisfy Tom's parents, and they moved on to their worry over David's health. After Sarah reassured them that he would be back to normal in no time, they brought up an equally uncomfortable subject.

"How're you doing with your finances, Sarah? I know the survivor's benefits aren't that great."

Under normal circumstances, she would've been relieved at the change of topic, but since she struggled in that area, she felt embarrassed to disclose her meager budget to her in-laws.

"The monthly annuity is not nearly as much as Tom's salary but moving here to the cottage reduced our expenses considerably. I appreciate your concern, but for now, we're fine. Thank you for asking."

"I'm glad it's working out. The boys seem to love it here, and I doubt they'll ever want to move. You will let me know in the future if you require assistance. Tom would want us to help you."

Sarah thanked them again for their concern. "I can't wait to meet your famous neighbor. Don't forget to call him." So much for wishing Mom Stuart would forget.

When Sarah reluctantly made the call, Alex sounded a bit too satisfied with himself when he agreed to come by the last morning of the Stuarts' visit. She felt uneasy, not knowing how he might react. She'd been embarrassed more than once by his brazen behavior.

When the final day of the Stuart's stay arrived, Alex came strolling up the beach. Instead of his usual self-confidence, he acted uncharacteristically shy and insecure when Sarah introduced him. As she relaxed in the presence of the new, reserved Alex, Mom and Dad Stuart assumed the role of grateful fans, complimenting his writing and discussing a favorite novel. Like a chameleon, the old Alex emerged along with his comfortable, self-confident attitude, causing Sarah to recoil and dread the outcome.

The boys were all over him with lots of stories to tell. They showed him the gifts their grandparents had brought, including more sand toys and play clothes. Alex, as always, responded with dramatic enthusiasm. He didn't overlook the babies as he cuddled them and told them how cute they looked in their new outfits. They relished his attention and then cried when he put them down. While he seemed quite at home with her family,

Sarah worried about her in-law's reactions and wished the lively man would take his intimidating personality and leave.

Alert to Sarah's discomfort, Alex stood to curtail his visit. He thanked the Stuarts for the invitation to meet him, then deeming this an appropriate time for honesty, he invited them to walk out with him. It took some convincing to keep the boys inside, but Alex promised to stop by the following morning.

When they were near the beach, Alex strengthened his resolve. "Mr., I mean Colonel and Mrs. Stuart, I appreciate your willingness to speak with me. Although this seems like an unusual request and slightly awkward, I'd like to ask your permission to marry your daughter-in-law. You see, I've fallen in love with your son's family, especially Sarah. She's perfect for me in so many ways. I promise to take care of her and the children and love them like I'm sure your son would have if he'd survived. Grandparents are important to children, and I want to assure you that Sarah and I will always include you in their lives."

Alex saw the colonel stiffen and grasp his wife's arm. He could only hope they had seen how much he cared for Sarah and her family.

Mr. Stuart spoke softly and slowly. "Well, Alex. As you can see, this has taken us by surprise. It's not that we disapprove, and we certainly noticed how much the children are taken with you. It's just a little sudden.

"Since Tom's death, we've been concerned for Sarah and the children. Sarah has rebuffed all our attempts to assist financially. I'm not sure how she manages on her own, but she's one independent, stubborn woman. You seem to have had better luck with her. Does Sarah return your love?"

"I believe she does, but she won't admit it. After the loss of her father and then your son, she seems afraid to let another man into her life. Also, she loved Tom and doesn't want anything to detract from his memory. I'll do my best to keep those memories alive where the children are concerned, but I want nothing to interfere with Sarah's love for me. I realize that Tom will always be the father of her children, and he'll have a special place in her heart, but I want to be her only love when we marry. I hope that doesn't seem selfish to you."

"Not at all. I think I understand how you feel. How long have you been waiting to be the father to my grandchildren, Mr. Caine?"

"Since the moment I first met her, sir. I knew then we were meant to be together, but when I delivered the baby girls, I fell completely under her spell."

Mrs. Stuart looked aghast. "You delivered the babies? Well, that's something Sarah failed to mention. She said they were born at home, but we assumed the midwife delivered them. I've never heard of such a thing."

Alex gave them the condensed version of Sarah's fall and the premature delivery. He explained how he'd stayed to make sure she recovered and then had her rushed to the hospital when she hemorrhaged. He told them about his mother and Anna coming to help, and that he'd returned to faith in God through all the trials and Sarah's rejection.

"You see, I've been staying away from Sarah the last couple of months until she invited me to the boys' birthday party. That's when we first noticed something wrong with David. I've been helping her since then. We need each other, and I'm not going to give up. I hope that won't be a problem for you. I'm fairly certain that Sarah won't move forward without your blessing."

"Thank you for sharing, Mr. Caine, and we wish you God's best. If it's his will for you to be Sarah's husband and the father to our grandchildren, Sarah will come around. Just continue to be patient with her. It's obvious the children love you. David seems to be especially devoted. Thank you for being with them when we cannot."

They bade Alex farewell, and he turned toward home, feeling satisfied with the conversation.

Sarah stood at the window and watched her in-laws as they listened intently to Alex. He looked too serious as he made his point with gestures. She was annoyed that he excluded her from the conversation. How did she allow them to go out alone? Enduring the visit when they were all in the cottage proved difficult enough without Alex asking for a private conference. She continued to stew until the Stuarts returned inside.

The colonel didn't waste any time in getting to the point. "That's one fine young man you have there, Sarah."

"Sir, he's not mine to have. I had a fine young man, and now he's gone. I still love Tom. Neither Alex nor anyone else will ever take his place."

“That’s true, Sarah, but there comes a time in our lives when we should put the past behind us and move on to the future. I’m not saying that Alex is the one, but I think you should seriously pray about it. God certainly brought him into your life for some reason, and the boys seem to think he would make the perfect daddy. Don’t write him off, Sarah. We’ll support you in whatever decision you make.”

Tom’s mother continued. “You know, Sarah, Alex asked our permission to marry you. Though highly unusual these days, it’s wonderfully romantic. Did you know he planned to do that?”

“You’re kidding me? I’ve never given him any reason to hope that we’d be together. How dare he? No matter how successful he is with his writing, he doesn’t seem to understand the word, ‘No.’ I don’t want to feel pressured into something when I’m not ready. I can’t believe the arrogance of that man.”

Sarah continued to fume over Alex’s audacity while her in-laws listened with knowing expressions. “Yes, honey, we understand how you feel and how hard it is to move on, but one day soon God will give you peace about Alex. Be open to what he has in store for you and the children. Always know that we love you no matter what happens.” They hugged Sarah, but continued to linger, as if hating to leave.

“Thank you. You’ve been the best, supportive parents to Tom and me. I miss him so much, and I know his death is hard for you, too. Thank you for coming and checking on us. Please keep in touch.”

When they’d said their final goodbyes, kissed the children many times and took about a dozen more pictures, the Stuarts got into their rental car for the trip back to Washington. The colonel would be assigned to the Pentagon the next few years, making it convenient to spend more time with the children. They were good people, and Sarah looked forward to frequent visits.

CHAPTER TWENTY-TWO

The next morning when Alex dropped by, Sarah opened the door for him but walked away without the first indication of welcome. "Well. Good morning to you, too."

She threw the dishcloth she'd been holding in the sink and turned around quickly with her hands on her hips. "Alex Caine, I can't believe you told my in-laws about all these grandiose plans you have for my life. How can I deal with all of this if you keep interfering? What possessed you to ask them for permission to marry me?" Her voice rose another octave with each accusation. "That's none of their business, and I've told you many times, I don't want to consider that now. I'm not ready. You make me so mad!"

Alex stepped back as if she'd slapped him. He returned the punch. "Whoa! You know, Sarah, I don't need or deserve this. I understand that you're upset and just recovering from the stress of David's trauma, but that's no reason to go berserk."

"Go berserk? Is that what you think is happening when I can't get you to leave me alone." Sarah stopped as soon as she realized what she said.

"Do you hear yourself? I hadn't been near you until you invited me to the birthday party. Then I came to your rescue during David's surgery. What is your problem? One minute you require my help, and the next, you want nothing to do with me."

"I'm sorry, Alex." All the anger disappeared from her voice. "I don't know what's wrong with me."

Alex studied her. "You know, I'm pretty confused myself right now. Perhaps I'm the one who needs time to reevaluate this obsession I have with you. Maybe I jumped the gun in talking to Tom's parents, but for some reason, I thought I'd earned the right to discuss our future with them. Forgive me, but I believe I've overstayed my welcome. Besides, I've neglected my book. It's almost finished, and I have to get it to the publisher before my agent disowns me. Tell the boys I'll see them out on the beach the first warm day." Anger rising, he couldn't resist a sarcastic barb. "Feel free to call next time you require my services. In the meantime, I'll *pretend* to be the good neighbor you claim to want."

Alex jerked the door open with more force than he intended while his heart pushed against his ribs. As he rushed from the cottage, he swiped at tears threatening to unmask his hurt. Sarah's stress didn't justify her irrational behavior. What happened to the patient, loving woman he admired and loved? Where had this angry version come from? Perhaps they weren't meant to be together after all.

When Alex reached the waterline, he looked out at the powerful display of crashing waves. The anger slowly gave way to guilt as he breathed deeply of the salty mist. Before today, he felt certain the main reason for Sarah's hesitation concerned the reaction of her husband's parents. Instead of waiting, he took measures into his own hands. Maybe the time had come to take a step back and trust God. A guy's pride could only take so much, and he'd about reached his limit with Sarah Stuart. That resolve sounded familiar to his declaration back in November when she'd given him the boot. Regardless, he planned to stick with it this time.

Before Alex reached home, he had resolved to finish his book and refocus on his career. He had mounted the steps to the deck when he remembered his promise to take the boys to Disney World. How would he ever keep his promise without speaking to their mother? How had he gotten himself into this impossible situation?

His cell phone rang as he entered the house. He would've ignored the call, but the ID indicated his mother. One of his parents might be sick, or perhaps something happened to Jana. On the fourth ring, he accepted with his usual greeting.

"Hello, Mother!"

"Alex, in the middle of my quiet time this morning, I felt compelled to pray for you. Is everything okay?"

"No, Mother, nothing will ever be right again. This week has been the longest of my life with so many ups and downs I don't know what's what."

"What happened?"

Alex told his mother about his hellish week, beginning with the birthday party and ending with his explosive conversation with Sarah. "Would you like to know what she named the babies? Elizabeth Anne and Hannah Grace. What does that sound like to you, Mother?"

"Oh, Alex. I'm so pleased. If she didn't care for you, she'd never have named one of the babies after me. She wanted to please you. Can't you see that?"

"Of course, I see it, and that presents the problem. One minute, Sarah declares how much she cares and appreciates me, and the next she pushes me away. I've decided I'm not going to put myself in that position ever again. That sharp tongue of hers cuts me where it hurts the most—in my fragile heart."

"You've said all of this before, Alex. The two of you bicker like a couple of old married folks. I don't think this is the final page of this story. You love her and the children too much. You must continue to be patient and pray. Is David healing well?"

"Yes, he seems fine. It's a challenge for him to slow down while trying to keep up with Jonathan, and that one has an unbelievable energy level.

"Which brings me to another dilemma. While in the hospital, I promised David and his brother a surprise when he fully recovered. They want me to take them to Disney World, and I've given them every indication that we'd go. How on earth can I plan a trip like that when I'm not even speaking to their mother?"

"I recommend you plan the trip when it's convenient for you and believe that God will restore the relationship. My experience over the years proves that a little time is all that's required to resolve most disagreements." Alex silently thanked God for his mother's words of encouragement.

"I don't know how to handle it, but I can't disappoint those boys. Please pray for me, Mother. I've had more difficulties since I became a Christian than I ever had as an unbeliever. I hope that isn't what's in store from here to eternity."

"I think you should read the book of James and pray for patience. James says that suffering brings patience, which builds character and maturity. God disciplines those he loves, Alex."

When he hung up, he thought about how often his mother returned his focus to God. He read the verses, as she suggested, and prayed for patience before opening the computer. No more whining, self-pity, or interruptions. As he immersed himself in the story, concerns over Sarah soon took a back seat to the creative scenes flashing through his mind.

Alex focused on the book and submitted the manuscript to his agent a few weeks later. "I'll have to say I was beginning to worry about you, Stephen, until I read the script. I think this might be your best yet."

"So, does this mean I'm out of the doghouse?"

Lori laughed. He'd worked with Lori Sharp for years and was confident in her ability to bring a book to publication.

With the manuscript delivered, now would've been a convenient time to go to Disney World. Lori, however, planned to keep him busy doing interviews and book signings for his teen boy series. He would oblige her without complaint. His island home that had been his refuge had become a place of emotional turmoil. The farther he removed himself from Sarah, the better. Eradicating her from his mind, however, would be impossible.

Before leaving town, Alex went by the cottage to say goodbye to the boys. He planned to act as though nothing had happened between him and Sarah. Opting for the additional exercise, he strolled up the beach and knocked on the back door. Sarah opened the door. "Alex?"

He heard the surprise in her voice.

"Uh ... It's good to see you. C-come in."

The boys rushed from the living room and tackled him from behind, throwing him into Sarah. He caught her before she fell backward. While Sarah composed herself, he greeted the boys.

"Hey, guys, slow down. You could've hurt your mother."

"Sorry. But you caught her."

"That's true. But I might not always be around. Just be careful.

"Other than being full of mischief, how are you? Are you feeling better, David?"

"I'm better. But we haven't been able to play out on the beach in the mornings. It's still too cold." David had good coloring and looked his normal healthy self.

"Yes, that's a bummer, but the afternoons are nice. Maybe you could play outside after your nap."

Jonathan looked at him accusingly, "It's no fun without you and Bailey. You didn't come back to play with us. We miss you."

"I know. I miss you, too. But you'll have to get along without me for a while. I'm sorry I didn't come over before, but I've been busy writing another book. Now, I'll be gone for a few weeks, and I wanted to see you before I leave."

Alex hugged the boys and stroked their backs while they wiped their tear-smeared faces against his shirt. "Do you have to go?"

"Yes, I'm afraid I must. But I'll come back as soon as I'm able." While trying to reassure them, he forced himself to ignore their mother who stood to the side listening. He was so angry with her—and himself—that keeping his distance shouldn't be difficult. But when he'd caught her—he had to catch himself, too. Being too close was a temptation he was finding more and more difficult to resist. This trip out of town couldn't come too soon.

"While I'm gone, perhaps your mother could plan a play date with some of your church friends. Wouldn't you enjoy that?"

"I guess, but we have more fun with you. What about our trip to see Mickey Mouse?"

"Well, I'm working on that. When I have some details, I'll talk to your mother and decide when would be the best time. You can count on seeing Mickey and Donald soon, but right now I must go away. When I return, the weather should be warm enough for me to play on the beach with my two best buddies."

He had all he could do to hold back tears as he hugged the boys. When would he see them again? As he lowered the boys, he saw two little girls crawling toward him. He picked them up, whispered baby talk in their ears and stroked their curls. They snuggled against him, kicking and cooing back at him.

Alex tossed the babies in the air a few times and planted gentle kisses on their foreheads when he caught them. Reluctantly, he put them down and started for the back door. His emotions felt as raw as if he were losing something precious. When he noticed Sarah, looking so lost and forlorn, he turned toward her uncertain of a response. Resisting the urge to hold her, he took her hand and kissed it. "Goodbye, Sarah."

"You're leaving because of me, aren't you?" Sarah whispered.

"Not entirely, but I must get away for a while." Alex looked around the cottage and rubbed the ache in his chest. The need to belong left him weak-kneed and helpless. Not a feeling he wanted to entertain for long.

"Besides, I have obligations with my publisher. We'll talk when I return." He again looked at the children. "Take care of my children for me, will you?" Alex turned away to hide his emotions as he walked out the door.

Sarah ran out on the porch to watch Alex disappear behind the dunes. No "I love you, Sarah." No "I'll miss you, Sarah." Merely, "Goodbye" and of course that part about her taking care of *his* children. She didn't mind after watching the way he treated them with such warmth and love.

In contrast, the man treated her as if she were an outcast. Wearing his feelings on his shoulders, he'd avoided her since that awful morning when she'd lost it. She was surprised that he bothered to come over at all. Now, he planned to leave for who knows how long, and Sarah couldn't blame him.

The fear of rejection rendered Sarah powerless against the formidable force of Alex Caine. Although he promised to talk upon his return, she wondered how they would ever restore their relationship enough to take the boys to Orlando. She wouldn't allow them to go without her, but unless the situation changed, it would be an awkward week.

Reconciling with Alex was difficult when he managed to turn any positive gesture into permission to call a wedding planner. What to do with the exasperating man? One thing for sure, she wouldn't have to worry about him for the next few weeks. Her relief lasted but a moment before rejection and hurt came rushing back with a vengeance. How would she survive without knowing that he waited for her down the beach?

CHAPTER TWENTY-THREE

While packing for his trip to New York, Alex received an excited call from Lori. She'd heard from a producer who wanted to make Alex's last novel into a movie. Despite Lori's enthusiasm for the proposal, Alex had mixed emotions about the prospect. Writing a screenplay would be much different than writing a book. And he refused to trust others with the contents of his work.

"I'll have to pray about it and get back to you, Lori."

"What? Are you crazy? This is what you've always wanted. I can't believe you're not jumping at this."

"I know. But I've changed over the past few months. Since I've become a Christian, I see things differently—as God sees them. Most of what comes out of Hollywood leaves me concerned about the message it conveys. I have to approach your proposal with caution."

The conversation ended with Lori baffled and Alex feeling the need for spiritual guidance. He scheduled an appointment with Pastor Mark and his wife before leaving town. The men would catch up over breakfast and then meet Deborah later at the church office.

After a quick search of the restaurant, he found Mark in a back, corner booth. He noticed a deep sadness on his friend's face. The two men had grown close over the last few months, meeting weekly as their schedules allowed. In that time, he'd never seen his friend look anything but upbeat and positive. Pastor Mark usually coaxed Alex out of his doldrums. This time, his pastor seemed to be the one with a problem.

Laying aside his own concerns, Alex greeted Mark with a quick hug and went through the motions of scanning the menu. He gave the waitress his usual order—the oversized, cholesterol-filled breakfast. Indulging in the delicious, greasy food was a guilty pleasure he enjoyed with the promise of a few extra miles on the treadmill.

"Okay, my friend, what has you so preoccupied this morning?"

"Alex, I know we usually talk about you and your problems, but today my heart aches for my son, Jonah. Deborah and I were so proud of him when he earned a full scholarship to the university. He'd made friends and seemed happy and content. Majoring in business and finance, he made the dean's list almost every semester. Out of the blue, he called last night and told us he's dropping out of college. He's nearly finished his third year, and now he's applying to the police academy. We can't understand what could've caused him to move from the steady, outgoing young man, to this confused, sad individual who hasn't a clue regarding his future.

"Trusting God with your children isn't easy, my friend. One of my twin boys is also going through a challenging time. Sometimes, I wonder if their mother and I are responsible for the way our boys withdraw when faced with major problems. They refuse our advice and support during the stormiest times. Chad left his church a couple months ago and completely disappeared. Even his twin brother doesn't know his whereabouts.

"And now, this with Jonah. To make such a decision without seeking our advice has me floundering. It's not like him at all. I'm at a loss as to how to handle the situation. Please pray for me, Alex."

Alex didn't quite know what to say. In the past, Pastor Mark reported nothing but impressive, glowing reports of his boys and their pursuits. Raised by godly parents, yet two of the three sons had issues. Mark's worried look pointed to a significant crisis for an otherwise stable family.

"I can't give you advice on fatherhood, Mark, but I do know that your boys are grown men with the ability to make decisions, whether good or bad. Knowing you and Deborah, I'm certain you've given them the right tools and training. Perhaps you should step back and let God deal with them as my parents did for me. A lot of prayers were uttered in those years while I struggled on my own. I might not have the answers, but we know someone who does."

At the close of their meal, the two friends prayed for each other, with much emphasis on Mark, Deborah, and their boys. Alex's concerns appeared shallow compared with the burden his friend carried. But at Mark's insistence, Alex mentioned the possibility of the movie deal and his desire for wisdom and discernment. Prayers were offered for his trip, including boldness to share his faith. The friends left the restaurant with lighter hearts.

As if they were not well-caffeinated, Deborah had a hot pot of coffee waiting for them at the church. She greeted Alex, then gave her husband a worried look, kissed him and lingered in his arms. Their unapologetic display of affection and their obvious concern for one another reminded Alex of Sarah. Words didn't seem necessary to convey their hearts. How he longed for that kind of relationship.

Not wishing to take an inordinate amount of time from their schedules, Alex got right to the point. "Thank you for agreeing to see me. Let me say at the outset how much I appreciate your work here. Your commitment and dedication to the parishioners impressed me from the get-go. Knowing your heart for mission, I have a suggestion that should benefit both the church, the community, and especially Sarah.

"Please don't think me unselfish when I came up with this idea. Sarah and her problems were foremost in my mind. She struggles both financially and physically. You may not see it, but I do, and she won't accept help from either her husband's parents or me. Sarah lives on such a tight budget that she can't afford preschool for the boys or even a babysitter to give herself a break. Lest she take unfair advantage of her friends, she hesitates to call. With her mother in the Raleigh area, that's not a regular option either.

"As I prayed about her situation, I felt God gave me a solution that would benefit Sarah and other young mothers in the church and community. I've observed only a few members attending with young families, but on the island, there are several unchurched families, along with those who travel to the mainland for worship. What I'm proposing is something on the order of a Mother's Day Out Program, two days a week. For us to help mothers like Sarah, we should provide both daycare and preschool.

"I know you'll tell me you don't have the resources. That's why I plan to fund the program in its entirety. We'd hire qualified teachers willing to work part time. After you hire a certified staff, we could solicit volunteers to assist and fill in the gaps. Perhaps our seniors might enjoy rocking the little ones or reading books to the toddlers. I'd even be willing to volunteer when I'm in town.

"I wish we had more time to discuss this further, but I have a plane to catch. Here are my notes and thoughts on the program. Let me know what you think when I return in a few weeks. To be realistic, I don't expect anything to happen before the beginning of the fall school term. I realize you'll need the approval of the church council and time to seek God's direction before making a final decision. Oh, one last thing. Please keep my involvement confidential. Sarah would refuse to participate if she thought I had anything to do with it. And that, my friends, would defeat the whole purpose."

Alex knew he bombarded Mark and Deborah with his spontaneous presentation, but he felt crunched for time.

"We don't know what to say, Alex, except this is something that God has also brought to our attention. Deborah noticed Sarah and others struggling to care for their children without any time for themselves. You're an answer to our prayers. Not only does this confirm God's plan for a new direction for the church, but you've provided the funds to make it happen. No church council would refuse such a proposition."

They prayed for the new venture before Alex rushed home to finish packing. He was scheduled to fly out of Raleigh in a few hours. He needed to hit the road. All the way to the airport, he thought about Sarah and her family. More than anything, he wanted to make life easier for the woman he loved. If only she'd love him with the same devotion.

Lori met him at the airport. Her first words sent him reeling. "Alex, I certainly hope you've thought seriously about this movie deal. You have a meeting with the producer on Thursday morning."

Except for the prayer with Mark, he hadn't had time to pray seriously about the offer. Regardless of his indecision, he agreed to the meeting with the stipulation that his lawyer, Jameson Reed, be included.

A few days later, Alex's driver maneuvered his way through Manhattan traffic toward the Bergman Building near Times Square. Lori and Jameson met him at the entrance. Together, they made their way to a suite of offices on the eighteenth floor. Engraved wood paneling, nautical prints, and oil seascapes lined the wide hallways. They checked in with the receptionists and were ushered into a massive conference room with similar ambiance.

Under normal circumstances, Alex wouldn't notice wall décor, but the seascapes captured his attention and made him homesick. The hustle and bustle of New York City contrasted greatly to the peace he usually found on Shell Island. Alex's anxiety over the meeting melted away as he focused on the serene prints.

The producer, Harry Vogel, seemed to overpower the room as he stood to introduce his staff. Alex cleared his throat and restlessly shifted from one weak leg to the other. The group standing before him represented some of the most talented men and women in the business—at least two lawyers, screenplay writers, and several directors with various levels of expertise. Alex felt outnumbered as he introduced his agent and attorney and breathed a silent prayer for wisdom and discernment.

Not far into the meeting, Alex realized the direction the production company intended to take. Vogel and his team wanted final control of the content with contracts giving them carte blanche. In return, they offered him more money than he would need in a lifetime. Alex studied the faces around the room before standing. He spread his hands on the massive table and leaned forward to speak—his voice steady and clear.

"I see you have put a lot of work toward securing the rights to my book and even proceeded to write the screenplay. A year ago, I might have jumped at this generous offer, but within the last few months, I've changed." Alex took a few calming breaths and prayed for boldness. "I'm no longer a self-serving, egotistical person with little regard to the influence of my writing. I have a responsibility to the message my books and perhaps movies might convey." Alex stopped and looked out the window. He thought of Sarah and the boys before continuing. "There's a great need for literature and films that families can enjoy without the embarrassment of immoral acts, filthy language, deceitful actions, and excessive violence."

The chair squeaked as the producer shifted uncomfortably. "Are you not happy with the offer, Mr. Jacobs?"

"No, the financial agreement is more than satisfactory. But, based on my recent return to the Christian faith, I desire to obey God in everything I do. I cannot, in good conscience, release control of the contents of a film based on my writing. I refuse to cede the screenwriting to others, and I insist on being involved in the editing before signing off on the final film version. If this isn't possible, then my latest book will not be available for marketing by the film industry."

The tense audience sat with their jaws ajar. "Since we're a long way from an agreement, I see no reason to prolong this meeting. If you feel we can work together under my terms, I'll gladly await a final contract or additional dialogue to further clarify my position."

The sound of shuffling broke the silence as Alex began gathering his papers. Lori grabbed his arm and whispered into his ear. "Do you realize what you're doing, Stephen? They've offered us a contract worth thousands, and you're throwing it out the window to make some kind of religious statement? I can't believe you'd do this to us."

"I can't allow money to dictate my actions, Lori. It may be unpopular, but I know I've done the right thing."

A warm peace filled him as he thought of the apostle Peter who declared in Acts, "We must obey God rather than men." Alex was thankful for the courage to stand for truth no matter the consequences.

The producer cleared his throat when he realized his potential client had concluded the meeting. "Mr. Jacobs. I'm not sure I understand your reluctance in accepting our generous offer, but I do admire your concern for the film's content. What you are suggesting, however, will take time on our part to research the feasibility in today's market."

"Take all the time you need. You may not understand my position, but I look forward to working with you in the future."

Alex hurried out of the room followed by Lori and Jameson. The elevator doors had barely closed before Lori unleashed her displeasure. "Are you out of your mind, Stephen Jacobs? I worked hard to get this contract, and you're blowing it off." She expressed her outrage all the way down and continued as she followed him outside, and he hailed a cab.

"Lori, it's okay. I know this is the right thing to do. It'll be a great movie, one we will both be proud of and one we can show our children one day. We'll discuss it later. Right now, I must dash to meet my sister."

Alex had set aside time to spend with Jana and Paul, if possible. He couldn't believe how his relationship with his sister had changed in the past few months. Jana came early for her weekend visit with her fiancé to have more time with her brother. Today, they were meeting at one of her favorite restaurants near Broadway.

When he departed the cab in front of the restaurant, his distracted sister failed to see him. He admired her as she scrolled through her iPhone. Jana wore a striking turquoise pantsuit with lines tailored to fit her slim figure. A healthy glow about her cheeks seemed to brighten her countenance.

"Hello, Jana. You look like a woman in love." Alex stood nearby with his arms crossed, shaking his head "Would that smile be for me or is it an afterglow from seeing that fiancé of yours?" He leaned close and raised an eyebrow. "Perhaps you're anticipating a June wedding? How are the plans, by the way?"

Jana laughed and flew into his open arms. "Alex, you're such a tease. I've never been happier, and you know it. I thought I'd miss going to work every day, but I've been too busy planning the wedding and spending time with Paul on the weekends to miss anything. It seems a lifetime ago when I helped manage a major company."

"Well, I'm happy for you, dear sister; perhaps a little jealous, but I wish you the best."

"Don't be jealous. I know God will bring you and Sarah together soon. I want you to be as happy as I am. By the way, how are Sarah and the children?"

"They were fine when I left the island a few days ago, but unfortunately, we didn't leave on good terms. I still miss them, but I refuse to let it keep me from the new peace I've found since surrendering to the Lord."

"I know what you mean, Alex. Paul's love for God has encouraged me to draw closer as well. We spend time studying the Bible and praying together. I'm so grateful to have found such a man." Jana stopped and studied him for a moment. "I won't ask you what you and Sarah disagreed on this time, but knowing you, you probably did something stupid like prematurely asking her to marry you."

Alex winced. "Not quite, but close. I don't want to talk about it."

Jana laughed, and the brother and sister continued to discuss their lives, including their hopes and dreams for the future. Alex recounted his meeting with the film producer.

"Wow. What an opportunity, Alex."

"I turned it down. It didn't feel right. Not now. Not with the way I've changed and what I'm trying to do with my life."

Jana put a hand on his arm. "That sounds like the right decision then."

"Thanks, Jana. I'm glad someone agrees with me.

When they left the restaurant arm in arm, a photographer snapped their picture and demanded the name of the blonde. Alex ignored them, helped his sister into a cab, and hurried to procure one for himself.

CHAPTER TWENTY-FOUR

A few weeks after Alex's departure, a morning news show provided background noise as Sarah finished washing the breakfast dishes. When a familiar name caught her attention, she turned off the water and hurried to turn up the sound. Her interest in everything Alex soon had her engrossed in the interview.

"We have with us this morning Stephen Jacobs, best-selling author of numerous historical novels. He's also considered to be one of the most eligible bachelors in America. Pay attention ladies—he's still available. After spending the last several years writing historical fiction, he has now written something totally out of character, and he's about to give us a preview. Let's welcome Stephen Jacobs.

"Good to see you again, Stephen. I must say, I was surprised when they gave me your latest release to review in preparation for this interview."

Sarah stared at the screen as she watched her recent nanny respond to the interviewer's question with confidence and class. Her Alex had never looked more handsome. She looked down at her stained sweatshirt and the faded leggings and tears of resignation filled her eyes.

"Can you share with us how this came about?" The TV personality seemed genuinely interested along with Sarah. Alex had told her his last book was different, but he never went into detail, or perhaps she was so wrapped up in her problems she didn't give him a chance. Shame on her for being so self-centered.

"It's a long story, but the gist of it is that I've had a renewal of my Christian faith in the past few months. When I considered when and how I'd walked away from God and the church, I realized my disillusionment started at about age fourteen. All these years, I felt comfortable with my agnostic viewpoint, living for myself without realizing that God waited patiently for my attention.

"I recently met two fascinating little boys. Their simple faith challenged me to reconsider all prior positions and led to a complete transformation. To my surprise, we became friends. They're four years old, but when they become teenagers, I'd like to see them avoid the mistakes I made in my adolescent years. Although they love God now, I'm praying they grow stronger in their faith, not lose it."

"Are they relatives of yours?" asked the attractive host.

"No, just a pair of cute twin boys I met while walking on the beach one day. At first, I thought they would provide some interesting material for my next novel, but they certainly surprised me with their convincing influence.

"As a result of this encounter, I decided to write a series of adventure books that would appeal to young teens and keep them focused as they enter those difficult, confusing, years. The first book in the series, *The Warriors*, is filled with adventure, battles, and challenges as the protagonists fight through adverse circumstances to retain their character, integrity, and faith."

"Do these little boys who mean so much to you have a special mother?"

"Somehow, I knew you'd ask that question," Alex laughed as he replied. "Yes, she's a special lady. Although I'd like for her to be more, she won't have me." He laughed again. "It's really not funny, but I don't think your viewers would appreciate seeing a grown man cry."

"It's hard for me to believe that any young woman in her right mind would not find you desirable and jump at the opportunity for a relationship. I'm rather surprised we haven't heard from the paparazzi regarding this woman."

"And you won't hear from them if I have my way. I appreciate my privacy, and I want that for her and her children as well."

"Well, a lot of your single fans will be disappointed if she finally says yes. When word gets out that there's someone special, you might have a media fight on your hands."

"You know, the interesting thing about this is that I've never actually pursued a meaningful relationship before now, but this one woman captures my heart like no other, and I hope to one day be the husband she deserves."

"Well, good luck with your love life and thanks for revealing so much for the first time here on our show. I guess we'll have to wait to find out about this lucky young mother who captured the heart of our popular guest. We wish you the best with this new series, Stephen. I found the book a real page-turner, and I'm sure your young readers won't be able to put it down. They'll be pounding on your door for the next installment. Does this mean you plan to discontinue writing adult novels?"

"Of course not. My next historical fiction is at the publishers as we speak. There's more to come for all ages."

"Will you return to the show when your new book is released?"

"I'd love to, Helen. Thank you for having me."

Sarah felt drained of strength as she sat down at the kitchen table. She used the dishrag to wipe away the tears trickling down her face. Who was this man who stole her heart, her family, and her life? Alex was a prince among men, and yet he felt unworthy of her. Who was he kidding? She didn't deserve him—the most patient man on the planet.

Alex longed to return to the island, even with its turmoil and unfinished business. Lori, however, had him booked solid with interviews and book signings.

One thing he liked about Lori—she wasted no time when a new book hit the market. She claimed the first few weeks were crucial to the success of a book, so he followed her from one event to the next. Though she was accomplished in many ways, Alex quickly tired of her company.

Lori continued to bring up the movie opportunity despite his instructions to place the deal on the back burner until he received positive word from the producer. His lawyer would review any new proposal before passing it on to him. When his calendar finally cleared, Alex made plans to leave the busy city. He couldn't wait to see Sarah and the children and feel the peace and serenity of his island home.

Upon Alex's return to Shell Island, he spent the first few days planning the trip to Orlando. Since Jana's big church wedding was scheduled for June, the month of May seemed like the best time for a touch of magic.

Before he left for his tour, David and Jonathan had already expressed their impatience. He should've waited until the last possible moment to promise such a surprise. Next time he'd know better.

Since Sarah and he remained at odds, he didn't quite know how to present his plan. He prayed about it, and when he worked out some details, he called about the time the children were napping. He was so happy to hear her sweet voice that he couldn't respond immediately. After the third "Hello," he managed to clear the longing out of his voice and answer.

"Hello, Sarah."

He would have preferred a warmer greeting such as, "I've missed you, Sarah," but he figured she wouldn't entertain such intimacy. Instead, he got right to the point.

"I've been working on the Disney trip for the boys, and I'd like to come over and discuss the details while the children are resting. Would that be all right?"

"Alex, I'm not sure that's a good idea."

"My coming over or the trip to Orlando? Sarah, I can't disappoint the boys no matter how uncomfortable the week might be for us. We must act like adults and make it a fun adventure for our boys."

Alex knew Sarah didn't miss the "our boys" remark, but fortunately for him, she chose to ignore it. "It seems to matter little if I agree or not. I'd be the mean old mommy if I didn't go along with your wonderful plans. You continue to put me in these uncomfortable positions, and I don't like it a bit."

"Sarah Stuart, I haven't seen you in several weeks. As you recall, the last we spoke we were still recovering from David's appendectomy. It's obvious that everyone is well and happy since I've not heard from you in a while." The snide remark was uncalled for, but he couldn't seem to react without remembering the hurt Sarah inflicted with her latest rejection.

"Perhaps I deserved that, but I'd rather not debate with you, Alex. You're right. We must get along for the sake of the children. They've missed you. When you come over, you should stay until the boys are up. Otherwise, they'll be disappointed—again. You walk into our lives, take charge and make everything better, then you disappear to who knows where for what seems like forever, and suddenly, you remember us, and here you are again."

"Sarah, you have the shortest memory ever. You are the one who keeps giving me the boot despite my winning personality." Alex had to tease her to prevent their conversation from turning into a full-blown, he said-she said argument.

"Well, it doesn't matter whose fault it is, you still need to spend time with the children. Somehow, you've managed to make yourself indispensable. They look up to you and love you no matter what."

"Yeah, yeah. I know–wonderful me. I wish their mother felt the same."

Before Sarah could respond in kind, Alex changed the subject.

"It's a wonderful day, Sarah, so I'd love to play on the beach with the boys. I'll bring Bailey, too, if that's okay with you."

"That's fine. You might as well come on down so we can get this over with as soon as possible."

"You sound like we're discussing a divorce or an inquisition of some sort. We're planning a trip to the 'happiest place on earth.' How about acting a little excited when I get there? If not for my sake, do it for the children. See you in a few."

Alex left Bailey on the back porch and knocked lightly on the kitchen door. The cottage had become as familiar to him as his own home and housed the family he loved most in the world.

"Come in, Alex. Would you like some coffee and cookies?"

"Thank you, Sarah. That would be nice. I haven't had any of your delicious cookies in quite a while."

With his finger, Alex captured every cookie crumb from his plate and sipped his coffee. He studied Sarah, who traced the edge of her cup with great interest. The polite silence was killing him. At the clearing of his throat, she looked up suspiciously.

"First, please forgive me for that last dig I got in over the phone. I don't know what possesses me sometimes. You seem to turn me into a vindictive monster. I don't wish to discuss what I said but to say I'm sorry, and I want us to be friends."

"I forgive you, but just let me say, you have a way of blaming me for everything, even your vindictive attitude. Do you ever listen to yourself?"

Alex hung his head. One minute he wanted to shake her and the next he wanted to grab her and kiss her until she couldn't breathe. She made him crazy. How would they ever survive a week in Orlando?

"You're right. No excuses, please forgive me. Perhaps before we begin, we should pray for peace."

Whether from the warmth of her hands or the nearness of her presence, Alex loved praying with Sarah. Unlike their earlier disagreement, they meshed into complete unity. His skin tingled, and heat rushed through his body as he concluded the prayer. He'd hoped to hold her hands longer, but she pulled them away so fast it felt as if she had poured a bucket of ice water down his back. He pressed his lips together, sighed heavily, and opened his notebook with the initial outline of the trip.

"Thank you, Alex, for reminding us to put God's will ahead of our own."

Alex looked up in surprise at her kind remark but chose to move on to the main reason for his visit. "I'm trying to decide if it would be better to rent a large van here and drive or to fly and rent the van with car seats at the Orlando airport. What do you think?"

"I know it's a lot of trouble driving to Raleigh to catch the plane, but it's a pretty long trip to Orlando. Flying might be easier on the children. The decision's up to you, but I'm concerned about the babies. They won't be able to endure long days at the parks. Also, what are your plans for sleeping arrangements?"

"How did I know you'd be concerned about that little detail?" Alex grinned while Sarah looked as if she'd deck him. He understood her concerns. An unmarried Christian couple didn't travel hundreds of miles together and spend a week in a hotel with four young children as chaperones.

"What would you think about inviting Anna and her grandson to come along? Mike's about twelve years old and would love a trip to Disney World.

"Anna can stay with the babies in the morning while you and I take the boys to the park. After lunch, we'll return and let Anna spend the rest of the day with Mike. After the children's naps, we'll return to the park and remain until after dinner. At least one night, we should stay out long enough to see the fireworks. I know it would be a late night, but perhaps we might sleep later the next morning."

"You've been away from us too long, or you'd remember that the boys never sleep late. They're usually stirring by six, regardless of what time they go to bed. Don't you remember?"

Alex laughed. “Wishful thinking, I suppose, or perhaps the hope that they’d grown out of that nasty habit.”

“I do like the idea of inviting Anna and her grandson. The boys would enjoy Mike. He could tag along with us in the morning and have a full day at the parks. But you haven’t answered my question about the sleeping arrangements.”

“They have beautiful hotels and resorts on the Disney property with three and four-bedroom suites. I thought I might take a bedroom with the boys while you share with the girls. Anna and Mike would share a room. You could even invite your mother if you wish. Does that meet your moral standards, Mrs. Stuart?”

Sarah hit him with her dishcloth before responding, but he saw the relief at his suggestions. “I guess so, but I still worry about our spending that much time together. It doesn’t seem right to me.”

Alex cocked his head to one side and raised an eyebrow. “What’s the matter, Sarah, do you think you’ll be unable to resist my lovable personality? Or, perhaps you’re afraid you might allow me into your heart?”

“I’m not discussing this with you again, Alex. You know how I feel. I’m praying, and I hope you are too. I’ll let you know if anything changes, but don’t keep bringing it up. And don’t spoil our trip by making it into something it’s not. Do you understand me?”

“I understand that you are one stubborn woman who scolds me as if I’m one of your children. Well, I’m not a child, but an impatient, grown man who loves you and will reluctantly wait forever if that’s what it takes. End of discussion.” Alex swiped his thumb and forefinger along his mouth indicating zipped lips. Sarah managed a weak smile.

Sarah sighed, “This is going to be a long week in Orlando. Do you think we’ll survive?”

“It’s going to be a wonderful week that our family will talk about forever.”

Alex continued without giving Sarah a chance to disagree. “The last question is, do you think we might go in about two weeks? I must leave again in about a month, and I can’t keep putting this off. It would’ve been a “nice” family honeymoon, but the boys might be teenagers before their mother says yes. I don’t think they’d appreciate the delay.” Alex smiled at his teasing remarks while Sarah rolled her eyes.

"My sister's getting married in June, and when I leave here for the wedding, I won't return for some time. My latest book is at the publishers. When it hits the market, I'm scheduled for a promotion tour."

"I didn't know Jana had wedding plans. When did all this happen?"

"At Thanksgiving, when I was in the doghouse with you. I guess I failed to mention it the few times we were speaking. The condensed version is that Jana came a day earlier than expected. Her boss had fired her, leaving her confused and angry. She'd worked closely with him for the past two years and had heard nothing but praise for her work. When he showed up moments before dessert with great remorse and a marriage proposal, we were all a bit surprised. The longer Paul worked with Jana, the more frustrated he became as he attempted to come to terms with his attraction to her. Not knowing how she felt, he feared repercussions if he acted unprofessionally. His dilemma was either to fire her or to marry her. He chose to fire her, but soon realized his mistake and drove about twelve hours to amend his decision. Over dessert, we planned a June wedding. See what you missed by ditching me."

"I can see that we have a lot of catching up to do. Maybe we can talk in Orlando. We missed Thanksgiving and Christmas together. I'm so sorry, Alex."

"Speaking of Christmas, you made me so angry when you sent that thank you note regarding my gifts. How could you say that you have nothing to give me when all I want is you? Of course, if you'd sent me a sweater, I wouldn't have taken it off." Alex smiled at her to soften his scold.

"Why do you take everything the wrong way? I attempted to thank you and apologize for my lack of a gift, and you turn it into a debate which reminds me of something a friend said recently to her husband, 'If I agreed with you, we would both be wrong.'"

Alex laughed. "I'm sorry I turned your note into an argument. I really like your little husband-wife joke. Despite having to concede all future arguments, I hope to spend many holidays with you and the children. I'll gladly let you win the disagreements."

"Alex, what happened to that zipped lip?"

"Oh, sorry!" Alex attempted remorse, but the joy of being with Sara had brightened his day.

CHAPTER TWENTY-FIVE

Alex took Sarah's advice, and they flew to Orlando. They arrived at the airport with time to spare. Anna and Mike drove in a separate car to provide space for the overflow of luggage, which Alex had failed to consider.

Although Sarah's mother turned down the invitation, Anna and Mike were thrilled with the offer. Anna had brought her grandson over to the cottage to introduce him and put the boys at ease. They loved the idea of an older friend willing to play on their level, "like Daddy." A few days after David came home from the hospital, Jonathan also picked up on the new title. Alex loved it while Sarah cringed uncomfortably each time she heard the endearing name.

Their first-class seating arrangements became a problem when the boys disagreed over who would sit with Alex for their first airplane ride. They reluctantly conceded to sit together in front of him. As soon as the plane reached cruising height, Jonathan and David escaped their seatbelts and crowded into the window seat to watch the miniature landscape below. They soon grew bored with the monotonous scene, snuggled in one seat, and fell asleep. Mike and Anna dozed across the aisle.

Alex entertained Hannah while Sarah nursed her sister. Hannah woke hungry, but his playful baby talk, butterfly kisses, and tickly bounce kept her occupied while she waited her turn. Soon after the girls were back in their car seats, Alex heard the announcement to prepare for landing.

"Why did you let us fall asleep? We wanted to see the clouds."

Alex chuckled as Jonathan returned to his seat. "You missed little, buddy. Just clouds and more clouds. You and your brother needed the rest to prepare for a week of fun and adventure." The quick reminder soon had them back to the excitement of their destination.

While they'd discussed security concerns earlier, Sarah remained apprehensive. "Aren't you a little concerned about entering a crowded place like Disney World? What will you do if someone recognizes you?"

"I'm praying that won't happen while you and the children are with me, but eventually someone is bound to connect Stephen Jacobs to Alex Caine. I suppose I should be prepared.

"It wouldn't be fair to the boys, however, to keep them hidden away on the island to protect my privacy. One day, I may have to hire guards, but I'd do anything to ensure their safety and happiness. Please don't worry, Sarah. With my baseball cap and dark shades, I should be able to mix well with the other tourists. If that doesn't work, my five young traveling companions should throw them off."

"You seem to be assuming a lot regarding our future, Alex Caine. I thought we agreed to discontinue such talk."

"I can't help myself, Sarah. You and the children invade every area of my life, including my thoughts and plans. At least let me enjoy this week with you and your family."

"Please don't set those plans in concrete without consulting me." Sarah's sass turned to concern. "I do hope we'll be able to move freely through the parks. Perhaps the other families will be distracted by the same attractions that our boys can't wait to see."

"See, you just admitted that we share the children. That means you also see me in your future."

Sarah hit him on the shoulder and groaned in exasperation as he pulled the van into the resort. While he checked in, his charges waited in the spacious lobby where cartoons played on giant screens, and Disney characters entertained the children. Alex thought about an entire week with Sarah and her family. He felt almost as excited as the children.

Jonathan and David bounced in anticipation as they entered the Magic Kingdom on Monday morning. Sarah and Alex rushed to keep pace with Mike as he walked between the twins. Considerable discussion ensued as they decided which ride should be first. When Mike suggested Dumbo, everyone headed toward the flying elephant.

"It looks as if Mike has done his homework. I can't believe that young man's patience with the boys. He acts their age when entertaining them, but at the same time, exhibits maturity and responsibility."

"Mike impressed me from our first meeting. Thank you for inviting him, Alex."

After Dumbo, the boys had them moving from one ride to the next. Their constant chatter only ceased long enough to pose for pictures with the roaming characters. During meals, Alex saw the joy on the children's faces as they described at length the rides, the parade, the shows, the fireworks, and even their introduction to cotton candy. He wouldn't exchange the experience for all the solitude in the world.

Alex made reservations for the Character Breakfast with Mickey Mouse on Wednesday. After the short walk across the landscaped garden, they entered the resort dining room filled with the squeals and laughter of happy children. All five children soon joined the fun.

Etiquette demanded Alex remove his baseball cap in the dining room. Taking one of the hostesses aside, he pointed to a table in a far corner where they would be less conspicuous. Regardless, two sets of twins attracted attention no matter where they dined. Here, they were even more visible with the boys dancing around the tables and Hannah and Elizabeth staring wide-eyed at the colorful, amusing rodents.

"You must eat your food, boys." Sarah encouraged.

Amid the distractions and activity, their delicious brunch grew cold and sitting still became impossible. Alex understood. While they interacted with the characters, he moved about the table, capturing candid shots and movies.

"Looks like you're also neglecting your food, Mr. Alex. Have you lost your appetite in favor of all this entertainment?" Sarah teased as she tried to interest the seven-month-old girls in their pureed fruit. It was a losing battle. They too were distracted by the music and colorful costumes.

Far past their bedtime that evening, the boys continued to talk about the fun breakfast with Minnie and Mickey, their new best friends.

Every day became an adventure. As Alex maneuvered the stroller through the afternoon crowds, the babies squealed with pleasure at the brilliant colors and spinning rides. Most of the characters delighted them until an occasional over-exuberant actor danced too close. A quick break with a few comforting words from Alex soon brought back their bright smiles.

To keep the boys from wandering away and getting lost in the crowd, Alex rented another double stroller for the afternoons. He and Sarah took turns waiting nearby with the girls or enjoying the amusements with their brothers. Often the rides were mild enough even for the babies, giving them an opportunity to board together. To the casual observer, they appeared to be an average family on vacation, but each evening when they returned to the resort, Alex felt relieved when another day passed without anyone recognizing him.

As the week advanced, Alex realized how much they depended on Mike. He entertained Jonathan and David with an array of sound effects and entered eagerly into their world of make-believe. Knowing he and his grandmother would enjoy the big rides later, he never complained about his mornings with the boys. For such a young man, he had a remarkable attitude.

In the evenings, the whole group enjoyed dinner at one of the many restaurants within the Disney complex. Mike entertained the boys with tales of his afternoon adventures. He made them feel as though their rides were as scary and fun as his had been. Alex saw the pride on Anna's face as she watched her animated grandson.

Upon their return to the resort, Alex was wiped out. On the other hand, Sarah, the "energized bunny," didn't know when to quit. While he rested and attempted to talk his body into a few more hours of "fun," Sarah found a multitude of tasks that couldn't wait.

"You amaze me, Sarah. Are you some 'Supermom?' I'm exhausted and about to crash, while you're up for a marathon. I feel like an old man compared to you."

"Yes, this is tiring, but I'm thankful my strength returned soon after the surgery, and I have the energy for this non-stop activity. Nap time is often the only break this so-called Supermom gets. Don't you remember how busy you were when you were overseeing my crew?"

Yes, he did remember the week of Sarah's hospitalization. This exhaustion felt similar, but with one exception—she was now by his side. Her presence alone strengthened him and kept him moving.

It never seemed to bother her that they had little time alone. Consideration and politeness governed their relationship. They acted more like an old married couple with insignificant conversations and mutual understanding. Alex didn't like the brief exchanges, but there seemed no way to alter the situation and time was running out.

At the end of the week, they had managed to visit all the Disney parks, including a couple of water parks. The boys picked out toys to commemorate the week, and Sarah chose stuffed animals for the babies. She bought her mother a pretty vase from one of the upscale shops. Alex didn't need a souvenir—he had a week's worth of memories and a SIM card filled with pictures.

When Sarah's van pulled in front of the cottage, Jonathan woke up from a short nap and recognized the familiar surroundings. "Look, we're home. That was the best week ever."

Alex and Sarah laughed, "You boys should thank Mr. Alex for such a wonderful time. You've made some great memories. Not many little boys get to spend a whole week at Disney World."

David spoke first, "Thank you, Daddy. It was great. Can we do it again sometime?"

"Yeah, some of those rides were awesome. Next time I want to ride the big roller coasters like Mike. Could we go back?"

"We'll see. It'll take us a while to recover. I can't speak for your mother, but you wore me out."

For the next few weeks, Alex came by on nice days with Bailey to play on the beach with the boys. Sometimes, he took them for walks, but only with their mother's permission. He ached to be with Sarah, but he didn't go inside the cottage. She trusted him enough to leave her watchful perch on the porch when he arrived, and that alone gave him hope.

Alex had little time to recoup before he had to leave for his next publicity tour, which coincided with his sister's wedding. Jana asked him about inviting Sarah and the children, but Alex declined. He didn't want Sarah to feel obligated. His pain and longing escalated as he thought of his sister exchanging wedding vows. It would've been torture with Sarah there with him, yet so far out of reach.

Jana's wedding moved him to tears. The white designer gown fell gently from her waist into a sea of shimmering silk. The cap sleeves complemented the pearl strewn lace bodice while her smile glowed amid the garden of white lilies. His sister never looked more radiant as their father escorted her down the aisle. Paul's look of love said it all.

The service itself, so rich in tradition and spiritual significance, drew the guests into worship and praise. He dreamed about sharing such an experience with Sarah, but he wondered again if they would ever be together. Discouragement and depression tormented him to the point of despair.

After the wedding and reception, he went back to his room at his parents' home. He slouched into a comfortable chair by the bed and lowered his head. Moistening his lips, he tasted salt from the tears. He'd vowed to put aside his own desires and seek only God, but he'd failed miserably. He longed for Sarah and refused to consider a substitute. Perhaps the book tour and interviews would take his mind off this unhealthy obsession, but he doubted it.

Alex hadn't fully recovered from the trip to Disney. He couldn't seem to shake the tiredness. When the tour came to an end, he planned to discuss his health with his mother and perhaps see a doctor in Northern Virginia. He hated to worry his parents, but he suspected he suffered from something more than debilitating grief over Sarah.

CHAPTER TWENTY-SIX

On the island, Sarah experienced similar grief intermingled with confusing thoughts about Alex. At times, she was angry with herself, feeling responsible for the way Alex had left. The beach seemed empty and lonely without him though she hated to admit it. The children missed him as well. When she went to the grocery store, his picture with some pretty woman glared back at her from the magazine rack. Jealousy wasn't an easy thing to deal with. She even envied her children for the way they freely expressed and received love from the man. Why couldn't she overcome her fears, swallow her pride, and just tell him how she felt?

Before their trip to Florida, Sarah had anticipated a bonding time for them. But shortly into the trip, she realized how close they were already. Conversation seemed unnecessary at times as they moved as a unit, often finishing a sentence or anticipating the desires of the other. Despite their disagreement over their relationship, Sarah acknowledged their compatibility on many levels.

Alex had somehow tempered his tendency to be in control. He respected and honored her, and she longed to spend time alone with him in the evenings. Though she suspected he used his exhaustion as an excuse—to avoid her and her acid tongue. It was her own fault. When they returned home, he distanced himself even further. She'd pushed him away one too many times.

Even as Sarah admitted that her feelings toward the man were changing, she continued to allow insecurity and fear to control her. Would she ever manage to move ahead with Alex or anyone, for that matter? Despite her inconsistent feelings, she chose to rely on God's faithfulness and be open to whatever he planned for her. If that meant a relationship with Alex, she wanted to be willing.

Regardless of her new determination, Sarah continued to feel sorry for herself and miss Alex. Her friends stopped by often, and her mother came for a visit, but no amount of coaxing reversed her foul mood.

Summer's arrival brought higher temperatures and a near-constant ocean breeze. The boys played outside almost every day and were delighted when Anna brought Bailey for a visit. Alex's housekeeper used the excuse that the dog missed Alex, but Sarah suspected the sweet woman came by for the boys, knowing they felt the same. Not a day went by that they didn't ask when "Daddy" would be home.

While her mother visited, Sarah spent time away from the children, shopping, running errands and even meeting friends for lunch. Waiting in line at the grocery store, she tortured herself by perusing the celebrity magazines. Her heart beat a little faster when she first recognized his familiar face. But the sight of the tall blonde clinging to his arm turned her elation to distress. The caption read, "Might this be the young mother who stole Stephen Jacobs' heart?"

Paralyzed, Sarah stared at the magazine and cried like one of her overtired twins who needed a nap but couldn't sleep. She wanted to rip out the picture of the floozy who'd taken her place. The other customers stopped what they were doing and gawked, including the woman behind her in line.

"Are you okay, honey?" People on the island were known for their gossipy ways, but they also respected a person's privacy. Sooner or later the word would get out, and all would be privy to the scoop. In this case, the woman would be disappointed. Sarah wasn't about to share her sad tale.

Pulling herself together, she addressed the woman as politely as possible. "Thank you for your concern, but I'll be fine. I sometimes overreact to sad situations. Forgive me."

After she managed to place her groceries on the counter and pay with her credit card, she realized her attempt to project calm didn't convince her island neighbors. Their sympathetic looks moved from the magazine back to her. Sarah jammed her cart through the door, raced to her van, and shoved the grocery bags into the rear.

All the way back to the island, between crying jags, she berated her stubborn, fearful self. Sarah took full responsibility that Alex had found someone else. She didn't deserve him. In calmer moments, she admitted that the woman in no way resembled a floozy, but the attractive, intelligent woman that Alex needed. When she entered the cottage, red eyes and streaks of telling tears remained. Her inquisitive mother wasted no time in asking what happened.

"I don't want to talk about it." And she didn't. What good would it do? Mother would probably say, "I told you so!" After seeing how much he cared for her and the children, Leslie had been pushing her to give Alex a chance. Her mother admitted that she declined the trip to Disney hoping they'd spend some quality time together and perhaps realize how perfect they were for each other.

"Might it have something to do with Alex's picture with the cute blonde on the front of that magazine?" Leslie asked with a knowing expression.

"How did you know? Have you seen the picture?" *How did her mother know about the picture?* "She's gorgeous, and he looks at her the way he used to look at me. How could he forget me so soon?"

"Sarah, listen to yourself. You practically beat the poor guy on the head to get him out of your life, and now you wonder why he's with someone else. Shame on you!"

Leslie let her suffer a few minutes longer before observing, "You know that cute blonde looks a lot like his younger sister, Jana. I believe she lives in New York with her husband. It wouldn't surprise me if he were having an evening out with his sister. He's that kind of guy you know."

"But if it were Jana, wouldn't the magazine know that?"

"Why would they? They only know his pen name. Jana Caine means nothing to them, nor does her new last name, whatever that is."

"Oh, Mother, do you think so? You don't know how I've punished myself since that day he came here to say goodbye to the boys. I should swallow my pride, tell him how I feel, and beg him to forgive me. If I find out he's home, I'm going down that beach and do everything possible to persuade him to give me another chance."

"I hope you know what you're doing. I'd hate to see you hurt again. Alex is a fine young man, but his life is so dissimilar from yours. He did tell me way back when you were in the hospital that he would someday be my son-in-law, so you'd better be prepared to marry him if you reveal how you feel. You know how persistent he is."

Sarah continued putting away the groceries and thinking about the man who dominated her thoughts. He refused to go away. Even the house reminded her of him. She remembered how he looked relaxing on the couch, playing on the floor with the children, and even sleeping in her bed.

If he ever came home, she promised herself she would ask his forgiveness and try to restore their relationship. For her peace of mind, she had to try at least. But as her mother suggested, he would interpret it as her being ready to commit, and she doubted she would ever be. He fulfilled every requirement of a perfect husband, yet fear of abandonment held her back, especially when she thought of giving herself completely to Alex. Friendship she'd accept, but she already considered him her best friend and even more.

After he completed Lori's exhaustive agenda, Alex left for Northern Virginia. By the time he arrived at the home of his parents, he could hardly move. Pain in his lower back kept him popping ibuprofen, and he ran a low-grade fever.

His appearance alarmed his mother. "Alex, you look so tired and pale. Are you ill?"

"Something's wrong. I don't think I've ever felt like this."

"That's not like you at all. I'm going to call our internist and see if he has an opening."

Alex considered himself in the peak of health. He rarely visited a doctor, but by nine o'clock the following morning, he sat on the examination table wearing nothing but a paper gown. After numerous questions and blood work, the doctor sent him to the radiology department at the hospital.

"After they run all their tests, I want you to stay in town until we have the results and can make an accurate diagnosis." Alex didn't have the energy to argue with the doctor.

Two days later, the doctor's office called requesting an afternoon appointment. He felt relieved when his parents insisted on accompanying him. The consultation resulted in a distressing diagnosis—Aggressive Renal Cell Carcinoma which had spread to the lymph nodes. While the doctors consulted on a course of treatment, he prepared to return to the island for a few days. When considerable protest from his parents didn't change his mind, his mother offered to drive him. Relief at the offer trumped any dread of the seven-hour confinement with a hovering parent.

His desire to see his friends on the island overcame his concerns over an information leak. He wouldn't let anyone know he was coming, and he'd limit his contacts to Sarah and Pastor Mark and Deborah. He wanted to finalize arrangements for the childcare program. And seeing Sarah and the children would give him the energy needed for the treatments that lay ahead.

Although he hadn't fully recovered from the exhausting road trip, and he looked terrible, Alex made an afternoon appointment with Pastor Mark. He didn't plan to disclose his diagnosis, but he wanted to spend time with this man who had both encouraged and challenged him throughout the past year.

After the initial greeting, overshadowed by Alex's attempt to disguise his poor health, they discussed the daycare program. Mark and Deborah had made excellent progress in carrying out his ideas and were planning a grand opening in the fall. Alex did his best to hide his disappointment. Attending the event would not be an option.

The men concluded the meeting with prayer without discussing anything personal. As he rose to leave, Mark insisted they meet for breakfast on Tuesday morning where Alex would again be forced to camouflage his weakness. He took the stairs from the church office in slow motion and stopped half-way up the steep flight of steps. Depression and guilt gnawed at his gut. He felt like a coward for not being honest with his friend.

CHAPTER TWENTY-SEVEN

Sarah hadn't realized he was in town until Susan dropped by with the news. She and Alex had crossed paths that morning in the diner. "When he asked about you and the children, he seemed sad and uncomfortable. It made me wonder if you've seen him since he's been home."

"He's home? And he hasn't even come by to see the boys. I suppose he'll never forgive me, but I'm not letting him get away with it. Susan, are you free to watch the children a few minutes? I have something to do that I refuse to put off any longer."

Sarah's determination to move past the fear and at least get back to the comfortable relationship they shared in Orlando sent her rushing down the beach. Halfway there, her sanity returned, along with a good dose of reality. If she poured out her heart to Alex, he'd ask for an immediate commitment, and Sarah knew that couldn't happen any time soon. Restoring their friendship was the best she could offer. *God, please help Alex understand.*

Sarah had driven past Alex's house and curiously glanced at it beyond the gated entryway, but nothing prepared her for the view from the beach. Rising four levels skyward, the mansion spread over more than one beachfront lot. The man who appeared so comfortable in her small cottage couldn't possibly live in such luxury. She gaped in disbelief and began doubting her impulse. If she didn't feel her mission so important, she'd flee to her small home where she belonged.

Intimidated by its size, she became frustrated when she couldn't locate an outside entrance. As she rounded the corner to try the street side of the house, a familiar male voice came from an intercom set so loud she heard it over the crashing surf. "Are you trying to break into my house, Mrs. Stuart?"

Sarah searched the many windows for Alex until she found him gazing at her from the third-floor deck. "You scared me half to death, Alex Caine, or is it 'Stephen Jacobs, now—the eligible bachelor who escorts beautiful women around Manhattan.' Let me in. How does someone get into this monstrosity of a house anyhow?"

Alex laughed. Give the man credit. He always lifted her spirits. She steeled herself and rehearsed what she wanted to say to the man who confused and intimidated her.

"Stay right there, and I'll come to you."

Sarah waited while Alex came down the outside stairs. By the time he stopped a few feet from her, she couldn't hide the tears. He must think her a basket case. Embarrassed that he should see her so vulnerable, she turned away and wiped the moisture with the hem of her sundress. When she regained some modicum of control and returned her attention to him, she saw that he had tears of his own.

"I've missed you, Alex," she whispered. "You've been home for two days, and you haven't come to see us. Did you think you could desert us, and we'd forget you? We spent a whole week with you in Florida, and you grew on us. Then you leave us for so long."

Alex gazed at her but made no move toward her. Sarah continued, "Say something. Please don't make me beg, Alex. You must forgive me."

"Oh, Sarah, I could never forget about you. It's almost as if I can't breathe without you. My life has never been the same since we first met, but even that proved difficult if you recall."

"I know, Alex. And it's mostly my fault.

"Nothing about our relationship has ever been easy for either of us. You don't know how much I missed you while I was away, but I can't allow you to keep hurting me. I'm not as strong as you are, Sarah, and it hurts too much. I do forgive you, but I'm telling you right now, you can't keep doing this to me."

When Alex finally opened his arms to her, she hesitated but a moment, then slowly came to him. "Can you forgive me, then, for all the times I've been rude to you? I want us to be friends, Alex. The boys love you so much and ..." As Sarah continued her little speech, she felt Alex slowly pulling away.

"I can't be just your friend, Sarah. This so-called friendship is almost more than I can bear. Have you not seen my heart? Have you not understood how I feel about you? Come inside. I want to show you something."

Alex led Sarah up two flights of stairs to a large deck with outdoor wicker furniture and through French doors into a sitting area. When Sarah looked around, she realized she'd entered a large master suite.

"I just realized, I've never seen your house. Would you give me a tour?"

"That's what I have in mind." Sarah had never seen Alex this serious. He frightened her. "We're in the master bedroom. I had it redecorated recently for the woman I planned to marry. Do you like it?"

"Who wouldn't like it? It's beautiful." Sarah ignored his comment regarding marriage. Her mother had been right when she warned her about being ready to commit if she gave Alex the slightest encouragement. "Did you have a decorator?"

"Yes, but I didn't do much in here. I thought my wife might want to put her taste into it."

Sarah admired the spacious room. The sitting area had upholstered lounge chairs with a reading lamp between them. A large screen TV hung above the marble gas fireplace. A half-wall separated the sitting area from the massive space dominated by a king-sized bed. Through an archway, the bath and dressing area featured a large jacuzzi tub surrounded by live ferns, giving one the feel of an outdoor garden. The fixtures, the Italian marble, the lighting, all spoke of money.

The drapes, furniture, and bed linens were coordinated in beautiful shades of rose, blue and green. She couldn't have decorated a room more suited to her taste. As the longing for him in her heart escalated, Sarah realized she'd made a terrible mistake. She shouldn't have come here. If anything, she learned one thing: They would never suit. He deserved one of those fancy women with their shining tans and expensive clothes.

For some reason, Sarah never thought of Alex leaving her through death as did her father and husband. Instead, she doubted her ability to compete with the many beautiful women, knowing it would break her heart when he chose one of them over her. He moved in circles that she knew nothing about and didn't care to know. She'd always been content with staying home and caring for her family. Even her career choice worked better for a wife and mother. Now would be the time to let him go. She shook herself as she tried to dislodge the choking sensation that followed her moment of truth.

"When did you have time for all this, Alex?"

"Last December when we were on the outs. Come to think of it, there hasn't been a shortage of opportunities the past few months to not only decorate my house, but write novels, do publicity tours, and spend time feeling sorry for myself. Alone, I might add."

"Oh, Alex, you do have it bad. How could you allow a woman with four children and too many problems to make you miserable? Why do you continue to wait for someone trapped in the past who is most unsuitable for the image your public demands?"

"Not long after we met, Sarah, I determined that one day you'd be mine. My whole life changed while I waited and prayed for the fulfillment of that dream. Now, I'm not so sure. As far as the public goes, I care little about what they think as long as they keep reading my books."

Sarah wallowed in remorse, hearing the defeat in his words and knowing she'd put it there. Despite her confused feelings for him, she looked at the perfect room and allowed herself to dream of sharing it with him.

As she looked out at the view, she saw an area she'd missed outside the French doors. She went back to take a second look. At the center of an outdoor seating area stood an enormous hot tub surrounded by planters and hanging baskets cascading with an abundance of color.

"Oh, Alex, it's so unbelievably beautiful. This space has to be one of your happy places."

"I suppose it is, but I'd hoped to share it with you. That would've made me extremely happy."

He noticed her discomfort and steered her back inside.

"I take this house for granted sometimes, but it is magnificent. There's no time to tour the other floors, but I'd like you to see a couple of bedrooms I remodeled with you in mind. The one next to the master suite was designed for the babies."

When Sarah entered the spacious room, she felt a sense of perfection, comfort, and pleasure. The tiny room at the cottage she shared with the babies seemed like an anthill compared to this beautiful space. Decorated in soft shades of yellow, an animal mural graced one wall. The same animal theme marched about the room atop the wide chair rail. Separate cribs, an oversized stuffed rocking chair, two chests, a play mat with a large open basket of toys and stuffed animals and, most interesting of all, two changing tables completed the furnishings.

"Looks like someone is counting on twins."

"It seems that way."

Sarah checked out the adjoining bath, which had every convenience imaginable to take care of infants and toddlers. The large playroom next door had shelving, cupboards, a television with a DVD player, comfortable chairs, an art area, a low table with four chairs, and two large open spaces with colorful rugs adorning the wooden floors. There were books, puzzles, and toys lining the shelves. Alex and the decorator had thought of everything.

"I know you must get back to the children, but just one more room before you go."

Alex ushered her into the boys' room, similar in size to the nursery, but decorated in an airplane theme with murals scattered throughout and model planes hanging from the ceiling. The boys each had a double bed covered with dark blue comforters and airplane accessories. They also had chests, bookcases, and shelves scattered throughout the room. Sarah knew the boys would love it. The aviation theme continued throughout the bathroom obviously designed to keep little boys soaking in the ample tubs, one at each end of the bath.

"Alex, the boys would love all this, but haven't you gone to a lot of expense when you don't even have a fiancée?"

"Maybe back in December I had more faith. Lately, I don't know if I'll ever need it. Maybe I should put the house on the market and sell it to someone who would appreciate it."

Alex looked so tired and sad Sarah had to get away from him. The upbeat man she'd come to know rarely allowed himself a negative thought much less a display of defeat and discouragement. What had prompted the abrupt change from the arrogant man she first met? How could she encourage him without giving false hope?

"I must get back to the children, Alex."

"Sarah, before you go, I must tell you something. I plan to leave the island for a few months." The thought of Alex leaving again almost paralyzed her. Instead of being relieved, her heart seized up in fear.

"Why are you doing this? I told you how much we missed you when you were away these past couple of months, now you plan on staying away even longer. Is it my fault? I thought you had forgiven me."

"Shush, Sarah, it has nothing to do with you. It's me. I'm required to be away. Don't be angry with me. I couldn't stand that. I want you to remember me as someone who loves you and cares about you and the children. I'll probably see the boys on the beach in the morning, but I can't stay long. I'm driving back to Northern Virginia tomorrow. Pray for me, Sarah. I need your prayers, now, more than ever."

"What's wrong, Alex? You're scaring me."

"I'm sorry, but I don't want to talk about it. Just pray for me."

"I hate for us to part like this, but I truly must get home to the children. I hope that when you leave this time, you'll keep in touch. Please, don't forget us."

"Come here, Sarah."

Alex took her in his arms and held her tightly. She encircled his waist and placed her head on his chest. She heard the rapid beat of his heart and knew it mimicked her own. It felt as if they were saying goodbye forever, and she didn't want to let him go. After a few moments, he released her.

"You'd better go, Sarah. The girls might be hungry. I'll stop by tomorrow to see the boys."

Before Sarah left, she took one last look at the beautiful master suite, doubting that they would ever share it. He sounded so final as if he never planned to see her again. What had she done? She had to get out of there before she did something stupid. As she headed up the beach, she ached deep inside as though grieving the loss of someone dear. When the pain reached her throat, she cried out in anguish, hoping no one heard above the sound of the ocean.

At the porch, Sarah stood for a moment, trying to calm her racing heart and wiping away her tears. Susan greeted her with a teasing grin. "Well, I suppose you straightened everything out with Mr. Caine?" Then she saw Sarah's distress and recanted. "Sorry, I guess not."

"I'm not sure what happened. I apologized, and he said he forgave me, but I can tell he doesn't trust me, as if I'm going to hurt him again. I think he's given up on our relationship. Oh, Susan, I have caused this. I kept pushing him away until he no longer wants me. Do you think he's found someone else?"

"No, I don't think he's found anyone else. You are his life. Most of your friends have known that for a long time. I'm glad you finally admit it to yourself. Give him time, Sarah. I know you guys are meant to be together."

"I hope you're right. I'm sorry I stayed so long over there, but Alex showed me some of the rooms he redecorated. Susan, you should see that house. It's amazing, but I felt lost in it. It's so foreign to anything I ever dreamed about. I wouldn't know what to do with something like that."

"Well, if it was my house, I'm sure I'd find a way to adjust rather quickly." Susan laughed as she made her point.

"I don't think it'll ever be mine. He even talked about selling it to a family who would appreciate it. I've never seen him so sad. When he insisted he had to leave again for several more months, I nearly lost it. I don't think it's business this time. He wants to get away from me, though I did everything but beg him to stay. He claimed it wasn't me, but him. What am I going to do? It almost sounded as if he never planned to see me again." Sarah paced the floor and wrung her hands as she told her friend a condensed version of what had happened.

"I'm so sorry, Sarah. Maybe he has a good, logical reason. We must pray for him and believe that God will work it out. I know you're disappointed after getting the nerve to go over there and confront him, but maybe he needs time to put everything into perspective. Right now, I've got to run, but I'll return in a couple days, so we can talk again and pray together.

"Oh, by the way, did you hear that the church is considering a childcare program for the fall? They would like to begin earlier, but it takes time to hire qualified teachers and helpers. I understand they have the curriculum and someone to fund the program. Can you believe that? For the older children, three and older, there will be a preschool two mornings a week. The babies will have a daycare with music and stories.

"The best thing I heard about the program is that mothers aren't allowed to volunteer, and an anonymous donor completely funded it. They hope to make an announcement at church on Sunday and start the registration. We can talk about it more next time. Sounds as if the babies are ready for their mama. Keep your chin up, girlfriend."

Sarah admired her energized friend as she left before Sarah had a chance to respond to the welcome news. Yet another thing to love about Community Church. What a blessing to have her boys in preschool, her girls in daycare, and two mornings a week free to do as she pleased. Sarah didn't even have to guess who the generous donor might be.

CHAPTER TWENTY-EIGHT

From the window of his study on the top level, Alex watched Sarah disappear up the beach. Rehearsing her visit and mulling over his circumstances, he let his eyes drift toward the water. In the distance, the ocean glistened like fine diamonds. Sandpipers played tag with the waves as they searched for food at water's edge. Occasionally, a pelican flew low with his eye on an unsuspecting fish.

Normally, this view brought peace and serenity to his spirit, but today he felt an ache so deep inside he could barely breathe. Cancer could be robbing him of all he loved, forcing him to leave this place and his beautiful Sarah. He'd never be happy without her, but with the challenge he faced, he couldn't have her now—maybe never.

When he met the boys on the beach the next morning, Alex saw Sarah sitting on the porch. He felt tempted to go to her and tell all. He knew he could count on his parents in the days ahead, but without Sarah, he might as well be alone. He longed to have her by his side, but what would it do to her and the boys if he didn't survive?

Jonathan and David were upset when he told them he had to leave again, but as he played with them in the sand, their happiness returned. He'd miss these good times. The boys were full of life and had years ahead of them, but as for him, he didn't know if he'd live to see any of them again.

Before leaving, Alex made a quick stop at the church office to verify plans for the daycare program with Pastor Mark. The business details seemed to be in order with Deborah agreeing to direct the program. As Alex stood to leave, Mark reminded him to pray. When Alex asked about

Jonah, the pastor shared that his son continued to struggle. Although the young man had returned home to sort out his life, he remained bogged down with grief and depression and refused to discuss anything with his parents.

Out of the blue, Mark looked at Alex with a concerned expression. "Alex, I know you've not shared much about what's going on with you personally, but in my spirit, I know something isn't right. If it's too private a matter, I understand, but you're continually in my prayers. Whatever might come your way, remember that God knows, sees, loves, and cares."

With that admonishment, Mark prayed for Alex, Jonah, and the families that would be reached through this new outreach program. Alex had never heard such urgency in a prayer. He longed for that kind of connection with God, yet he was confident that the pastor's prayers were effective even if he didn't know the whole ugly story.

Driving back to Northern Virginia with his mother, Alex worried about the toll this ordeal might take on his parents, but there seemed to be no other way. Their proximity to the medical facility and their loving support would be necessary throughout the extended period of treatment and recovery. The one person he desired most continued to plague his mind, but she could never be an option.

He wanted to forget about his dream of a life with Sarah and her children, but he didn't think he could. For their sake, he had to at least try. When he considered how abandoned she felt when both her father and husband died, he knew he couldn't put her through another loss. Regardless of her lack of commitment to him, he knew in his heart that for him to desert her through death would devastate her further.

The last time they were together, Alex felt Sarah's love for him and knew she came close to sharing her heart. After all these months of praying and waiting, she had finally moved within reach. And now, he couldn't have her. Nothing seemed fair in this life. The only thing he could count on was eternity.

Alex regretted showing Sarah his home. Did he think that would repay her for the way she treated him for months—giving him hope, then jerking it away? He doubted even he would see the house again, so what exactly had he accomplished? He remembered how upset she acted when she left. They should have talked out on the beach and left as friends. Common sense never seemed to prevail when it came to Sarah.

Confused and disheartened as he was, one thing he did know: If he should survive cancer, he couldn't expect Sarah to live with a man carrying a death sentence over his head. It wouldn't be fair, especially for someone who had already lost so much.

The hospital oncologist classified his cancer as treatable, though the doctor seemed concerned with the designation of "aggressive." The regimen meant additional chemotherapy to ensure that the cancer wouldn't rear its ugly head in some other part of his body. The loss of a kidney was bad enough without the monster taking one organ at a time until he had nothing left.

Back when his patience grew thin waiting for Sarah, his mother suggested he read in the Bible where James encouraged believers to consider it joy whenever they faced trials. If cancer were an example of one of these trials, he'd cease praying for patience, and for the life of him, he had yet to discover an ounce of joy in this ordeal.

Alex identified more with Job in the Old Testament. The poor man lost everything including his children, health, and possessions. Though he didn't have a family to lose, Alex felt as if he'd been stripped clean. Little remained but God, and yet at times, even he seemed out of reach. When tempted to doubt, he remembered two quotes from Job, "Though he slay me, I will hope in him" and "As for me, I know that my Redeemer lives."

Jana called wanting to come down for the operation, but he discouraged her. She and Paul were expecting their first child, and he didn't want anything to jeopardize his sister's health or her pregnancy. She'd broken down in anguish when she heard the initial diagnosis, and he didn't wish to cause her further distress. His desire to be alive long enough to become an uncle seemed a distant hope.

The operation was scheduled for the following week, but his calendar filled up with pre-op appointments. He tried to keep a positive attitude—a necessary ingredient in the fight against cancer. Along with good doctors, the experts also suggested a dedicated support system comprised of people who loved the patient and would pray regularly for his recovery.

Every time he thought of contacting his friend, Mark, he rejected the idea. He couldn't think of anyone or anything on Shell Island without thinking of Sarah. She would be devastated to learn of his diagnosis, and he couldn't take that chance. When his church family heard of his illness, he prayed they'd understand and forgive him. The prayers of his family and their churches would have to suffice.

Although he tried to stay positive, he soon wearied of the effort and preferred death to the darkness that enveloped him. Much of his attitude stemmed from feeling cut off from Sarah. He longed for her presence, but he couldn't impose this bleak situation upon her. If she knew, she'd come, and that's why he'd do everything to keep it from her.

The doctors declared the operation a success, and after a few weeks of recovery, Alex began chemotherapy. When he breezed through the first week of infusions, he mistakenly thought he had the situation made. But he'd been warned the buildup in his body might not be felt until after a few treatments. When the side effects did hit him, weakness and nausea took over. He couldn't eat, and if he did, he threw up. The little gold pill refused to live up to its name, and death seemed his only escape.

Shortly after treatment began, his hair fell out in clumps, leaving him stripped of much that had previously defined him. He had often received compliments on his thick, light-colored hair. Now he refused to look in the mirror. The person staring back in no way resembled the "handsome bachelor every young single woman would love to date." What a laugh, but also a fact he'd taken for granted.

As anticipated, the side effects of the chemo weakened Alex. When he entered the hospital for the fifth time, fighting infections and blood clots and battling to survive, he made a decision that could end his life. He gave up. Now that he'd made peace with God, he preferred heaven to the hell that awakened him every morning and plagued him into the night.

Alex could barely speak when the doctor stopped by his room early the next morning. The weakness had taken its toll, but he determined to have a serious conversation with the man.

"Dr. Franko, I can't take any more. Please, no more treatments. I would rather die than continue like this."

"I agree with you, Alex. I just went over your latest blood work. You're at risk of a shutdown of major organs. With your immune system so low, you're subject to even more infection. To prevent further damage to your remaining kidney, I've discontinued the treatments. If you feel like going through another regimen after a few weeks, then we'll reconsider. But right now, your body has reached its limit. I hope the treatments you've had are sufficient to keep the cancer at bay. Prematurely discontinuing is a gamble, but in your case, may be our only recourse."

"When might I go home? I'd eventually like to return to my beach house. It's a place where I've always felt at peace, and if I'm going to die, I'd rather it be there."

"Would you have help?"

"I'll hire someone, if necessary. One thing I do know is I don't want to continue living like this."

"If we see improvement within the next couple of days, I'll consider releasing you, but right now your prognosis isn't good. We'll give you something to boost your immune system, and hopefully, arrest this latest infection. Perhaps then we'll consider dismissing you to return to your parents' home, but I'd prefer you not leave the area for a while."

"I welcome anything designed to improve the way I feel. Although the treatments were meant to save my life, they certainly felt as if they were killing me. I appreciate all you've done, but I'm thankful you're discontinuing the chemo."

After the doctor left, Alex's thoughts returned to Sarah. No matter how much he tried, he couldn't erase her from his mind. Thoughts of her lingered throughout the day and invaded his dreams at night. Always right there with him, but never close enough. Even without hope of a future together, he had to see her when he returned to the island.

He heard a tap on the door, and his mother stuck her head inside. She had an amazing knack for showing up when he needed her most. "May I come in?"

"Of course, Mother. You're always welcome. Have I told you how much I appreciate you and Dad? You never fail to support me even when you disagree with my decisions, but now you're doing so much more. How will I ever repay you for such sacrifice? You look tired—like you're not getting enough rest."

"I'm all right, Alex. All the thanks I require is to know that you'll be okay."

His mother had been a rock throughout the illness, but he couldn't ignore the worry lines that increased after his diagnoses. Walking with him through this trial had taken its toll, and he felt responsible.

"I'm going to be okay, Mother, whether I live or die. I don't want you or Dad to worry. Just keep praying. I told the doctor to stop the treatments. They're killing me and making me miserable for the time I have left. You and Dad have been so strong for me, but it's time to let me go. I want to go home to North Carolina and feel the ocean air on my parched skin. I don't really want her to see me like this, but I must see Sarah and the boys one last time. Please understand."

His mother attempted a smile through the flow of tears. "Please don't give up, Alex. Your scans all reveal the treatments have helped."

"I haven't given up, Mother, but I don't think my body will take much more, and Dr. Franko agrees."

"It's hard for your dad and me to see you struggle like this."

"I know, Mother. Keep praying for me and trust God to restore my health. He's my only hope."

He wanted to continue the fight to please his parents, but he didn't have the strength or the determination. His mother had been his biggest cheerleader, but of late, her cheer had almost vanished.

"Oh, Alex. Please don't give up. Let me call Sarah. You need her, and she'll be so upset when she finds out from another source."

Alex shook his head. "No, please don't call her. I can't let her see me like this. I'll see her when I return to the island, but until then, I don't want her upset. There's no hope of a future with her, and I refuse to put her through another loss. Promise me."

"When you love someone, Alex, you don't have to have a wedding band to feel the loss."

He knew his mother's words were true, but Alex couldn't face Sarah. Maybe pride drove his decision, but more than anything he wanted to protect her and the children from seeing him so weak and vulnerable. Although Grace argued the case for Sarah, she reluctantly agreed to honor his wishes.

Alex held his mother while quietly praying for her comfort and strength. He wanted to tell her that the treatments were successful, and he'd live many more years, but he couldn't give her false hope. Not when his life seemed to teeter on the edge of death.

CHAPTER TWENTY-NINE

By October, most of the summer residents had returned to their winter homes sporting tans and boxes of salt water taffy. Sarah felt as empty and abandoned as the island looked. Alex hadn't contacted anyone since June. Whatever happened couldn't be good.

The church daycare program became a beacon of light. Since the grand opening in early September, Sarah enjoyed freedom two mornings a week without any expense. She knew Alex was responsible. The generous man found a way to help her while contributing to the entire community.

The freedom, however, did nothing to heal her wounded spirit. To the contrary, it provided additional hours of uninterrupted worry. The last time she'd seen Alex, he'd appeared weak and defeated as he asked for prayer. Sarah berated herself for not expressing her feelings. She should've fallen on her knees and begged him to marry her. Her heart ached for the sensitive man and the love he expressed so freely. How could she be so stubborn? What if something terrible happened?

On one of those lonely, worry-filled days, the island buzzed with word of a hurricane coming up the East Coast. The locals evaluated the situation from many angles with the senior citizens comparing the storm to those before and the younger people relying on the doppler and barometric pressure changes. What to do—evacuate or stay and ride out the storm?

Amid the hoopla, Anna called to say that she'd heard from Alex. News of the storm reached him, wherever he was, and he was worried about Sarah and the children. With his tendency toward preparedness and attention to detail, he'd made reservations for her family on the mainland, fifty miles from the path of the storm.

"If he felt so concerned, Anna, why didn't he call me? I don't understand. He's been gone forever, and suddenly he appears on the radar along with the hurricane."

At Sarah's insistence and further questioning, Anna admitted that she hadn't personally talked with Alex. The message, delivered through his agent, Lori Sharp, confused Sarah further. "Well, I couldn't accept his offer, so it doesn't matter who relayed the message. If I decide to leave, I plan to go to my mother's in Raleigh."

Sarah appreciated Alex's concern, but even when he demonstrated his concern for her and the children, he managed to aggravate her. Why was he avoiding them? Couldn't the man even pick up the telephone to call her?

Storm reports continued to come in. Most of the residents decided to stay and ride it out. At her mother's insistence, Sarah planned to drive to Raleigh. She didn't want the children frightened by the wind and rain. Also, with the cottage situated near the beach without elevation, the possibility of flooding became a factor. While they were away, Susan's husband, Sam, promised to keep an eye on their house. The dear man showed up earlier with a friend to put up storm shutters and secure the outside furniture.

As she packed the car with enough clothes for a few days, the landline rang. She rushed inside and picked up the receiver. "Hello." There was no response. "Hello." She raised her voice. Perhaps there was a bad connection with the storm approaching. "Hello," she yelled. "I don't have time for this," she muttered and pulled the earpiece away from her ear. Just before she hung up, she heard a weak clearing of the throat. "Hello, Sarah."

Alex. Warmth spread through her, followed quickly by annoyance. "Well, if it isn't the disappearing celebrity down the beach. Are you back in town for the storm party?"

"Sarah, I don't have time to argue. I merely wanted to make sure you're safe." Alex's voice sounded scratchy and weak.

"Don't concern yourself with us, Alex. We were on the way out the door when the telephone rang. We're going to Raleigh to stay with Mother a few days. Is that okay with you?"

"As long as you're out of harm's way. I couldn't stand it if something happened to you or the children."

"Speaking of concerns, Alex. Where are you? We've been so worried about you. No one seems to know what's going on. You've completely disappeared from the media. Are you okay?"

"I'm fine, Sarah. I called to check on *you*. I must go. Be safe."

Before Sarah could question him further, he ended the call. She groaned in frustration at the man and her lack of caller ID. She would've called him right back whether he liked it or not. Even though he'd broken the silence to check on her family's safety, he continued to avoid her as though he couldn't wait to finish the conversation. Instead of his usual confidence and control, he sounded distant and unsteady. What happened to the teasing, attentive man who loved to be with them?

Thoughts and concerns for Alex bombarded Sarah as she traveled to Raleigh. She felt as if she'd lost something precious with no means of recovery. She continued to blame herself. Fear and panic seized her as numerous, disastrous scenes played through her mind. When she felt unable to drive safely, she pulled off the interstate at the next exit.

With the children asleep, she placed her head on the steering wheel and cried. A quiet voice whispered into her troubled mind—"When I am afraid, I will put my trust in You"—the words she'd read in Psalm 56 that morning. In place of the unwelcome, distressful videos playing through her head, she asked forgiveness for the fear and unbelief. Her thoughts returned to Alex, and she prayed for his protection and comfort. After a brief time, she found the strength to re-enter the highway and continue the trip. Her confidence restored, her thoughts turned to praise and worship, which shortened the time considerably.

The rejected, fearful Sarah who had departed the island a few hours before had been replaced with a confident, trusting woman who navigated the car through her mother's neighborhood. When she pulled into the driveway, her mother came running out of the house with the unmistakable evidence of relief. The dear woman must have been worrying for hours.

After Leslie greeted them and the children were settled, her mother wanted details concerning the preparations for the storm. Sarah told her about Sam coming over to secure the house and even mentioned Alex's phone call. At the reference to his name, the conversation shifted to the mysterious author and his sudden reappearance.

"You say he sounded weak and unlike himself? I wonder what's going on. There's been nothing mentioned about him in the entertainment news. Since he called you, I suppose that means he's around somewhere. At least he still thinks of you, Sarah. If you ever get another chance with that man, I certainly hope you take it. Alex is a good man, brought up by parents with faith, and now that he's turned his life over to the Lord, he'd make a perfect husband and father."

"I know, Mom, but I wish he'd let me know where he is and what's happening. We're a sad little family without him. It would've been better if we'd never met than for him to be so near and yet so far away. It feels almost like losing Tom all over again."

The two women continued to speculate about Alex's whereabouts and situation. Sarah tried to put him out of her mind and enjoy the time with her mother. They visited the museums in downtown Raleigh and walked a nature trail through the park. The boys were full of questions, especially the creatures of the wild. Much to their grandmother's objection, snakes dominated the conversation.

"Where do the snakes live, Mommy? Do they all live at the museum?"

When they observed the snakes feeding, the boys wanted to know if they ate people, too. After being assured that most snakes were harmless, they put in their request for one.

"I don't think that's a possibility. I thought you wanted a dog?" which had to be the worst possible response.

"We haven't seen Mr. Alex and Bailey in a long, long time, Mommy. Where is he?" Jonathan looked and sounded as if he'd lost his best friend.

"He's our daddy, Jonathan, remember?"

"I know you boys miss Mr. Alex, but he's away and extremely busy right now. He called as we were leaving to make sure we'd be safe from the storm. So, you see he hasn't forgotten us and still cares. Keep praying for him, and I bet we'll see him in no time."

As the boys agreed, Sarah prayed that her little pep talk spoke the truth. She didn't know anyone she'd rather see right now than Alex. A sigh escaped her lips as she struggled to believe her words.

With her friends checking on the house in her absence, Sarah opted to stay a few more days. Finally, after all these years, she and her mother had reached a comfortable place in their relationship. Leslie blamed herself for their past problems, but Sarah wouldn't allow her to take all the responsibility. As she prayed about their relationship, she realized how little she knew her mother and how much she desired to remedy that situation. When she put aside selfish desires and listened, Sarah recognized her mother as a dear parent who loved her daughter and wanted the best for her. She regretted the many years they'd wasted.

Returning to the island felt bittersweet. She'd miss the camaraderie with her mother, but she longed to return to the seashore where she felt the strong presence of both God and Alex. The boys were anxious to see their friends at the church preschool. Even the babies seemed content in their class. They giggled and clapped when they saw the other children. Thoughts of the preschool brought Alex—who undoubtedly was responsible—to mind. When she did finally see him, she wouldn't know whether to greet him with grateful kisses or berate the man for putting her through such misery.

CHAPTER THIRTY

Sarah couldn't get Alex out of her mind. As the days grew shorter and the cold north wind kept the furnace hot, she imagined every negative reason for his leaving the island. Her young, fragile heart had been shattered when both Tom and her father died. They had each, in turn, planned her life, protected her, loved her, and then deserted her. Although she had committed her life to God, at her darkest hour, she felt abandoned by him as well.

Sarah revisited the many discussions with Alex when he attempted to rush her into a commitment. From the beginning, he had felt certain they belonged together, yet she pushed him away. She hesitated to entrust her heart to him, and in so doing, refused to trust God. How ironic that she feared Alex's rejection when she was the one rejecting him.

Sarah couldn't go on feeling abandoned. She needed someone to help sort it out and pray with her against the paralyzing fear. Desperate for direction, she made an appointment with Pastor Mark and his wife. Susan agreed to watch the children.

Pastor Mark and Deborah each greeted Sarah with affectionate hugs as she entered the office. They had become two of the many supportive friends she'd found since moving to the island. With Deborah sitting next to Sarah on the love seat, Pastor got right to the point. "Sarah, I know you've been struggling since your husband died. I'm glad you came to see us."

"Thank you for your time. It's been difficult, coming on the heels of my father's death, but I'm doing much better now. There's another reason for my coming to see you."

"I hope I'm not being presumptuous, but would Alex Caine be your concern?"

Sarah hesitated a moment, surprised that the minister read her so well. "How did you know?"

"Alex and I have become friends over the past few months making me privy to much of his involvement with you and your family. He didn't hesitate to express how much you mean to him. It's obvious, Sarah, that you think highly of Alex as well.

"Regardless of how you feel, I suspect that you have wounds that aren't quite healed, wounds that perhaps keep you from moving forward. Deborah and I have been concerned and felt compelled to pray for you. It would've been difficult enough if you were alone, but you have those four children to consider. How can we pray for you, Sarah?"

Sarah felt Deborah move closer and put an arm around her. "I'm a stubborn woman, Pastor Mark. God has placed a wonderful man in my life, but I've continued to push him away. Alex helped me through some challenging situations that would've been impossible alone. I was devastated by the loss of my father and my husband, but I'm determined to move past it and get on with my life. The problem is that when I finally came to that conclusion, Alex must have given up on me. He left the island, and I've not heard from him in months. He even missed the babies' birthdays. Perhaps he's annoyed with me, but he'd never neglect the children. Have you heard from him?"

"I'm sorry to say that I haven't. Deborah and I have both found that unusual. In the past, Alex kept in touch at least once a week while out of town, but this time, nothing. When I call his cell, it goes directly to voice mail, and he has yet to return a call. I don't know what to think."

Sarah felt too rejected even to attempt calling Alex. His failure to respond would've devastated her further, and she didn't think her heart could take it. Pastor Mark's worried look did nothing to alleviate her fears.

"We're also concerned about Alex and have been praying for him. It's obvious that you know no more than we do. It's almost as if he completely disappeared. The last time I met with him, I felt a great urgency to pray. I don't know what's going on, but I know that God does, and he has Alex in the palm of his hands. Let's pray."

They took turns praying for Alex, but when Sarah left, she felt worse than ever. The concern of her friends confirmed that something was wrong. Though she went home to her children, Alex remained heavy on her heart. She longed to go to him, but how would she ever find him? Would he even want her?

Thanksgiving and Christmas came and went without a word from Alex. It didn't seem right to celebrate without him. She missed him and regretted the frustration she'd caused him.

One morning, when she felt especially discouraged as if she'd lost him forever, a familiar face filled the television screen of the morning news program.

"Stephen Jacobs, renowned author and known to his family as Alex Caine, is reported to be in the hospital suffering from a life-threatening infection following cancer treatments. His last two book releases are *New York Times* bestsellers. Our thoughts and prayers are with you, Mr. Caine."

Sarah doubled over and muffled the agonizing scream in the tail of her shirt. *Oh, Alex, why couldn't you tell me. I would've been there for you like you've always been here for me.*

Soon Sarah's telephone started ringing. First Susan, then Pastor Mark, and then her mother. All were devastated by the news. In the middle of the fourth call, Sarah realized something—Alex hadn't told any of her friends. He hadn't wanted her to know. Why would he want to suffer alone? She knew why. He did it for her. It was his way of protecting her from further pain while not giving her false hope for the future.

How could she keep pushing him away with his love so obvious? In the darkest place of his life, he thought of her over his needs. He kept the darkness from her. That kind of love seemed impossible, yet he offered it freely to her.

But now that she knew, even Alex couldn't keep her away. Sarah wiped her tears and proceeded to make plans to find that magical love she'd tried so hard to escape. She called her mother and asked her to stay with the children. She'd weaned the babies a few months back and knew they'd be fine. The children loved her mother and enjoyed the frequent visits now that Leslie felt free to return to the beach cottage.

Next, Sarah contacted Grace Caine. Under the circumstances, she felt certain he'd be staying with his parents in Northern Virginia. When she made the call, his mother answered the phone sounding so tired and discouraged. "Grace, it's Sarah. I heard about Alex's illness on the news, and I must come. Please don't keep me away."

"Oh, Sarah, of course you may come. We need you. We need to do something for Alex. He's lost the desire to live. He stopped the treatments and wants to go home to the island as soon as he's strong enough. Although the chemotherapy seemed to be working, his lack of hope yields the opposite effect. I would've called you long ago, but he wouldn't agree. I prayed daily that God in his mercy would allow you to find out. Please come and bring some encouragement with you. I could use a good dose myself."

"I'm sorry he didn't tell me when he came home from his last tour, but I think I know why. I'm mostly to blame, but part of it was Alex trying to protect me."

"None of that matters, Sarah; all we want is for him to get well and come back to us."

Her mother arrived in a couple of days, and by then Sarah had the children prepared for her departure. The boys looked sad and confused when she told them about Alex, but after she explained his sickness on their level, they seemed to understand. Still, they were too young to grasp how long it might take for Alex to be well.

"You can just kiss him and make him better, can't you, Mama?"

"We always feel better after you kiss our owies."

Sarah kissed the tops of their heads and shot a pleading look at her mother. Leslie would have to explain the delay in Alex's homecoming.

They weren't the only ones looking forward to his return. The whole town rallied in prayer for him. Being here by the sea had been good for her and Alex. They'd each experienced spiritual and emotional healing in this peaceful environment. Now, she prayed it would become a place of physical healing as well.

Before leaving, Sarah made a quick run to the grocery store. The trip turned out to be anything but quick with everyone stopping her to inquire about Alex. One elderly woman from church voiced her anger toward Pastor Mark. She felt certain he knew of Alex's cancer and failed to share it with the emergency prayer chain. Sarah assured her that wasn't the case.

When she finally escaped the store, she was stopped by a stranger in a dark suit, asking for a moment of her time. "I'm sorry, but I'm in a hurry to leave town. Maybe someone else might help."

"That's probably true, but I believe you're the one with the information on Stephen Jacobs or should I say, Alex Caine? Mrs. Stuart, isn't it?"

Sarah felt violated as the man pushed a microphone into her face. "I'm sorry, but I can't help you. Please let me pass."

"Just tell me what your relationship is to Mr. Caine."

"He's my neighbor and friend, and that's all I plan to tell you. If you don't leave me alone, I'll ask the clerk to call the police. We take care of our residents in this town, and they wouldn't appreciate your bothering me, especially when I'm in a hurry."

Sarah had her fill of the intrusive man and sent the mike flying. He fumbled to retrieve it as she rushed past him and jumped into her van. Was this what Alex put up with all the time?

Later that day, Sarah left the island in her mother's car, a necessity since Leslie would require the van to transport the children. Before departing, she alerted the police to the snooping media and warned her mother of the possibility of inquiring visitors. Chief Haines assured her that they'd keep a watch out for her mother and the children. He said to tell Alex not to worry about anything except getting well and coming back where he belonged. She drove straight to Northern Virginia, making one stop near Richmond for gasoline and a cup of coffee. Grace said that Alex had been unable to eat. Whether from sympathy for him or nerves, she had no appetite and preferred to avoid further delay.

With the detailed directions Bill Caine gave her, she found the house with little trouble. Grace met her at the door and enveloped her in her arms while releasing a long breath that felt a lot like relief. "I didn't tell him that you were coming. He would've worried the whole time. I know you're anxious about how he'll receive you, but I have a feeling you're the medicine he can't live without. I predict he'll be happy to see your pretty face."

"I hope you're right. When I saw the news bulletin, I was so frightened for him. We've lost too much time due to my stubborn insistence on having my way. When I finally realized how much I loved Alex, it was too late. Now, here we are with this heavy cloud hanging over us, and Alex struggles to find a way through this haze without me. I pray he won't turn me away."

"Well, you may have to do some convincing, but I have the greatest confidence in you, my dear. Besides, I prayed for you to come, and I believe

God sent you just in time. Go to him. He's in the second room on the right down the hall."

Sarah knocked lightly on the door, and then entered when she heard no response. She gasped when she saw his bony frame, a mere skeleton of the healthy man she remembered from a few months before.

When he turned over in bed, Sarah had to grab hold of the chest to keep from falling. Sad, lifeless eyes looked back at her. Dark bruises marred his once healthy glow, and his thick blonde hair had disappeared. She'd promised herself she'd be strong, but when she made that resolve, she had no idea what she'd be facing.

Alex looked at her with contempt and fury and turned away. She heard him mumble, "I didn't want you to see me like this, Sarah. I don't need this now. Just take your pity and go."

"That won't work with me, Alex Caine. You know how stubborn I am." She climbed up on the bed with him and molded her frame to his.

"What are you doing, Sarah. Are you crazy? Leave me alone. I can't deal with you; I can't stand myself like this."

"Oh, but I can stand you. When you left me that last time, I felt lonely and abandoned. The longing for you caused me to pray about our relationship seriously. Peace came, along with God's assurance that you're the man of my heart. I think I always loved you, but fear kept me from accepting the gift God so patiently wanted to give. Please forgive me, Alex, for not trusting you or God with our future. I love you."

"I'm afraid it's too late, Sarah; there can't be any hope for us. I may not live to see another year, and that wouldn't be fair to you or the children."

"You're wrong, Alex. You'll not only live, but we'll grow old together. Do you hear me? I don't want to hear any more of this talk about dying. I will not lose you."

Sarah's arm draped over his shoulder, and he finally pulled her hand toward his heart. He never could ignore her, even when she infuriated him. How ironic that, after all his waiting and praying, he finally had her attention, yet he had no strength to respond.

"You have such a big heart, Alex. Might I tell you a story about two lonely, mixed up people?"

"I'm sure you plan to tell me whether I wish to hear it or not." Alex couldn't help himself. He loved to tease her and wait for her witty response.

"It's a delightful story. You may want to take notes. It might have book potential," she teased back. He'd never be disappointed with her.

Alex felt Sarah squeeze his hand. "Once upon a time, this handsome young writer moved to the seashore, so that he might live in a quiet, lonely world with few distractions. While he wrote these wonderful novels, he considered himself satisfied and perfectly happy. But God saw that deep inside, the man longed for something more. He survived a few years in this empty fantasy until he met a young family up the beach.

"The young mother also pretended to be satisfied and demonstrated her independence. Unlike "the dog man," as her boys first called the writer, she didn't choose to move to the island. She had no other options. Although she often denied it, she needed someone to rescue her from impossible situations. So, that big, generous-hearted man reached out to this frightened young widow. He didn't shy away from getting involved, even though she turned out to be a piece of work with two toddlers in tow and two more babies on the way.

"This needy mother didn't realize it at the time, but she had descended into the darkest hole imaginable. She lived in anger and bitterness toward her father and husband who had both died and left her with mountains of responsibility. For a while she even turned against God, thinking he'd abandoned her as well. All the while, God had a plan to rescue her through this handsome, caring man. Instead of accepting God's best, she continued to reject the man along with his love and care. When he left, she realized how much she loved him.

"When she finally understood her own heart and the sacrificial love of this man, she knew she'd loved him from that first meeting on the porch. But, she'd waited too long. He left her and didn't plan to return. He wanted to shield her from more pain and sorrow. When she realized his intentions, she couldn't let him get away with it. And he, knowing how stubborn she was, knew he had no choice but to allow her to walk with him through his dark tunnel."

The love flowing from Sarah's body to his gave Alex hope for the first time. He could resist her no longer. He turned over and pulled her into his arms. Their closeness and intimacy felt so right, as though he'd come home.

As he cried in her embrace, his body trembled with relief and gratitude. For months, he'd longed for her, and God sent her when he needed her most.

"Alex, it's going to be all right. I know I've hurt you many times, but believe me, I will never purposely hurt you again. I've often been incapable and weak, but I promise to be strong for you now. Please don't turn my love away."

"I know I should send you home, but I never could resist you, Sarah Stuart. I have nothing to offer you, yet I need you. When you're near, I feel alive and at peace. Thank you for loving me."

Their tears flowed together as Sarah held him and prayed for God to strengthen their faith enough to believe for a miracle. No longer would Alex struggle alone. Although she didn't deserve to be loved by such a fine man, she longed to be that woman.

Sarah pulled away slightly so she could see his face. She'd come to love that adoring look and wasn't the least bit surprised by his next words. "Sarah, you have to marry me as soon as possible. After I found out about the cancer, I decided that I didn't want you to go through this, but now, I realize that you're as necessary as any part of my body. This probably doesn't make sense to you, but it feels as though you exist simply for me. I don't have the strength or desire to live without you. You give me hope for the future—a future that held no promise even an hour ago. I love you."

"Alex, you said it so well. It's exactly the way I feel. You're going to beat this disease, and we refuse to entertain doubts or fears. I won't lose another loved one before we see our children grow up and give us grandchildren."

Sick as he was, he couldn't help but believe Sarah's prophetic words. God had brought her at a time when he'd lost all hope. The hopelessness he felt without her seemed to vanish as he pulled her to him, relishing the feel of her and the warmth of her love.

"I agree, Alex, we should marry soon. I don't plan to spend too many more nights without you. I want you sleeping near my heart." With that, she kissed him on the mouth with so much passion it nearly took his breath. When he returned the kiss and felt his body responding, he pushed her away.

"I may be sick, Sarah, but I'm still a man. I think you'd better get out of this bed right now before we do something we might regret." Even in his weakened condition, his desire for her stirred something deep within, a need like he'd never experienced before.

"No way, Alex. Turn over so I can rub your back and pray for you. You'll fall into a peaceful, healing rest while you think about getting well, seeing your babies, and becoming my husband." Sarah kissed him again and then helped him turn over.

Alex didn't think he'd be able to sleep with Sarah hugging his back, but with his strength depleted, he felt himself relax under her tender care. His heart filled with gratitude to God as he listened to her quiet prayers. Sarah correctly described the ordeal as a dark tunnel. That's exactly how it felt. Now, beams of light pierced the darkness and he no longer struggled alone. God had sent his Sarah, and she brought real hope for the first time since this ordeal began.

CHAPTER THIRTY-ONE

When Grace came into the room, she found them asleep with Sarah snuggled against Alex's back. Tears of relief slid down her face as love and gratitude flooded her spirit. Her son's heart would no longer ache. *Lord, you are so good.*

During her many prayers for Alex, she'd often felt compelled to call Sarah, but Grace reluctantly honored her son's request. Although the newsworthy revelation of his identity would create future problems, she refused to allow worry to rob her joy. This battle required a host of prayer warriors. If a public announcement got Sarah here and rallied the troops, so be it. Smiling at the love those two shared, she adjusted the covers and left them in peaceful, healing rest.

Sarah woke confused. The positive attitude she'd displayed for Alex now gave way to fear and doubt. She stumbled from the bed and searched for the guest room where Mr. Caine had put her luggage. The lovely room held no appeal as she fell onto her knees and wept her anguish out to God. *Help me, Father. I can't lose another good man; Alex looks so frail and hopeless. I know I confessed your healing, but though my mouth spoke the truth, one look at his cancer-ravaged body flooded me with doubt and discouragement. Only you can bring us through this darkness.*

When she'd exhausted herself with tears of anguish, a verse from Philippians came to mind, "Be anxious for nothing, but in everything by prayer and supplication with thanksgiving let your requests be made known to God. And the peace of God, which surpasses all comprehension, will guard your hearts and your minds in Christ Jesus." With that reminder, she turned her thoughts to gratitude for Alex and the blessing he'd been to her family. She thanked God that this wonderful man could love a woman in her situation. As she quietly worshiped, she felt strength building her faith and conquering her fears.

Her prayer spent, she got up and looked in the mirror. She hardly recognized the disheveled figure staring back at her. Opening her luggage, she found clean clothes and entered the adjoining bath, in hopes that a shower would improve her appearance. The peace prevailed as hot water washed over her tired body. When she felt refreshed and presentable, she returned to Alex. He'd awakened and looked more himself, relaxing comfortably on a stack of pillows.

"Sarah, come sit so I can hold you." He patted the bed next to him, opened his arms and pulled her to him.

"Well, you must feel better since you're back to bossing me around."

"When I turned over, and you weren't here, I felt disappointed that I was dreaming. After all, you do seem to show up in most of them. Then, I shamefacedly remembered our conversation and that most unromantic marriage proposal. Forgive me, Sarah. May I please have another chance?"

Sarah laughed at his remorse before drawing him to her. "Never would I consider you unromantic, Alex Caine. You made me so happy that anything resembling a proposal would've worked. But, if you prefer a second go of it, I'm always up for romance."

"I regret that we're not at a nice restaurant or that I'm unable to kneel, but this is the best I can do." Alex held her face in his hands and rubbed his thumb over her lips. He kissed her gently on her eyes, both cheeks and then her lips. Sarah was so hungry for him she wanted to prolong the kiss, but he moved his lips near her ear. She felt breathless.

"Sarah Stuart, I love you more than words could ever convey, and I know that God brought us together. My desire is to love you, honor you, and take care of you and your children. Will you allow me the pleasure of becoming my wife?"

Alex retrieved a ring box from under his pillow. "I purchased this months ago and brought it with me when I left the island. I planned to return the ring to the jeweler, but I'm so glad I waited. Please accept this token of my love and commitment to you. Marry me, Sarah."

Tears filled her eyes as she viewed the diamond solitaire. Even his choice of a simple, unpretentious stone spoke of his knowledge and understanding of her. When she returned her attention to Alex, he looked disappointed and sad.

"It's okay, Sarah. I understand if you're afraid. I've asked too much of you. Please ..."

Sarah put her hand to his mouth. "Nothing would please me more than to be your wife, Alex. These are tears of gratitude for the man who knows me so well, he picked out the perfect ring."

Sarah had never been able to control her emotions when expressing love. After Alex slipped the diamond on her finger, she pulled his head down and kissed him passionately. He opened his mouth to her and returned the kiss with equal fervor. When he started to squirm under her, she realized she was practically on top of him. "Oops. Sorry, Alex. I tend to be a bit passionate with the men I love."

"I'm not the least disappointed with that revelation, but I suggest we wait until after the wedding. You have no idea what you do to me. This isn't the first time I've needed to put some distance between us."

The man was so adorable that she felt tempted to move back into his arms. Instead, she gave him a peck on the nose and tickled him briefly under his arms. Their romantic interlude turned into laughter, teasing, and incredible joy.

"I want to call the boys, Sarah. Do you think now would be a good time?"

Sarah loved his renewed determination and felt he'd cleared a hurdle. He was livelier and seemed stronger by the minute. She checked the time on her watch. "Sure, they'd love to talk to you. They were worried when I told them you were sick."

Sarah noticed the pillows had become somewhat askew during their roughhousing. When she'd finished the fluffing and straightening, she gave him a quick kiss and stood to inspect her efforts. His expression brightened.

"What a stubborn fool I've been to deny myself this attention. You plan on spoiling me as much as you do the children?"

"Don't become too comfortable with it. As soon as you're better, it's back to changing diapers, wiping up spills, and supervising children on the beach." Sarah delighted in that banter she'd longed to hear.

"I'd love to be playing dump trucks with my boys on the beach."

"Just so you understand, the girls will require a prince to build their sand castle. They aren't into construction equipment."

As the man burst into laughter, Sarah ignored the sick room and looked heavenward in anticipation of a future that brightened more every moment. She felt peace deep inside and recognized the renewed hope in Alex's expression.

Suddenly, Alex became quiet and solemn. "Sarah, I'm blessed beyond imagination. Not only are you beautiful and fun, but you challenge me to be a better person. Can't you see what a great life we'll have if I can beat this sickness?" Alex stopped to control his emotions and then continued with a husky voice. "Sorry. These are grateful tears, but before I become a slobbering fool, go ahead and dial the number. I want to talk to your mother first."

Sarah wondered what he was up to but did as he asked. She then relaxed in the comfortable chair near his bed and took a moment to observe the man she would marry. Seeing him through eyes of love, she realized that even with the cancer treatments emaciating him, he remained handsome. She would never get enough of him, his teasing, or his attention. How could she have denied his love so long?

"Hello, Mrs. Warren. It's Alex Caine." Sarah worried about the tiredness in his voice as she listened to his side of the conversation.

"Thank you for asking. I'm feeling better since Sarah arrived. You should've sent her long ago. She has that healing touch, you know." Alex smirked sweetly at her.

"I must ask you something, Mrs. Warren, which probably won't come as a surprise. I would like to marry your daughter, but I can't wait until I'm well enough to come home. It's hard to explain, but when she's near, it translates into healing for me. Would you and the boys mind if we married here? I regret that you and the children won't be with us, but the trip would prove difficult without the risk of alerting the public. Under the circumstances, the ceremony must remain private. Please understand."

She didn't have to hear her mother's response to know she'd be disappointed. Sarah wanted to protest but realized the complications involved for everyone, including Alex. When his expression brightened, she knew her mother had agreed to his plans.

"Thank you, Leslie. I'll let you talk to Sarah in a few minutes, but may I speak with the boys first? I appreciate your care of the children."

Alex put the phone on speaker so Sarah could participate in the conversation. “Mr. Alex, is it really you?”

“It is, and your mommy is here with me. Is David on the other phone?”

“Daddy?”

“Hello, David. How are you guys doing?”

The boys answered with their usual, “Fine.”

“Thank you for sending Mommy to see me. I know you miss her, but I need her.”

“We miss you, too. Where’ve you been? You’ve been gone a long, long time. You even missed the babies’ birthdays and Christmas again,” Jonathan reprimanded.

“I’m sorry to have been away so long, but I haven’t been well. I spent some time in the hospital like you did, David. But ever since your mommy arrived, I’ve felt better. When your mother and I get back, I never again want us to be away for so long.”

“If you’re sick, you should come home so we can pray for you. When we pray for Mommy, she gets better. When are you coming home?”

“I’ll be there as soon as the doctor gives me permission to travel, but you don’t have to wait until I return to the island to pray for me. With you and Jonathan praying, I’m sure I’ll be well in no time.”

“We told Mommy to kiss you and make you better. Tell her, in case she forgot.” That had to be Jonathan, the expert with his multitude of boo-boos.

“I’ll make sure she follows your orders, Jonathan, as soon as we get off the phone.” Alex grinned at Sarah as she rolled her eyes at him.

“Before I let Mommy talk, may I ask you both a serious question?”

After the boys gave their approval, Alex continued. “Before we come home, I’d like to marry Mommy. I love her, and I want us to be a family. Do you know what that means?”

“You’d come live with us all the time?” Alex laughed at Jonathan’s logic, knowing his love of the beach cottage.

“Since that’s your grandma’s house, I would prefer that you live with me. Would that be all right with you?”

Jonathan always had to have all the details. He wanted to know where they would sleep, if they might play on the beach at the new house, and if Bailey would be their dog now that “they were all getting married.”

Alex answered as best he could, but when Jonathan wanted to know where his Mommy would sleep, he paused to think of an appropriate response. He wanted the boys to feel comfortable when he and Sarah kissed or hugged in their presence.

"When I marry your mommy, we'll be husband and wife, and married couples sleep in the same bed, so they can love and cuddle each other. Will that be all right with you and David?"

"Will the babies sleep with you, too?"

"No, the babies are old enough to have their own room now, but Mommy and I will share a room not too far from you guys. How does that sound?"

"Good, if the babies don't cry all the time," practical Jonathan replied.

"You're really going to be our daddy, aren't you?"

"Yes, David, I am. You are special boys, and I'll love you and your sisters always. So, are you okay with me marrying your mother?"

The boys answered affirmatively and then attempted to prolong the conversation. At that point, Sarah intervened, probably seeing his fatigue as he tried to mask his weakness and answer their unending questions.

"Hey, guys, it's Mommy. I miss you, but we'll have to stay here for a few more weeks. Are you helping Grandma and being good for her?"

"We're being real good like you said and helping her with the babies, aren't we, David?" Sarah laughed at the quick response from the one most likely to cause trouble.

"Okay, I'm counting on it. Daddy and I will call every day to check on you. I'm so glad you agreed for me to marry Mr. Alex. He loves us all and will take care of us. Please don't forget to pray for him."

"Did you kiss him like we said?"

"I certainly did, and I'm pretty sure he liked it." Sarah sent Alex a mischievous look. "I must talk to Grandma before you hang up. I love you guys."

"And I love you, too," Alex inserted, "I do miss playing with my special buddies. We'll talk tomorrow. Be good for Grandma."

While Sarah talked at length with her mother, Alex thought of the difficulties caring for the children alone. Though the church childcare program would be available, Leslie could use additional help. He took the telephone back from Sarah.

"Leslie, it just occurred to me what a burden this has placed on you. Would you mind if I ask Anna to come over in the afternoons? She can help care for the children, assist with chores and run errands—whatever you need. It would give you time to rest or even get out of the house occasionally. I hope you won't be stubborn like your daughter and insist on going it alone."

Sarah's mother laughed before answering, "No, I'm not the least stubborn when it comes to accepting such a generous offer. I love my grandchildren, but, as you know, they can be a handful. Sarah told me about Anna after your trip to Florida, and I look forward to meeting this superwoman."

"You'll love her, and the children seem comfortable with her. I'll give her a call right away. Thanks again for this sacrificial gift. I know Sarah feels more at ease with you there."

After Sarah and her mother discussed a few more details regarding the children's schedules, she ended the call and returned her attention toward him. "Alex, you're exhausted."

Alex wanted to continue making plans with Sarah, but he acknowledged the truth. Sarah removed some pillows and helped him get more comfortable. Instead of leaving him as he expected, she returned to her position on the bed behind him. With her quiet prayer and gentle touch, he felt himself drifting. His last conscious thought overflowed with peaceful intimacy.

Though Alex improved daily, Sarah realized it would take time and patience for a full recovery. The same chemicals designed to fight cancer also destroyed good cells, leaving him weak and vulnerable. Knowing that God had created bodies to restore themselves, Sarah constantly prayed for Alex to be healed.

By the end of the week, Alex wanted to move forward with wedding plans while Sarah worried about his susceptible immune system. Even a simple, low-key service would tax him to the limit. At his insistence and despite Sarah's protest, Grace called her minister and arranged for a private ceremony the following week. The service would convene in the chapel of the church where his family worshipped. His parents would be their only guests. Part of the service would include a rededication of Alex's life to God. He'd strayed away so many years before and desired a formal recommitment. The wedding ceremony would conclude with communion, their first act of worship together as husband and wife.

On the afternoon of the wedding, Sarah dressed carefully in the tea-length, ivory dress that Grace insisted she order. Never before had she spent so much money on one item, but she liked the way the silk fabric felt against her skin. The dress was worthy of the man she would marry.

Sarah drove herself to the church and stood at the back surveying the small sanctuary. Light from the candelabra flickered and reflected a warmth off the baskets of white roses on each side of the altar. Alex's mother knelt at the front left pew—another praying mother. Sarah felt blessed. Grace's head came up at the same time Sarah noticed Mr. Caine pushing his son through the side door. She ached for her groom who could hardly hold his head upright. His frustration at being stuck in a wheelchair nearly broke her heart. Early that morning he'd told her how much he wanted to stand with her during the ceremony. She wanted to run to him but forced herself to wait for the signal.

Though the organ stood silent and she treaded the aisle alone, Sarah walked with confidence toward Alex, a surprising gift from God. When their tear-glazed eyes met, warmth filled her, and all else faded into the background. The sweet combination of love, forgiveness, and the presence of Jesus filled the sanctuary.

Never had she considered the possibility of finding another love comparable to that of her children's father, but this dear man had swept her off her feet amid mountains of protest and obstacles. She knew the journey ahead would be difficult, but they would walk together from this moment forward. Despite his weakness, Alex slowly stood when she reached out to him.

The vows they recited seemed surreal, "in sickness and in health, to love and to cherish until we are parted by death." Amid the fear that swept over her, Sarah inwardly cried out to God. The declaration she made when she first saw the gaunt Alex came back to her along with renewed hope: By faith, they would grow old together. She looked with pleasure at her groom and tightened her hold, allowing him to draw from her strength.

Their vows completed, Sarah felt Alex sinking as he collapsed into the chair. She knelt beside him with their hands intertwined for the prayer of blessing and the Eucharist. The communion seemed to strengthen him enough to give her a gentle kiss at the close of the service. When she started to push him down the aisle, he pulled her from behind the chair and onto his lap. She laughed with joy and relief.

"Since I can't walk with you, Sarah, you must ride with me." Sarah savored the ride as Alex's dad pushed them out together. Loving Alex had always been a roller coaster ride, but she chose to believe that the future held fewer hills, curves, and bumps in the road for the two people who had finally become one.

EPILOGUE

Seven Months Later

Another fall arrived along with a Nor'easter that had kept Alex indoors for the past few days. When the chilly wind and rain moved offshore, the sunshine broke through the lingering clouds enough to warm the deck where he sat waiting for Sarah. His contemplative mood turned his thoughts toward his family and the many changes that had occurred since Bailey discovered David and Jonathan playing on the beach that day.

As he gazed out on the ocean, he thought about the shallow person he used to be, a self-serving celebrity with no real friends and no understanding of love. That lonely, arrogant bachelor saw himself fulfilled and successful with little thought beyond another best seller. Oblivious, he'd been on a highway of self-ambition, leading toward a dead end. The disruptions he feared seemed mild compared to the pleasure of this new adventure. Those two little boys put a hunger in his heart for something greater than himself, and he'd found no rest until he'd surrendered his mind, soul, and body to God.

On their wedding day, he had been so sick and weak, it was all he could do to stand for the vows. If not for her presence and strength, he would've collapsed in Sarah's arms. He smiled as he remembered the joyous wheelchair ride from the sanctuary.

Alex thought about how nervous he felt as they prepared for their first night together. Sarah nearly took his breath when she entered the room in an iridescent white gown, revealing enough of her to set him on fire. Knowing he had the strength of a fly, he wondered how he would survive the torture. Near panic, he remembered Pastor Mark's recommendation.

After a passionate kiss, Alex pulled out his e-reader and read from Song of Solomon using The Message version, "You've captured my heart, dear friend. You looked at me, and I fell in love. One look my way and I was hopelessly in love! How beautiful your love, dear, dear friend—far more pleasing than a fine, rare wine."

Nothing could've explained his feelings better. Her tears wet his bare chest as he held her and prayed, "Father in heaven, thank you for this dear woman you've given me. How blessed I am! Please give me the strength to love her as she deserves."

Alex warmed from more than the sun as he remembered the kindness and gentleness of his wife that evening. He'd never experienced such love and romantic pleasure.

Despite the debilitating treatments, Alex's health improved daily. After the first week of therapy, Sarah took over as drill sergeant insisting he work harder. Their trips through the house became walks in the garden, and soon she escorted him toward a nearby park. Though it took a few days to accomplish the mission, she pushed until he succeeded. He felt thankful when he saw his father waiting to drive them home.

With encouragement from Sarah, the doctor soon released him to return to Shell Island. The trip seemed long and unbearable until they crossed the bridge over the Intercoastal Waterway. His energy level soared as he rolled down the window and breathed deeply of the moist, salt air. He laughed aloud thinking how he felt the last time he saw the ocean. Then, he'd had no hope of ever returning, but God allowed him to come home.

The children reacted with a combination of fear and concern when they saw him. They soon warmed to his greeting, however, and rushed into his arms. They piled on his bed while a little girl snuggled under each arm, and the boys grilled him about the wedding.

"We missed you, Daddy. We need you here with us. How long before we can play on the beach?"

"Mommy and I have missed you, too. I'm feeling better all the time. Keep praying for me."

Every day with the prayers of his family and Sarah by his side, he felt stronger and more at peace. Although the latest scans had come back negative, he realized the "C" word would be a constant companion. Regardless of the circumstances, he felt thankful for each new day.

As Alex continued his reflective mood, he heard the door open behind him. *Sarah.* He didn't have to see her to feel her presence. Her sweet perfume, combined with the scent of the sea, enveloped them as she wrapped him in her arms. His grateful heart merging with the warmth of her love brought tears sliding down his cheeks.

Sarah circled the large wicker recliner and moved into his lap. When she saw the moisture on his face, she frowned, "Oh, Alex. What's wrong?"

"Nothing really. I've been sitting here thinking about us and how happy I am with you. Makes me wonder how you ever fell in love with such a reprobate like me."

"Well," Sarah said with an amusing look, "you wore me down with the chase. How soon you forget, my love."

Before he could respond, she reached for him and kissed him so passionately he felt it down to his toes. Alex recovered long enough to say in a husky voice, "I hope the children are taking an excessively long nap. I think a little 'nap' would be perfect right now."

Sarah laughed as she jumped up and pulled him toward their bedroom, a place where this passionate woman completed him and warmed his heart. Nothing he'd ever written compared to the real life he experienced with Sarah.

Whether he lived one more day or many years, he would always be thankful for that particular morning. The morning that initiated a series of encounters ordained by God to change his life forever. That morning not so long ago, when he went walking by the sea with Bailey.

ABOUT THE AUTHOR

Claudette Sharpe was raised on a dairy farm in South Georgia. While attending Lee University in Cleveland, Tennessee, she met and married a fellow student, Charles Renalds. They moved to fast-paced Northern Virginia where she worked at the Pentagon. Five years later, she left to become a housewife, mother, and Christian education volunteer. As their children grew older, she accepted a full-time position as Director of Children's Ministry for Church of the Apostles, Fairfax, Virginia. When Claudette retired in 1994, she had time to indulge in her love of reading Christian fiction, and her desire to write surfaced when she and her sister compiled their mother's biography.

Claudette's writings are included in compilations by the Northern Virginia Christian Writers Fellowship: A devotional, entitled "Treasures of the Sea" was published in Whispers, 2015; "My Proverbs 31 Mother," in Characters We Know and Love,March 2016; and in Short Story Revival, April 2017, her submission, "A Touch of Regency," sends the reader back in time with a love story set in England. In June, 2018, NVCWF will publish an anthology entitled Legacy. Her submission, "The Legacy of Prayer,"describes the impact her grandmother's prayer had on her family. *By the Sea* is her debut novel. She and Charles live in Haymarket, Virginia.

45213995R00149

Made in the USA
Middletown, DE
16 May 2019